CHRISTOPHER
THE CASE OF THE MISSING MINUTES

CHRISTOPHER BUSH was born Charlie Christmas Bush in Norfolk in 1885. His father was a farm labourer and his mother a milliner. In the early years of his childhood he lived with his aunt and uncle in London before returning to Norfolk aged seven, later winning a scholarship to Thetford Grammar School.

As an adult, Bush worked as a schoolmaster for 27 years, pausing only to fight in World War One, until retiring aged 46 in 1931 to be a full-time novelist. His first novel featuring the eccentric Ludovic Travers was published in 1926, and was followed by 62 additional Travers mysteries. These are all to be republished by Dean Street Press.

Christopher Bush fought again in World War Two, and was elected a member of the prestigious Detection Club. He died in 1973.

By Christopher Bush

CHRISTOPHER BUSH

THE CASE OF THE MISSING MINUTES

With an introduction
by Curtis Evans

DEAN STREET PRESS

INTRODUCTION

THAT ONCE vast and mighty legion of bright young (and youngish) British crime writers who began publishing their ingenious tales of mystery and imagination during what is known as the Golden Age of detective fiction (traditionally dated from 1920 to 1939) had greatly diminished by the iconoclastic decade of the Sixties, many of these writers having become casualties of time. Of the 38 authors who during the Golden Age had belonged to the Detection Club, a London-based group which included within its ranks many of the finest writers of detective fiction then plying the craft in the United Kingdom, just over a third remained among the living by the second half of the 1960s, while merely seven—Agatha Christie, Anthony Gilbert, Gladys Mitchell, Margery Allingham, John Dickson Carr, Nicholas Blake and Christopher Bush—were still penning crime fiction.

In 1966--a year that saw the sad demise, at the too young age of 62, of Margery Allingham--an executive with the English book publishing firm Macdonald reflected on the continued popularity of the author who today is the least well known among this tiny but accomplished crime writing cohort: Christopher Bush (1885-1973), whose first of his three score and three series detective novels, *The Plumley Inheritance*, had appeared fully four decades earlier, in 1926. "He has a considerable public, a 'steady Bush public,' a public that has endured through many years," the executive boasted of Bush. "He never presents any problem to his publisher, who knows exactly how many copies of a title may be safely printed for the loyal Bush fans; the number is a healthy one too." Yet in 1968, just a couple of years after the Macdonald editor's affirmation of Bush's notable popular duration as a crime writer, the author, now in his 83rd year, bade farewell to mystery fiction with a final detective novel, *The Case of the Prodigal Daughter*, in which, like in Agatha Christie's *Third Girl* (1966), copious references are made, none too favorably, to youthful sex, drugs and rock and roll. Afterwards, outside of the reprinting in the UK in the early 1970s of a scattering of classic Bush titles from the Golden Age, Bush's books, in contrast with those of Christie, Carr, Allingham and Blake, disappeared from mass circulation in both the UK and the US, becoming fervently sought (and ever more unobtainable) treasures by collectors and connoisseurs of classic crime fiction. Now, in one of the signal developments in vintage mystery publishing, Dean Street Press is reprinting all 63 of the Christopher Bush detective novels. These will be published over a period of months, beginning with the release of books 1 to 10 in the series.

Few Golden Age British mystery writers had backgrounds as humble yet simultaneously mysterious, dotted with omissions and evasions, as Christopher Bush, who was born Charlie Christmas Bush on the day of the Nativity in 1885 in the Norfolk village of Great Hockham, to Charles Walter Bush and his second wife, Eva Margaret Long. While the father of Christopher Bush's Detection Club colleague and near exact contemporary Henry Wade (the pseudonym of Henry Lancelot Aubrey-Fletcher) was a baronet who lived in an elegant Georgian mansion and claimed extensive ownership of fertile English fields, Christopher's father resided in a cramped cottage and toiled in fields as a farm laborer, a term that in the late Victorian and Edwardian era, his son lamented many years afterward, "had in it something of contempt....There was something almost of serfdom about it."

Charles Walter Bush was a canny though mercurial individual, his only learning, his son recalled, having been "acquired at the Sunday school." A man of parts, Charles was a tenant farmer of three acres, a thatcher, bricklayer and carpenter (fittingly for the father of a detective novelist, coffins were his specialty), a village radical and a most adept poacher. After a flight from Great Hockham, possibly on account of his poaching activities, Charles, a widower with a baby son whom he had left in the care of his mother, resided in London, where he worked for a firm of spice importers. At a dance in the city, Charles met Christopher's mother, Eva Long, a lovely and sweet-natured young milliner and bonnet maker, sweeping her off her feet with a combination of "good looks and a certain plausibility." After their marriage the couple left London to live in a tiny rented cottage in Great Hockham, where Eva over the next eighteen years gave birth to three sons and five daughters and perforce learned the challenging ways of rural domestic economy.

Decades later an octogenarian Christopher Bush, in his memoir *Winter Harvest: A Norfolk Boyhood* (1967), characterized Great Hockham as a rustic rural redoubt where many of the words that fell from the tongues of the native inhabitants "were those of Shakespeare, Milton and the Authorised Version....Still in general use were words that were standard in Chaucer's time, but had since lost a certain respectability." Christopher amusingly recalled as a young boy telling his mother that a respectable neighbor woman had used profanity, explaining that in his hearing she had told her husband, "George, wipe you that shit off that pig's arse, do you'll datty your trousers," to which his mother had responded that although that particular usage of a four-letter word had not really been *swearing*, he was not to give vent to such language himself.

Great Hockham, which in Christopher Bush's youth had a population of about four hundred souls, was composed of a score or so of cottages, three public houses, a post-office, five shops, a couple of forges and a pair of churches, All Saint's and the Primitive Methodist Chapel, where the Bush family rather vocally worshipped. "The village lived by farming, and most of its men were labourers," Christopher recollected. "Most of the children left school as soon as the law permitted: boys to be absorbed somehow into the land and the girls to go into domestic service." There were three large farms and four smaller ones, and, in something of an anomaly, not one but two squires--the original squire, dubbed "Finch" by Christopher, having let the shooting rights at Little Hockham Hall to one "Green," a wealthy international banker, making the latter man a squire by courtesy. Finch owned most of the local houses and farms, in traditional form receiving rents for them personally on Michaelmas; and when Christopher's father fell out with Green, "a red-faced, pompous, blustering man," over a political election, he lost all of the banker's business, much to his mother's distress. Yet against all odds and adversities, Christopher's life greatly diverged from settled norms in Great Hockham, incidentally producing one of the most distinguished detective novelists from the Golden Age of detective fiction.

Although Christopher Bush was born in Great Hockham, he spent his earliest years in London living with his mother's much older sister, Elizabeth, and her husband, a fur dealer by the name of James Streeter, the couple having no children of their own. Almost certainly of illegitimate birth, Eva had been raised by the Long family from her infancy. She once told her youngest daughter how she recalled the Longs being visited, when she was a child, by a "fine lady in a carriage," whom she believed was her birth mother. Or is it possible that the "fine lady in a carriage" was simply an imaginary figment, like the aristocratic fantasies of Philippa Palfrey in P.D. James's *Innocent Blood* (1980), and that Eva's "sister" Elizabeth was in fact her mother?

The Streeters were a comfortably circumstanced couple at the time they took custody of Christopher. Their household included two maids and a governess for the young boy, whose doting but dutiful "Aunt Lizzie" devoted much of her time to the performance of "good works among the East End poor." When Christopher was seven years old, however, drastically straightened financial circumstances compelled the Streeters to leave London for Norfolk, by the way returning the boy to his birth parents in Great Hockham.

Fortunately the cause of the education of Christopher, who was not only a capable village cricketer but a precocious reader and scholar, was taken up both by his determined and devoted mother and an idealistic local elementary school headmaster. In his teens Christopher secured a scholarship to Norfolk's Thetford Grammar School, one of England's oldest educational institutions, where Thomas Paine had studied a century-and-a-half earlier. He left Thetford in 1904 to take a position as a junior schoolmaster, missing a chance to go to Cambridge University on yet another scholarship. (Later he proclaimed himself thankful for this turn of events, sardonically speculating that had he received a Cambridge degree he "might have become an exceedingly minor don or something as staid and static and respectable as a publisher.") Christopher would teach in English schools for the next twenty-seven years, retiring at the age of 46 in 1931, after he had established a successful career as a detective novelist.

Christopher's romantic relationships proved far rockier than his career path, not to mention every bit as murky as his mother's familial antecedents. In 1911, when Christopher was teaching in Wood Green School, a co-educational institution in Oxfordshire, he wed county council schoolteacher Ella Maria Pinner, a daughter of a baker neighbor of the Bushes in Great Hockham. The two appear never actually to have lived together, however, and in 1914, when Christopher at the age of 29 headed to war in the 16th (Public Schools) Battalion of the Middlesex Regiment, he falsely claimed in his attestation papers, under penalty of two years' imprisonment with hard labor, to be unmarried.

After four years of service in the Great War, including a year-long stint in Egypt, Christopher returned in 1919 to his position at Wood Green School, where he became involved in another romantic relationship, from which he soon desired to extricate himself. (A photo of the future author, taken at this time in Egypt, shows a rather dashing, thin-mustached man in uniform and is signed "Chris," suggesting that he had dispensed with "Charlie" and taken in its place a diminutive drawn from his middle name.) The next year Winifred Chart, a mathematics teacher at Wood Green, gave birth to a son, whom she named Geoffrey Bush. Christopher was the father of Geoffrey, who later in life became a noted English composer, though for reasons best known to himself Christopher never acknowledged his son. (A letter Geoffrey once sent him was returned unopened.) Winifred claimed that she and Christopher had married but separated, but she refused to speak of her purported spouse forever after and she destroyed all of his letters and other mementos, with the exception of a book of poetry that he had written for her during what she termed their engagement.

Christopher's true mate in life, though with her he had no children, was Florence Marjorie Barclay, the daughter of a draper from Ballymena, Northern Ireland, and, like Ella Pinner and Winifred Chart, a schoolteacher. Christopher and Marjorie likely had become romantically involved by 1929, when Christopher dedicated to her his second detective novel, *The Perfect Murder Case*; and they lived together as man and wife from the 1930s until her death in 1968 (after which, probably not coincidentally, Christopher stopped publishing novels). Christopher returned with Marjorie to the vicinity of Great Hockham when his writing career took flight, purchasing two adjoining cottages and commissioning his father and a stepbrother to build an extension consisting of a kitchen, two bedrooms and a new staircase. (The now sprawling structure, which Christopher called "Home Cottage," is now a bed and breakfast grandiloquently dubbed "Home Hall.") After a falling-out with his father, presumably over the conduct of Christopher's personal life, he and Marjorie in 1932 moved to Beckley, Sussex, where they purchased Horsepen, a lovely Tudor plaster and timber-framed house. In 1953 the couple settled at their final home, The Great House, a centuries-old structure (now a boutique hotel) in Lavenham, Suffolk.

From these three houses Christopher maintained a lucrative and critically esteemed career as a novelist, publishing both detective novels as Christopher Bush and, commencing in 1933 with the acclaimed book *Return* (in the UK, *God and the Rabbit*, 1934), regional novels purposefully drawing on his own life experience, under the pen name Michael Home. (During the 1940s he also published espionage novels under the Michael Home pseudonym.) Although his first detective novel, *The Plumley Inheritance*, made a limited impact, with his second, *The Perfect Murder Case*, Christopher struck gold. The latter novel, a big seller in both the UK and the US, was published in the former country by the prestigious Heinemann, soon to become the publisher of the detective novels of Margery Allingham and Carter Dickson (John Dickson Carr), and in the latter country by the Crime Club imprint of Doubleday, Doran, one of the most important publishers of mystery fiction in the United States.

Over the decade of the 1930s Christopher Bush published, in both the UK and the US as well as other countries around the world, some of the finest detective fiction of the Golden Age, prompting the brilliant Thirties crime fiction reviewer, author and Oxford University Press editor Charles Williams to avow: "Mr. Bush writes of as thoroughly enjoyable murders as any I know." (More recently, mystery genre authority B.A. Pike dubbed these novels by Bush, whom he praised as "one of the most reliable and resourceful of true detective writers"; "Golden Age baroque, rendered remarkable by some extraordinary flights of fancy.") In 1937 Christopher Bush became, along with Nicholas Blake, E.C.R. Lorac and Newton Gayle (the writing team of Muna Lee and Maurice West Guinness), one of the final authors initiated into the Detection Club before the outbreak of the Second World War and with it the demise of the Golden Age. Afterward he continued publishing a detective novel or more a year, with his final book in 1968 reaching a total of 63, all of them detailing the investigative adventures of lanky and bespectacled gentleman amateur detective Ludovic Travers. Concurring as I do with the encomia of Charles Williams and B.A. Pike, I will end this introduction by thanking Avril MacArthur for providing invaluable biographical information on her great uncle, and simply wishing fans of classic crime fiction good times as they discover (or rediscover), with this latest splendid series of Dean Street Press classic crime fiction reissues, Christopher Bush's Ludovic Travers detective novels. May a new "Bush public" yet arise!

Curtis Evans

The Case of the Missing Minutes (1937)

THE GREAT AMERICAN detective novelist Ellery Queen (actually two American cousins, Frederic Dannay and Manfred Lee) once recalled being introduced to an adult education class on "The Mystery Story" by hard-boiled crime writer Dashiell Hammett with the following provocative question from Hammett, concerning the proclivities of the author's brilliant amateur sleuth (who also happens to be named Ellery Queen): "Mr. Queen, will you be good enough to explain your famous character's sex life, if any?" In a later essay, entitled "The Sex Life of a Gentleman Detective" (which likely was written in the 1940s, though it first appeared in book form in 1957), Ellery Queen used the recollection of Hammett's impish query to reflect on the question of what constituted the proper sex life for a fictional sleuth of the contemplative, clue-puzzle school. Queen concluded that there were already plenty enough crime-solving couples (what he termed "conjugal criminologists") in circulation at the moment: "Books, magazines, radio, movies—the woods seem to be full of them, and of all types. . . ." Following leads from Dorothy L. Sayers (Lord Peter Wimsey and Harriet Vane) and Hammett himself (Nick and Nora Charles), mystery writers had responded to what they (and their publishers) perceived that an increasingly feminine mystery reading audience wanted in a detective novel: a humanized Great Detective, someone who lived a life which did not entirely revolve around searching for stray clues in the billiard rooms of bludgeoned baronets.

Up until the late 1930s Christopher Bush's brilliant amateur sleuth Ludovic "Ludo" Travers, seemed, like the fictional Ellery Queen, to lack not only a sexual or romantic life, but much of any sort of personal life to speak of as well. Of course there is Travers' loyal manservant, Palmer, who was with his master's family since Ludo was but an infant in the pram; yet Ludo's father, Major Travers, who had briefly appeared in *The Plumley Inheritance* (1926), the original mystery in the Ludovic Travers series, has, we find in a later novel, passed away. About Travers' mother or any other relatives we learn nothing, outside of a briefly mentioned uncle, Sir George Coburn, Chief Commissioner of Police (evidently retired now), sister, Helen, with whom Ludo regularly weekends at her and her husband Tom's pleasant country house, Pulvery, in Sussex (the county where Christopher Bush himself resided). Travers seems to have resigned his directorship in the mammoth consulting and public relations firm known as Durangos, Ltd., but both the royalties from the books he has authored (which include his widely-known financial tome, *The Economics of a Spendthrift,* and his recent true crime study, *Kensington Gore: Murder for High-brows*) and, presumably, a hefty inheritance from the late Major, allow him to reside comfortably in a posh London flat belonging to a building which he himself owns. His greatest friend seems to be his frequent partner in criminal investigation, Superintendent George "the General" Wharton, though he is on good terms with a great many policemen, including Major Tempest, Chief Constable in Seabourne, the lovely but seemingly murder-ridden resort town in Sussex where Travers has helped solve two particularly baffling slayings, as chronicled in *The Case of the 100% Alibis* (1934) and *The Case of the Chinese Gong* (1935). Yet despite the existence of these productive inter-personal relationships, Travers still seems an essentially solitary sort of person, like so many Great Detectives separated, on account of his egregiously exceptional intelligence, from the common human herd, despite having a vastly more ingratiating personality than Sherlock Holmes. However, in the sixteenth Ludovic Travers detective novel, *The Case of the Missing Minutes* (1937) (*Eight O'Clock Alibi* in the US), we begin to see more of Ludo's personal side, a development that deepens significantly in two subsequent Travers tales, *The Case of the Leaning Man* (1938) and *The Case of the Green Felt Hat* (1939).

Significantly, Travers is brought into *The Case of the Missing Minutes* at the behest of his charming sister Helen, who comes to Ludo's flat in London to tell him about the strange and fearful tidings she has received in a letter from her former personal maid, Lucy, a highly respectable woman. Lucy and her husband,

Fred Yardman, had left service to manage a pub, but, having lost their money during the Slump, the couple recently accepted employment as cook-general and house-parlorman with a gentleman named Quentin Trowte at his domicile, Highways, located in the sleepy little Sussex village of Seabreak, outside Seaborough, the town where Travers, as mentioned above, so kindly and keenly aided the police in the solutions of two murders. Helen persuades Ludo to visit the Yardmans at their bungalow on the grounds of Highways (they are restricted from the main house at night), so that he can try to get to the bottom of their problems with their employer.

Once Travers, his man Palmer in tow, is on the scene in Seabreak with the Yardmans, they unfold to him a disturbing tale of bizarrely eccentric behavior on the part of Quentin Trowte and Jeanne, the strange, ten-year-old granddaughter who resides with him (though at first the servant couple had thought Trowte "a nice old gentleman, sir," as they deferentially explain to Travers, ". . . . plenty of money, though he wasn't one of the real old gentry like yourself"). Then there are the mysterious upstairs locked room at Highways and the unearthly shrieks that emanate from the dwelling in the dead of night. From his questioning of the Yardmans, Travers determines that Trowte does not mistreat Jeanne (to the contrary, the couple maintains that the old man positively fawns on the girl), so who—or what—could be the source of those horrid shrieks?

So far this might seem like the prologue to a melodramatic Edgar Wallace thriller. As a bored Travers, hopefully scenting a juicy mystery in the Yardmans' dark confidings, tells himself, ". . . crime and melodrama were generally the same thing. Only a fool, for instance, would deny from the available information the possibility that the Seabreak house might be a den of counterfeiters, or a nest of spies, or a filthy, furtive shrine of black magic and unholy intercourse."

Yet night shrieks notwithstanding, *The Case of the Missing Minutes* is a true detective novel—one of the best, indeed, that Christopher Bush ever wrote. Not far into Travers' investigation on behalf of the Yardmans, a dead body turns up at Highways, and this death unquestionably is due to foul play. Travers himself discovers the body, at—and this is most important, dear reader—eight minutes to eight in the evening, but naturally he is not suspected of any untoward activity by the Seabourne police force, whose chief constable remains Ludo's friend Major Tempest. In tandem with Tempest and Tempest's underling Inspector Carry, Travers is soon investigating the most poignant case of his career to date, one in which he reveals his humane side to readers as he comes to realize that helping the innocent and the good matters more than merely solving some intriguing chess problem, even if he finds himself at odds with authority, in the imposing form of Superintendent Wharton of the Yard. As the reviewer for the *Times Literary Supplement* noted at the time, "[t]he human interest" in *The Case of the Missing Minutes* "is refreshingly different from that of the general run of detective novels. . ."

Aside from the marked character interest in *The Case of the Missing Minutes*, however, there is, as ever with Christopher Bush, a teasing puzzle element for the reader's delectation. As the title suggests, *The Case of the Missing Minutes* involves a slew of suspects with seemingly iron-clad alibis--some of the strongest, indeed, that Travers has yet encountered. As the gentleman sleuth declares at one point, the culprit has "not only committed a murder," but "also committed a miracle." In this complex case Travers and the team of police investigators (both local and from the Yard) have encountered a killer who seemingly can make time vanish at will, leaving Wharton to complain, "It's that damn ten minutes that's got us all beat. If that murder had only taken place at eight o'clock, everything would fit in right as rain." Can you, dear reader, find those missing minutes? Put on your best sleuthing cap, and give it a try--at the very least you should have fun in the attempt!

I
SOUNDS BY NIGHT

Ludovic Travers's sister Helen took advantage of the wonderful spell of summery weather which arrived in early April, and drove herself from Pulvery to town. In the morning she did some shopping, then met Ludovic as arranged. Over the coffee after lunch he suggested a matinée, but Helen said she was returning at once. Travers blinked in amazement behind his huge horn rims.

"But the day's only beginning!"

"I'm sorry," she said, "but it was really only an excuse my coming to town at all." She smiled. "I don't mean I'm doing anything underhand, but I told Tom I should leave early and come back by the coast road. He thinks I want to view the scenery—poor dear!"

Just like Helen, Travers thought, making the strangest statements in the most matter-of-fact way. His fingers went instinctively to his glasses, which was a trick of his when at some mental loss or on the eve of discovery.

"Let me get this right," he said. "You've come to town so as to go back forty miles out of your Way, and it isn't because you want to admire the scenery."

She smiled. "That's absolutely right. I really want to go to Seabreak."

"Seabreak?" He frowned for a moment. "Oh, yes. Just this side of Seaborough. A village, isn't it? Or would you call it a town?"

"I'd call it an anachronism," Helen said. "It's a sleepy little place that's never been built on or ruined, because it's all privately owned."

"I remember it," Travers announced triumphantly. "Some charming old houses all round a square, and little straggly lanes along the cliffs." He hooked his glasses on again. "But why this sudden passion for Seabreak?"

"I want to see Lucy," she said.

"Lucy?"

"Lucy Brown, that was. Lucy Yardman, as she is now."

"But their pub isn't at Seabreak?"

"Of course it isn't," she said. "If you remember, they lost their money during the depression and went back into service again. She's cook-general and he's house-parlourman. This is their second place and they've been there about eight months. It's with a Mr. Trowte, at a place called Highways. What are you smiling at, Ludo?"

"Was I?" said Travers, and shook a reminiscent head. "I was trying to recall a certain conversation you and I had years ago on the subject of servants. I remember putting it—wholly unwarrantably—into a book."

"And wasn't I right?" she challenged him. "I lose fewer maids than any one in Sussex. Lucy was with me for ten years—"

Travers laughed. "I know all the list. They regard you as a mother and write to you like a friend. All the same, I don't see why you should be going to work in this highly Machiavellian way. I don't mean that you haven't some perfectly good reason."

"I have," she told him quietly. It was strange, he thought afterwards, that she should glance quickly round, though there was no one but Palmer in the flat. "I'm worried about Lucy, and she's worried too. There're all sorts of things I don't understand. And she suggested herself that I should speak to you. She's seen your name sometimes in the papers."

"Good Lord!" said Travers, and blushed.

"I'll tell you just what I know," Helen said. "Lucy acted as my personal maid for a time—that's no news to you—so I know her very well indeed. She is a superior sort of girl, and most trustworthy and reliable. Not the kind, I mean, to talk nonsense or lose her head. Her husband, Fred Yardman, I've never met, but I should say he's very much Lucy's sort. I heard from her first after they'd had trouble and thought of going into service again, and she wrote me to know if I'd act as a reference. Then I heard no more for three years, till last October when she wrote from Seabreak. I kept the address but burnt the letter, and I'm awfully sorry now that I did, because I can't remember just what it was that worried me. She said the pay was good and the work not too hard." She paused there to frown, and gave a shake of the head. "Yet I got the impression that something was wrong, and I remember I wrote back and said if there was anything I could do, she was to let me know at once." She reached for her bag and brought out a letter. "Then two days ago I got this."

> HIGHWAYS,
> SEABREAK,
> *April 7th*.

DEAR MADAM,

I hope you will not think I am taking a liberty and I would not have done this if you had not said I was to write if anything was wrong and you could help.

Fred and I are very worried and we think something is wrong here that ought to be seen into, but we dare not let on to anybody for fear of what might happen to us and we cannot afford to lose our job. I dare not write anything but if you could come this way at any time and see us it would be a mercy for everybody and we would always thank you for what you have done.

We are not allowed to have letters come to the bungalow but Mr. Trowte has them come to the house and then gives them to us. Dear madam, if you could come on a Thursday afternoon, it is my afternoon off. Fred says leave the car in Seabreak and come by road, which is only a little way, and do not go to the house but come to the bungalow, where I shall be on the lookout.

I know you will excuse the liberty I am taking. I have told Fred about Mr. Ludovic when we saw his name in the papers about that murder in Seaborough, and Fred says would Mr. Ludovic come if you cannot come yourself.

I hope you are all well, especially the children. I would love to see them all again.

> Yours respectfully,
> LUCY YARDMAN.

Travers gave his glasses a polish, then read the letter a second time.

"Very curious," he said, and handed it back. "Lucy was a level-headed sort of soul, wasn't she?"

"Very," Helen said.

Travers shook his head. "I don't like it at all. The vagueness of it, and the secrecy. And that rather curious reference to myself." He shook his head again. "I don't think Tom would like you to go."

She smiled. "I know. That's why I didn't tell him."

"You'd like me to go down with you?"

"I don't think so," she said. "After all, I'm only paying a kind of friendly visit to an old servant. I mean, if there is anything really wrong—"

"Criminally wrong?"

"Yes, criminally wrong. If there is, then Lucy will tell me and I can tell you. I can ring you up here some time later. If it's just panic or nerves, then there'll be no harm done." She rose. "I think perhaps I'd better be going now. It's quite a long way and I don't want to be too late."

"Just one minute," Travers said. "I'm not at all sure you ought to mix yourself up with this. And haven't you any more information at all?"

"None whatever," Helen told him calmly. "Lucy wants to see me, and I'm seeing her. As far as any possible outsider is concerned, that's all there is." She smiled. "It may be some kind of mare's nest, after all."

"Yes," said Travers thoughtfully, and fumbled for his glasses. "But this bungalow business. I thought they were indoor servants? What one calls a married couple?"

"Oh, I can explain that," Helen said. "There's a tiny bungalow in the corner of the grounds, quite near the house, and the Yardmans sleep there and have their own personal things. I remember that from Lucy's first letter."

"The man, Trowte. Old, is he?"

She frowned. "I think so. An author, or scholar, I seem to remember. Oh, and his initial's Q. It struck me as rather strange at the time. Q. Trowte, Esquire, Highways, Seabreak. That was the address." She remembered something else. "There's a grand-daughter. A girl of ten, called Jean, or Jeanne, I forget which. . . . Only those two in the house; at normal times, that is. I don't know about guests."

Travers drew in his long legs and hoisted himself from the chair.

"It's happened so abruptly," he said, and gave yet another shake of the head. "Honestly, Helen, I'd rather you didn't go. Let me run down instead."

"Rubbish!" Helen said. "Even if anything serious were wrong—which, most likely, there isn't—I'm quite capable of looking after myself." She smiled. "Besides, I'm simply bursting to hear all about it."

"Hm!" went Travers, and pushed the bell for Palmer, his man. And when Palmer had gone to bring round the car, his mind was made up.

"It's just a quarter to two now," he said. "You should be at Seabreak by four. Say you stay for an hour, that gives you time to ring me up before half-past five. If you haven't rung me up by six o'clock, then I shall come down there myself."

She laughed. "But how dramatic! You surely don't think—"

"It's a funny world," Travers cut in. "And either you accept my ultimatum, or else I go down with you now."

"As you like," Helen told him. "It's very thoughtful of you, and very sweet of you too, but just a bit unnecessary. After all—"

"And one other thing," Travers broke in. "When you leave the car in Seabreak, be sure to let some one know where you're go-ing. You'll have to ask the way in any case."

"Oh, dear," she said, and laughed. "I almost wish I'd kept it all to myself and not told you a thing. You'll really begin to make me nervous if you keep on talking as you do."

"Sorry," said Travers. "Perhaps I am being a bit too mournful. But you'll do as I said?"

She nodded. "Finger wet, finger dry."

It was in the last moment or two before the car moved off that he thought of something else.

"Now I come to think of it, there can't be any possible harm to yourself, or Lucy wouldn't have asked you to come."

"But, my dear," she said, "I never for a moment thought there would be. I was just humouring you when you were being so melodramatic."

"I don't know," he said. "If anything serious is going on down there, you might get involved in it. In any case, it's a tricky business inquiring into the private affairs of private people, even at second hand. Which reminds me. Let me have that letter of Lucy's, will you?"

"You're making me even more inquisitive than ever," she told him, and handed the letter over. "Now I must fly or I shall never get to Pulvery before dark, and you know what Tom is like."

"Just one second," Travers said. "Better be safe than sorry. You know Major Tempest, the Chief Constable at Seaborough, don't you?"

"Of course," she said. "I lunched with him here. Don't you remember?"

"That's right," he said. "Then do this if you really do judge that something very fishy is going on down there. Call and see Tempest, and mention my name, as you go through on your way home. You can phone me from there. You see," he explained, with the most patent insincerity, "it may be something much more in his line than mine. Seabreak comes within his orbit, so to speak."

"Oh, dear," she said, and laughed. "This is getting worse and worse." Her hand went to the lever. "You're going to have a terribly anxious afternoon."

"Don't you believe it," Travers told her. "And don't go thinking about Lucy and taking your eyes off the road."

She made a face at him at that, and the car moved off. A hand emerged and waved at the turn into St. Martin's; Travers nodded heavily at where the car had been, and with a shrug of the shoulders went back to the life.

Superintendent George Wharton of Scotland Yard, who had long been associated with Ludovic Travers—or to whom Travers had very frequently attached himself—in the solving of certain problems of murder, was accustomed to remark with a cynicism beneath which admiration was faintly apparent, that the one thing missing from the vocabulary of the said Travers was the word "inexplicable." Travers, moreover, said Wharton—and again with admiration rather than malice—was the only Know-all and genuine Walking Encyclopedia.

Wharton himself had little reason to discount either the theorizing or the knowledge, from both of which he had frequently profited. Travers would have described the knowledge as of the superficial, cross-word solver's kind, whereas to Wharton—limited in tastes and background—its queer ramifications were a source of perpetual astonishment. "The camel," he was accustomed to say, "has a supercilious look because he alone of all creation knows the hundredth name of Allah. Mr. Travers could probably tell him the hundred-and-first." As for theorizing, Travers, still according to Wharton, could at a second's notice account for such oddities as the larynx of Balaam's ass or the gullet of Jonah's whale. As for the obvious, it never satisfied him. The fact that there are two sides to every question was for him merely an incentive to hunt for a third. And the source of his handsome income, Wharton would say, was probably hush-money paid as a guarantee against exposure by the International Society of Escapologists and Illusionists.

But when Ludovic Travers settled down in his chair that afternoon to puzzle out from her letter what lay at the back of Lucy Yardman's mind, he could find no satisfying answer. He remembered her well: a pleasant, homely, eminently sensible woman, not likely to give way to panic or exaggerate trifles. But what Travers was seeking in the letter was employment for the time that was on his hands and the rust that was settling on an over-leisured mind. That was why he had rejoiced at Lucy's queer reference to the Seaborough murder, though the quick anticipation had expressed itself in no more than the series of precautions which Helen had found so melodramatic. And yet, as Travers hopefully assured himself, crime and melodrama were generally the same thing. Only a fool, for instance, would deny from the available information the possibility that the Seabreak house might be a den of counterfeiters, or a nest of spies, or a filthy, furtive shrine of black magic and unholy intercourse.

Travers, in fact, was fearing the best and hoping for the worst, however much he might disguise it beneath the specious assurance that the sooner the Yardmans were free from anxiety the better for their own and Helen's peace of mind. By the time five o'clock had come, he was almost wishing that Helen would not ring. At a quarter to six, he told himself, he would tell Palmer to pack and have the car ready, and be on the road for Seabreak before Helen could exercise her woman's privilege of being late. Then as he fetched his large-scale map to make certain of the route, the telephone bell went.

"I'm ringing from Seaborough," Helen began, and Travers had a sudden thrill. "Not from Major Tempest's—from some friends of mine. I didn't want to be cut off at the end of my three minutes."

"Didn't anything happen, then?" Travers's thrill had as quickly gone.

"Yes—and no," said Helen, with an irritating reflectiveness. "It's all very vague, and queer. I think I'd have been frightened if I'd stayed very much longer after all the things she told me."

"Why frightened?"

"I don't know," she said. "I'm psychic, I think. I've often meant to tell you so but you'd only have laughed. I sort of felt little shivers in my back."

"Give me some facts," said Travers. "God forbid I should deny the psychic business, but let's begin with facts."

"I can't," she said. "It'd take hours. There're all sorts of—well, underhand, suspicious sorts of things. And every week or so they hear the most awful noises. Enough to curdle your blood, Lucy says. Like somebody absolutely terrified or gone raving mad."

"That's interesting," Travers told her. "Where do the sounds come from?"

"The shrieks? From the house, they think."

"Who's they?"

"The Yardmans. There's no end of a story attached to it, and you'd better hear it from them."

Travers's spare hand went to his glasses, then fell again.

"You really think I ought to run down and see them?"

"My dear, I do wish you would. But about the shrieks. Anybody would think it was the girl—the one I told you about, the granddaughter—but apparently it can't be."

"Why can't it be?"

"Well, her grandfather—the Trowte man—absolutely dotes on her. They'll explain all that down there."

"The shrieking is definitely human?"

"Of course it's human. You couldn't make a mistake about anybody shrieking. It's a kind of muffled shrieking. That's why they think it comes from inside the house."

"Hm!" went Travers. Then, as if dubious: "Do you think Lucy would be startled if I turned up straight away?"

"Oh, my dear, I'd be so glad!" Travers imagined he beard the sigh of relief. "I told her you'd be down, and she said it didn't matter when. But it must be after a quarter to eight. And at the bungalow—not the house."

"Why that peculiar precaution?"

"They'll explain all that," Helen told him hastily. "Now I must stop. I seem to have been talking for hours. But about the bungalow. It's at the east end of the grounds, by the track along the cliffs, all among some trees."

"I'll find it," said Travers. And, somewhat lamely, "Good-by, then. I'll let you know just what turns up."

"I think it's wonderful of you, and most unselfish—"

Travers cut hastily in with, "Don't you think you ought to tell Tom?" But the line was dead. Helen had hung up.

Travers made his way to his chair again and, with long legs outstretched and lean fingers intertwined, began to think things out. Various queer happenings and only one fact—shrieks that came from the house, presumably at night. No occupants of the house but the old man and the child, and therefore, in spite of the Yardmans' objections, the child it must be.

And Helen, saying the place gave her the shivers. Premonitions were queer things and not to be laughed at; faint, atrophied remains, as he thought them, of those spiritual visions and apprehensions which in some dim past had been the natural endowment or sixth sense among men. But in Helen's case it had probably been the gloom of the trees and some loneliness of the spot that had led to the uneasiness; an apt setting for Lucy's story of shrieking that came in the dark.

Then his eyes fell on the clock, and he rang for Palmer and gave him his orders. Palmer showed no surprise. He had valeted Travers's father and had known the infant Ludovic in his first pram. The eccentricities and disregard of convention had long ceased to bewilder or amaze, and behind the old man's diffidence and meticulous respect there were admiration and affection.

"Just one moment," Travers called to him at the door. "Just why does a child shriek?"

"Shriek, sir?" He rubbed his chin. "On account of pain, perhaps, sir. When—er—chastised, for instance."

"Yes," said Travers. "I hadn't thought of that. A parent or guardian is fully entitled to punish a child, and the child's entitled to its shriek."

"Exactly, sir." He gave that quaint, incipient bow of his. "And sometimes, if I might suggest so, sir, it's sheer temper."

"So it is," said Travers. "I hadn't thought of that either."

"Then there are dreams and nightmares, sir. If you'll pardon the liberty, sir, you yourself were very subject to nightmares. And afraid of the dark, sir."

"Was I?" said Travers, and smiled. Then he gave a queer shake of the head. "Curious—isn't it?—but that's precisely how I was feeling just now."

But that faint disquiet passed as Travers threaded the car through the early evening traffic. The suburbs were passed, and the outer, mushroom ring, and the Rolls slipped along towards Tonbridge and the coast. It was a quiet, luminous April night, finer and more warm than many a night of June, though there were signs of later mist and heavy fog, maybe, out at sea. The sun was low as they came into Seaborough, but dusk was in the air when those last three miles were over and Seabreak came into sight on its perch behind the low cliffs.

A modern hotel stood back from the huge square of green among the ancient timbered houses and their bowers of darkening trees. Then, as he stretched his legs and took a breath or two, he smelt the sea air, and his ear caught the sound of waves that lapped the shore below. There was another sound from somewhere of a piano being played, but it came as a kind of after-sound of which he was not quite aware.

The rooms were taken and a late supper arranged for; then Travers had a word with Palmer upstairs.

"I'm going out first," he said, "and you will follow me after a minute or two along the road that skirts the coast out there. I don't quite know what the lie of the land's like, but you'll pick me up and then follow me till I go into a little bungalow that stands in the grounds of a house. You go on to the house itself—as near as you can get to it—and, without making yourself conspicuous, keep an eye out for anything you see. If you should by any chance hear a shrieking sound, try to note down just where it comes from."

So Travers came out first from the hotel porch and stood for a moment facing the darkening square of open green. Then, as he moved off along the grass sidewalk, he noticed that people were standing at the doors of houses, and little groups were on the green itself. Then it suddenly came to him why they were there, and he halted for a moment to listen.

The sound of the piano was coming from an upstairs window of an unseen house along the road which he was about to take; and whoever the player was, there was no doubt about his virtuosity. The notes rippled and cascaded, yet each was clear as a silver bell.

"Lovely, ain't it?"

"Ever so much nicer than on the wireless."

Two women were talking at the door of a cottage as he went by, and he caught the words. Then, as he came to the last house he saw a young couple listening.

"Could you tell me who it is that's playing?" he asked the man.

It was the girl who answered. "It's a famous pianist who's staying here. What was his name, Jack?"

"Milovitch," the man said. "Ephraim Milovitch. The man who sometimes plays on the wireless."

"Very delightful," said Travers, by way of thanks and farewell. The wireless interested him little, and it was only faintly that he recalled the pianist's name.

"Last night he played right till ten o'clock," the girl said. "Ever so many people were listening. Just like on a summer night, it was—people standing about."

Travers smiled in courteous acknowledgment and moved on. The house of the pianist, and its high encircling wall, were passed. There were a big house or two standing back from the road, and then all at once the road dipped, and Travers was at a fork.

He glanced back and caught a movement that would be Palmer, then moved on again along the open, narrow track that skirted the widening wood that lay in an immense triangle between the track and the main road which he had left. Almost at once there were trees on both sides and the track rose through the wood, turned more south and dipped again, and just beneath him Travers could hear the splash and see the faint white of the incoming waves. Then the track petered out. On his right was a narrow strip of land that topped the low cliffs, and there on his left among the trees was what looked like a house, with a tall hedge of cypress towering like a wall.

Beneath that dark wall of hedge Travers now moved on. For a hundred yards it ran unbroken; then all at once there was a gap, and a low gate, and beyond it a short path and a building which was certainly a bungalow. But for a minute he made no move to open the gate, but listened intently, and watched the low blackness beneath the cypress arch. From the windows there was never a sign of light, and there was no sound.

Then suddenly there was a sound, and Travers stayed motionless by the dark hedge and held his breath. Then it went, and he could neither place it nor say what kind of sound it was; but as he strained to listen, it came again. It grew to a shriek—a muffled sound that was distant and yet curiously near. It came again, longer drawn-out, like the frightened shriek of a woman at the sight of a mouse or rat. Then it was gone, and the night was uncannily still, as if the silence had never been disturbed.

Then as suddenly there was another sound—the opening of a door. A dim light was along the path, and silhouetted against the brighter light behind her was a woman. Her head was sideways and, like himself, she was listening motionless.

"Is that you, Lucy?"

He saw her start at the sound of his voice, and as he groped for the latch of the gate she called in a kind of frightened whisper:

"Who is it there?"

"It's all right," he said; "it's Travers—Ludovic Travers."

He closed the gate behind him and came quickly along the path.

"One step, sir," she said, and her hand felt for his arm and drew him through the door. In a moment the door was closed, and he was aware that the hand which had guided him had been shaking like a leaf.

II
TRAVERS THEORIZES

THE THREE were in a small room on the right of the tiny entrance hall and, even before she introduced her husband to Travers, Lucy was apologizing for the cramped space and the bad light.

"You don't mind, sir, if we leave the lamp a bit low?" Fred Yardman said. "And we mustn't talk loud, sir. You never know who's about."

Travers liked the look of the man; quiet-spoken, efficient-looking and obviously reliable. He was of the butler type, with a colour inclined to reddish purple. That, thought Travers, might be a relic of his years of retirement. His age would be about sixty-five, but he carried himself like a man of fifty.

"You haven't aged much, Lucy," Travers told her, with a friendly smile that recalled innumerable things.

"That's because you don't know, sir," she told him quietly. "Let Mr. Travers have that chair, Fred. He always likes a low chair." And as Travers made a half-hearted protest: "If you only knew how glad we are to see you, sir."

"And I'm glad to see you," Travers told her. "My sister telephoned me soon after she left here, and I thought it would be as well if I came."

"Can I get you something, sir?" Yardman broke in. "There's only beer in the house, sir, but we can get you some tea."

"Nothing, thank you," Travers said. "I may not have a lot of time, and I'd like to hear all about these troubles of yours."

"You heard the shrieking, sir?"

"Yes," said Travers, with deliberate reflection. "I did hear what might be taken for shrieking. But let's leave that—do you mind?—and begin from when you came here. I'd like to visualize the house itself and your employer and everything."

Yardman began the story, and Travers, always somewhat puzzled why he should be made the depository of other people's secrets, was unaware as ever of the qualities that invited them. But he was always the perfect listener, charmingly mannered and supremely well-informed. For all his disregard of diehard convention and his occasional quaint mannerisms, one knew oneself assuredly in the company of a man of breeding; a man with a rare insight, with whom confidences would be safe and to whom sharp practice was an abominable thing.

The Yardmans had come to Highways for an interview with Quentin Trowte before they accepted the poet, and considered him a genial kind of crank. He had had the bungalow specially built for a married couple, and in consideration of the extra work it would involve for Lucy—keeping it clean and preparing some sort of late meal for her husband and herself—he had offered twenty-five pounds a year more than they could possibly have expected elsewhere. His little granddaughter Jeanne, whom he had just adopted on the death of her parents, would make no extra work, for he proposed to look after her himself to the extent at least of a man's abilities. There was a gardener also employed, but their only contact with him would be concerned with vegetables for the kitchen.

"We thought him a nice old gentleman, sir," Yardman said. "A bit queer in his ideas perhaps, but plenty of money, though he wasn't one of the real old gentry like yourself. What really struck us as unusual was the arrangement for the evening. There was to be a kind of late high tea or early supper at seven o'clock, which would be over at half-past. Then we were to clear away and, whether washing-up was done or not, we were to be out of the house by a quarter to eight, and we weren't on any account to have anything to do with the house till half-past seven next morning; just as if we'd gone clean away for the night."

"I understand," Travers said. "Just as if you were living in the village."

"That's right, sir," Yardman said. "And the reason he gave was that he liked to have a short time to find out what Jeanne—that's the granddaughter—had been learning during the day; and also he was a great reader and hated to be disturbed. A learned old gentleman, we took him for, who might be writing a book."

"The granddaughter was there during your interview?" put in Travers.

"Yes, sir; he called her in. He kept pinching her cheek and calling her pretty names—you know, sir, like he would do to a child. She looked a bit nervous of him, sir; almost frightened, you might say. We put it down to how she was shy, just having come there, and we put it down to him. A rather unusual-looking man, Mr. Trowte is, sir, and we reckoned she hadn't got used to him."

"And those two have always been the only occupants of the house?"

"Never a guest at all, sir. There's a tutor, a Mr. Howcrop, who comes mornings and afternoons, and he's a queer one too. I reckon this place has got on his nerves like it has on ours."

Travers knew that latter for himself. For all his tactful greeting of Lucy, she had changed from a buxom, fresh-coloured young woman to something he would hardly have recognized. Her fresh colour had gone; the hair was greying at her temples, and she looked nervy, worn and tired. And her age, as he quickly reckoned it, would be little more than forty; and it was only eight years since he had seen her last.

"Now tell me about the shrieking," Travers said. "When you heard it first, and at what times, and so on."

Yardman went to a chiffonier, unlocked a drawer and came back with a paper.

"I've got it all written down, sir, as near as we can remember it. The first time we heard it was a fortnight after we got here, which was the end of last September. We'd just settled down in here at about eight o'clock when we both heard it. 'That's Miss Jeanne,' Lucy said, and I thought the same, because we knew she went to bed at a quarter to eight, and her room's at the side, facing this way. Awful, it was, like some one being murdered, and off I ran to the house and hammered on the door—"

"The shrieking was still going on?"

"No, sir, it stopped just before I got there. I waited a bit and I tried the door, which was locked, and, as far as I could see, the whole place was dark as pitch. Then all at once the door opened and Mr. Trowte was there. I told him what I'd heard and asked if anything was wrong. It was moonlight, sir, and I could see him plain as he stood in the door, and I never saw any one's face like it. I thought he was going to spring on me, sir, and get his two hands on me and strangle me. And didn't he let me have it? Reckoned he hadn't heard a noise, and if there was one it'd come from the road back over there. And he reckoned that if I ever made a fool of myself and him like that again he'd sack us both at a minute's notice. Next morning he acted as if nothing had happened; but that shrieking came from the house all right, sir. It was too near to come from the road."

Travers nodded. "I'll have a look at the lie of the land to-morrow. Meanwhile, may I take a copy of that list?"

There were three occasions, with varying intervals, when the shrieking had been heard at about eight o'clock, not counting the sounds that had been heard that very evening, which, Lucy said, were as nothing compared with the horror of the others. Then there were two occasions when the shrieking had occurred before the Yardmans went to bed, which was at about half-past ten, and three occasions when one or the other had been wakened up by it during the night.

"Now," said Travers, "I want us to work this out together. Would you be prepared to swear on oath that the sounds came from the house? . . . You would. Then let's try an analysis of possible causes. You have given me to understand, Lucy, that the child is frightened of—or, shall we say? over-awed by—her grandfather. We'll go into that later. But let's arrive at it this way. From anything in the child's conduct that you have observed, is her grandfather likely to punish her? Thrash her, to put it crudely."

"She's a wicked child," Lucy said, and shook her head with a vicious determination. "She's crafty, and a liar and a tale-teller—"

"That's enough to go on with," said Travers dryly. "Then did her grandfather punish her in such a way that she shrieked with fright or pain?"

"She never was punished, sir," said Lucy with conviction. "I have to see to her clothes and her bath, and her body's never a mark or bruise. And he'd never punish her. He encourages her, if anything, and he makes you sick to hear how he talks."

"And how does he talk?"

Lucy looked at her husband, and he took up the tale.

"You wouldn't understand it, sir. It's a sort of'-there he spread his hands as if imitating a cringing man—"a sort of leering, you might call it. 'Wouldn't my little girl like to do this?' or, 'I'm sure my little Jeanne wouldn't do that.' He sort of pleads with her. Like as if he was humouring her." He shook his head. "I can't explain it any more, sir. It's just as if he fair doted on her. Always smiling and grinning and bowing. And you ought to see them of an afternoon, when he takes her for her walk. Holds her hand just as if she was a toddler."

"Yes," said Travers. "I think I begin to see. Her name is Trowte?"

"Yes, sir. The only daughter of the old man's only son—that's how we've worked it out."

Travers leaned forward in the chair. "Dotage, as you say. And yet—tell me if I'm right—there's something disagreeable about the relationships between the two."

"It gets on your nerves," said Lucy. "You see, sir, when we came we were told that we weren't to talk to the child at all, which, I may say, we thought rather peculiar. We'd never have dreamt of making ourselves familiar, but we weren't to speak to her at all. Everything necessary had to be done through him. Once I whispered something to her up on the top landing, and she went and told him."

Yardman broke in there. "You see, sir, it's like this. It gets on your nerves because it sort of goes on and we don't have anything to do with it. There's him and her, like we said, and all we do is hear it. She's as if she wasn't there at all as far as we're concerned, except when you meet her on the stairs or anywhere and she scowls at you or sort of cringes out of your way."

Travers shook his head. "A peculiar business, as you say. But about the shrieking heard later in the night. Is she likely to suffer from nightmares?"

"I don't know, sir," Yardman said. "Cunning as a weasel is how she strikes me. Always looking shifty-like."

"I think perhaps she might have nightmares," Lucy said. "Once or twice, as Fred knows, I've seen her all of a shake, when she didn't know I was looking. Making the most awful faces, like as if she was going to cry, or have a fit."

"That trouble she had with her inside might have caused that," Yardman said contemptuously.

"Trouble?"

"Two bad bouts of sickness," Lucy said. "Over-eating, I shouldn't be surprised—"

"Oh, no," Yardman cut in. "She hardly eats enough to keep a sparrow alive, unless the old man forces her. I will say that for her. Not forces, exactly. He sort of wheedles her into it. I'm always hearing him when I'm in and out."

"What's wrong with her is growing pains," Lucy told him. "That's one thing I do agree with Mr. Trowte in."

"What did the doctor say?—if they had a doctor."

"They had a doctor—Doctor Mannin," Lucy said. "Him and Mr. Trowte regular had words. Mr. Trowte was positive it was one thing and the doctor another. That's what I thought, though I wasn't supposed to hear."

"Well, we're getting off the track," Travers said. "Let's go back to the reasons for the shrieking. Is the child afraid of the dark?"

"There isn't any dark, sir. There's electric light in her room, and it's always in order, far as I know."

"Hm!" went Travers, and thought for a moment. "Let's leave the shrieking and talk about Mr. Trowte. What's wrong with him, except his fads and his apparently absurd dotage in the matter of Jeanne?"

There was a moment or two's silence, each looking at the other. Lucy opened her lips, then closed them. Then Yardman gave a little nervous clearing of the throat.

"It's funny to say, sir. Everything's peculiar about him and the house too. We're just like two sort of slaves working about the place, and everywhere's quiet and—well, it's as though nothing was happening, really, and something underhand was going on. There's that peaky-faced child sort of watching you, and the old man watching you, and the tutor watching you and never saying a thing." He shook his head. "It's all unnatural, that's what it is, sir. Like living on the edge of a volcano, as they say."

"Ever any visitors at night? I mean, any glasses dirtied or signs of any one having been in?"

"Never, sir."

"Then the tutor," Travers said. "Tell me all about him."

"Mr. Howcrop, sir? Well, he comes at half-past nine every morning except Sunday and stops till twelve. Afternoons he comes from two till three. Him and Miss Jeanne work in the morning-room and you never hear a sound. I take in a cup of tea for him and a glass of milk for Miss Jeanne at eleven, and they're both like dumb images, peering at me as it I was going to steal something. Once or twice I've given him his hat and coat when he was leaving, and all he's done is grunt and look at me under his eyebrows as if I was dirt."

"What age man is he?"

"About fifty, I'd say, sir. He's a gentleman, sir, I'll say that for him. Any one can tell that."

"You ought to know," Travers said. "But to go back to Mr. Trowte. You said he watched you."

"And so he does, sir," Lucy said. "You can feel his eyes behind your back. Then there's that listening to tales. That first time I was so wild I almost packed up and went."

"No use talking like that," her husband told her. "What chance do we stand of getting anything else, at my age? You've got to grin and bear a lot in service, sir."

"Yes," said Travers, "I'm afraid that's only too true. But just what was that first occasion you were referring to, Lucy?"

She gave a little indignant sniff. "One day last October, sir, when he sent for us both to the dining-room and Miss Jeanne was there. He said he'd been informed we'd made certain remarks about both him and her which he wouldn't overlook a second time, and he quoted some of our very words we'd spoke in the kitchen."

"It was the child who'd been listening?"

"Who else could it have been, sir? No one else come near the kitchen, I will say that for him." Another indignant sniff. "Then it happened another time soon after, just like it did before; and if we'd had any self-respect we'd have packed up and gone, after how he spoke. Ever since then we've had to watch every word or talk in whispers, and if that wouldn't get on your nerves, sir, what would?"

"I've even had an idea that he comes round here sometimes at night," Yardman said. "We keep the blinds drawn tight, sir, and we save our talking for when we're in bed."

"And what about that room upstairs he keeps locked?" Lucy said. "Shuts himself in there, and we're never allowed to set foot in it or tidy up or anything. Even the keyhole's stopped up—the old keyhole, I mean—and he's got a Yale lock on the door that no one can't see through."

Travers drew in a deep breath and let it slowly out. Then his fingers were fumbling at his glasses and he was shaking his head.

"I think perhaps I'll leave it at that, for the present." He smiled. "You see, it's all somewhat confusing to me, being a stranger to the place and the conditions, and so on. Not that you haven't told me a lot—and very clearly." He got to his feet. "I think perhaps—"

"Not so loud, sir, please."

"Sorry," said Travers, and lowered his voice to a whisper. "Tell me, at what time does the tutor leave? Midday, wasn't it?"

"That's right, sir."

"And at what time does Mr. Trowte take the child for a walk?"

"At three-fifteen to the dot, sir. They go out the front way, if it's fine, and down the steps to the beach."

"Then I'll make it my business to run an eye over them all some time to-morrow," Travers said. "I'll also look at the lie of the grounds and make a few very discreet enquiries. And I think I know a way to call on Mr. Trowte some time to-morrow night, after eight o'clock. That's the vital time."

"The vital time, sir?"

"Yes," said Travers, and instinctively sat down again to take his theorizing at his ease. "But let me say this first. Whether anything wrong is going on, I don't know. I'm certain that something remarkably curious is going on, and I'm prepared to stay down here till I'm certain that the remarkable isn't the reprehensible, so to speak." He smiled. "Sorry, but I'm rather anticipating things. Let's get back to the vital time—which is eight o'clock and after. And I'll tell you I'm pretty sure about it."

Yardman nodded, eyes never leaving Travers's face.

"Take this bungalow, built specially to house your two selves. There's plenty of room in the house, isn't there, for you to sleep?"

"There's two bedrooms, sir, that used to belong to the staff."

"Exactly!" said Travers triumphantly. "You were not wanted in the house after eight o'clock; I'll even go so far as to say it was urgent that you should on no account be there after eight o'clock. The excuse that he didn't want to be disturbed is a preposterous one. Indoor servants needn't disturb. All he had to do was banish you up to your room with strict instructions to stay there—that is, if he was faddy about being interrupted in any special work he was doing."

"You're right, sir." His hand rose as if to give a confirmatory thump. "Mr. Travers is right, Lucy. It's plain as a pike-staff."

"Then there's—"

But suddenly Travers broke off. His hand went to his glasses and off they came, and he was polishing away and snapping his eyes in the light of the lamp.

"I'm going to suggest something," he said. "Something you might call dangerous, and which we'd better dismiss from our minds as soon as we've talked it over. This locked room. Where is it, precisely?"

"Upstairs, sir," Yardman said. "A room that was once a bedroom, I should say."

"It'd be a biggish room," added Lucy.

"Ever hear the least sound from it in the daytime?"

"No, sir," said Yardman promptly. "Mr. Trowte, he goes up there and stays there all the morning. At least, that's where I think he goes, because I never see him about."

Travers nodded. "Then I put it to you," he said, "that in the circumstances it's most strange that the shrieking noises should on various occasions have begun as soon as you were definitely out of the house. You see the implication?"

Yardman shook his head and looked at his wife.

"Then I'll approach the matter from another angle," Travers said. "Are we so sure that those noises are made by a child? Mightn't they be made by a woman? Or even any demented person?" He shook his head dolefully as he hooked back the glasses. "I'm afraid that lets the cat out of the bag."

"My God, sir, you may be right," Yardman said. "There might be some one up there we don't know about."

"Yes," said Travers. "That person might be under a hypodermic all day and be allowed to come to as soon as you two are out of the house." He got to his feet. "But dismiss it all from your minds. At the moment it's too dangerous even to think of."

Lucy half rose, fingers to her lips and eyes staring.

"I daren't stay there, sir. I daren't."

Travers's hand went to her shoulder. "Oh, yes, you dare. There's nothing to be frightened of—either of you. Act as you always do, whatever happens."

She shook her head. "I can't stand it much longer. I can't, sir. If only we could get away from here."

"That's all right," Travers smiled at her. "You'll go on sticking it out for a day or two till we can clear things up. Besides, I may know of something that may suit you both."

Her face lighted up. "Oh, sir, if you could!"

"She'll be all right, sir," whispered Yardman as Travers moved towards the door.

"I know that," Travers told him, and then more loudly. "Expect me to-morrow night, somewhere about this time. Good night to both of you—and, no worrying."

Yardman's hand went out, and the door opened. Travers stepped cautiously out to the faintly lighted path, then at once the door was closed behind him and he was in the dark. He stood for a moment listening then moved forward shufflingly to the gate.

"That you, sir?"

Travers's heart gave a leap, and it was a moment or two before he spoke.

"It's me all right, Palmer. Keep in close till we get back to the road."

In a minute or two his eyes were used to the dark. The hedge was left behind, but it was not till they came to the fork that Travers halted.

"You heard those shrieking sounds while I was waiting at the gate before I went in? Where'd you think they came from?"

"From the house, sir."

"A child, was it, do you think?"

"Perhaps it was, sir, if I may say so."

"It couldn't have been a woman?"

Palmer thought for a moment or two, and then thought that it might have been a woman. Travers nodded complacently into the dark.

"Something happened while you were inside the bungalow, sir," Palmer said.

"Something happened? What was it?"

"Well, sir, I waited a bit while you were inside, then moved along the hedge. I'd come to the conclusion, sir, that you might be engaged for a considerable time—"

"Yes, yes," Travers told him impatiently. "But what was it that happened?"

"I was coming to it, sir," said Palmer imperturbably. "I went along the hedge, sir, groping, as you might say, till I came to the main gate, and just as I got there, sir, I heard some one coming, so I crouched down, sir, afraid to breathe, in a manner of speaking. It was a man, sir. I could see him against the sky."

"Go on," said Travers. "What happened then?"

"He stood there quite a time, sir, then gave a grunt and opened the gate cautiously. That's all I saw of him, sir—or heard either, till about ten minutes before you came out. I'd moved back there, sir, waiting for you, when I heard a noise again, and then I saw a match struck and there was a man having a quick look at something. His watch, I think it was, sir."

"The same man?"

"That I can't say, sir, but I know he came out of the grounds, because I heard a noise like some one breaking through a hedge."

"You'd recognize him again?"

"I think so, sir. He had a long sort of face, and something queer on his head like a big hat. Of course, if I may be allowed to make the observation, sir, I only saw him for the flash of the match, as you might say."

"Right," said Travers. "To-morrow we'll make a tour of the village and see if you can pick him up." Then suddenly he gave a little grunt. "I don't know, but I've got a remarkably curious feeling inside."

"Emptiness, if I may suggest it, sir," Palmer said. "Your last meal, I believe, sir, was at one o'clock."

"And what's the time now?"

"Just gone ten, sir. I rubbed a phosphorous match on the wet palm of my hand, sir, and looked at my watch."

"Did you, by Jove!" said Travers, and then remembered. His voice lowered. "Better get back to the hotel and do our talking there."

III
TRAVERS EXPLORES

Travers woke next morning with a vague uneasiness at the back of his mind, but long before Palmer came in with early tea he knew precisely what the uneasiness was.

Palmer had been positive that the unknown man had come through the hedge beyond the bungalow, which, Travers gathered, was the extreme east corner of the grounds. Two problems of vital importance had therefore to be immediately considered. The first—that the unknown had followed himself and Palmer from the village—was possible but extremely unlikely; though, in the rare event of that quick espionage, a new gravity and a new mystery were only too obvious.

More likely was it that the unknown was either a caller at Highways or making an investigation by night for some unlawful purpose. As for the former, Palmer was again positive that there had never been the faintest sign of a light from the house, as of a door opening, for instance, when the man was admitted. But that, argued Travers, might only show that the man was admitted in the deliberate dark, which made the call something of tremendous significance.

But the chief danger, as Travers saw it, was that the man had emerged from the grounds near the bungalow, which implied, if it implied anything at all, that he had been listening at the darkened windows. And yet, thought Travers, what could he have heard? Voices, save for a moment's forgetfulness, had always been low, in fact, little more than a murmur. Perhaps the best thing to do would be to make a test. That evening, when he paid his second visit to the bungalow, after calling on Trowte, he would get Lucy and her husband to talk inside and listen himself at the outside window.

As for the identity of the man, Travers saw no point in speculation. But one point in connection with his nocturnal prowling did strike him as particularly interesting. The visit to the grounds of Highways had been furtive and stealthy. *X,* therefore—the unknown man—had to avoid recognition. And yet he had run the risk of flashing a match to see the time. A flash it had been, and no more, but yet the risk had been there. Why, then, had X taken that risk? *Why was it so necessary for him to know the time?*

But Travers had no uneasiness in his mind when he came down to his first Seabreak breakfast. There was mist in the air, but the sun looked like breaking through for another day of premature summer. And the day before him was the kind in which his soul delighted. There he was in complete charge of a case; not a murder case, but something which had endless possibilities, and on his old friend Tempest's very beat. A case to one's self, with no hampering officialdom and obvious routine. The Seabreak world, in fact, his oyster, which he was proposing to spend a day in prizing open.

The hotel was a modern one, with a spacious lounge in the corner of which was the bureau of the manageress. Only two other guests were in residence, and Travers had the lounge to himself when he installed himself there with *The Times* and waited for the manageress to put in an appearance. Then he changed his mind and approached what looked like the hotel's handyman, who had the air of a native and an old inhabitant.

"Just a moment," he said, "but do you happen to know the village well?"

"I ought to, sir," the man told him. "Except for five years in London, I've been here all my life. In the West End I was, sir."

Travers allowed himself to be suitably impressed.

"Then you're just the man I want. You know a place called Highways."

"Highways? Yes, sir. Just along the Rye road, sir, about a quarter of a mile."

"Is my old friend Giles still there?"

"Giles?" He stared. "I never heard of any Giles, sir. A man named Trowte lives there now. Been there just over a year. A Colonel Staithe had it before him. Died about two years ago, which was why it was sold."

"Staithe," said Travers, and smiled. "I used to know a Staithe. Between sixty and seventy he'd be. A tallish man—"

"That wouldn't be him, sir," the other cut in. "Colonel Staithe what had Highways was a little, short man, and only about fifty he was when he died. Something he got in the war, so they reckoned."

"A pity," said Travers, by no means dissatisfied. "But you said the place was sold. Now, I understood the whole of Seabreak was in one ownership."

"So it is, sir," the man told him. "The Vendors have always had it. Sir Anthony Vendor it is now. That's why they haven't allowed the place to be altered—ruined, I ought to say—like them other places all along the coast."

"I see," said Travers. "The various properties are let on lease, with definite restrictions."

A half-crown changed hands, and Travers went back to his chair. Now the last part of his day's work was arranged for, and he began imagining the scene. That child went to bed at a quarter to eight. Immediately after that would be time to call, and it might be better to approach the house from some easterly direction, as if he had come in from Rye or Winchelsea. That might invite a certain delay, and maybe the offer of refreshment.

So Travers saw himself knocking at the door, and ultimately the queer-looking Trowte opening it.

"May I see Colonel Staithe?"

And with that imaginary ball set rolling, Travers left it. The rest of the conversation would arise out of that one question, after which it would be up to him to manage an entry and have some talk with Trowte. As for the earlier work of the day, Travers had it planned; and since ten o'clock was zero hour, he settled to the cross-word and a first pipe with the perfect detachment of one who knows each situation well in hand.

Ten o'clock came. Travers laid aside his paper stretched his legs, and made for the porch.

"A lovely day, sir," the manageress said.

"Yes," said Travers. "If this goes on, you'll soon have the hotel full."

"I don't think it will last," she said. "If you ask me, we're going to have fog. Quite thick, it was, early this morning."

Travers smiled. "I'm afraid I can't confirm that. But you get pretty bad fogs here?"

"All the year round," she told him. "Kind of sea mists they are really."

Travers went out to the porch, and stood there for a time, taking deep breaths of the morning air and finding a strange contentment in the scene. Very English and peaceful, he thought it, and saddening curiously in the memories it evoked. An anachronism, perhaps, as Helen had said; or was it that the rest of England—like that gaudy south coast—was the anachronism? Nothing modern lay beneath his eye save the colourful globes of the petrol pumps at the little garage by the school. Half a dozen shops seemed reticently hidden as if careless of custom. But a scarlet pillar-box in front of what must be the post office—that was modern, and yet somehow it was not. And there was the police station; that red-roofed house with "EAST SUSSEX CONSTABULARY" conspicuously displayed. A pity those massed trees concealed the church, he thought; and then wondered what children were doing, playing on the green, till he remembered that it was just after Easter and their holidays were still on.

There was a sound behind him, and all at once Palmer came through the door. In his ceremonial black and with his fine features and silver hair, he had the look of an archdeacon in mufti.

"A lovely morning, sir. If I may say so, a perfect morning."

"It is," said Travers, and broke off to stare. "Who's that queer bird coming round the corner there?"

The queer bird was a man of medium height, wearing a velvet jacket, over which was a flowing cape, and a voluminous tie. A black sombrero hat seemed perched on the head, so enormous was the mass of hair. With him was a woman; tall, smartly dressed, scarlet-lipped and altogether very chic and modern.

There was the sound of the door again, and the manageress came out. As Travers turned to make the question, she supplied the answer.

"Oh, look! There's Milovitch, the pianist!"

"So that's the pianist," said Travers.

"I wish he was staying here." The smile had all the wistfulness of a fan.

"Good publicity for you," Travers said. "But he's living at a house on the edge of the village, isn't he?"

"At Channel View," she said. "They've taken it furnished for a week."

"And who's the lady?"

"Well,"—she was all at once girlish—"they say it's his secretary."

"Splendid," said Travers. "Then we'll say she's his secretary too. But they're coming this way. I think I'll get in."

So Travers reclaimed his *Times* and went up to his room. Before he had been there a couple of minutes there was a tap at the door, and Palmer was in the room. Something had happened, for he was blowing a bit from a quick rush up the stairs.

"That man, sir—the pianist!"

Then as Travers waited, he gave his little bow.

"I beg your pardon, sir. But the pianist, sir. He's the man I saw last night."

Travers flew across to the side window that overlooked the square. But nothing could have been in sight, for he was back at once.

"You must be mistaken," he said. "It's ridiculous. I mean, a man like that prowling about at night and getting through hedges! He looks as though he'd faint if he felt a draught."

Palmer listened impassively and with dignity.

"If I may take the liberty, sir, I would venture to insist, sir, that he was the man I saw."

Travers smiled and shook his head.

"The flash of a match in the dark. You're wrong. You must be wrong."

"I still regret to insist, sir—"

Then Travers did a rare thing—he cut in with a sudden impatience.

"Heavens, man, can't you ever be direct?"

Palmer drew himself up.

"Then it's you who're wrong, sir. I tell you it was the man."

Travers stared for a bewildered moment, rather like one who has been suddenly savaged by a pet rabbit. Then he laughed, and he clapped the old fellow on the shoulder.

"Splendid, Palmer, splendid! We'll take it from now on that he was the man. But—er—any unquestionable reasons?"

"Merely his face, sir," Palmer said. "It was a long face, sir, and rather white, and a big nose."

"Yes," said Travers reflectively. "A big nose. Semitic, shall we say? And you said he had something big on his head. That would have been his mop of hair; it couldn't have been a hat." He frowned. "That rather upsets things, in a way. Yet I don't know. Perhaps you'd better bring round the car as arranged."

Palmer departed, and Travers took another squint through the side window. Then he frowned. For a long minute he appeared to be thinking hard, then he gave a shrug of the shoulders.

For all Palmer's delicious and rebellious insistence, he himself was very far from convinced. And yet, a furnished house taken for a week—there might be something in that. It might not be unprofitable some time later to ring up a certain party in town and ask for full information about Ephraim Milovitch. Milovitch—Semitic—his secretary—long face; the thoughts went round and round, and ended at another shrug of the shoulders. If the day itself ended with no definite disclosures, then Travers was deciding to call in some extra aid and keep both Highways and the house of the pianist under observation.

But other work was in hand, and he made his way down to the car. Palmer drove, and slowly. At the last houses of the village Travers cocked an eye up at Channel View. Quite a small house, it seemed, and little more than a cottage. Glass in the roof, however, which meant a studio, and that had doubtless appealed to the pianist.

The last house was left, and Travers surveyed and tried to memorize the countryside. The car drew up at the fork, and along the right-hand edge of the triangle of woods he could follow the track he had taken in the dusk and mark the wild, uncultivated land with its patches of gorse and little white outcrops of chalk. Then the car moved on again, with woods still on the right, till all at once there was a gap.

"Draw up and then back," Travers said.

From where the car was stopped he saw the gap was a private road, weedy and narrow. At the far end, two hundred yards away, was a splash of red, which would be the roof of Highways.

"It mightn't be a bad idea to come down this way to-night," Travers said. "Gloomy, perhaps, at a quarter to eight, but not too dark to see. Move on again and keep it slow."

That main road all at once turned towards the coast, and Travers gave the sign to stop.

"Take the car on where you like," he said, "provided you're back by lunch. And if you should happen to go into a pub and there's any one with any intelligence in the saloon bar, bring the talk round to our friend Milovitch."

The car moved on, and Travers slipped at once into the open wood. Almost at once it thinned, and he was out on the chalky cliffs with the line of coast so brazenly and unexpectedly before him that he felt a kind of nakedness. In a moment he was behind a handy clump of gorse. From the village to where he was, the coast made a perfect bay, so that to go back by the shingly beach would be a short cut. Boats were moored in under the undulating cliffs, and there were the steps which Lucy had mentioned. There was Highways, a bare three hundred yards away, with its tall cypress hedge. No sign of the bungalow, but that would be hidden in its trees. Concealment of some sort would almost certainly have been made a condition under which Trowte was permitted to erect it. About a couple of acres of ground, there looked, or maybe three; protected by the wood at the back, and facing due south. An oldish house, by the look of it, and much smaller than he had thought. A man on the green patch between hedge and house, and pushing something. The gardener, it would be, rolling the lawn. A lot of work for one man, and no wonder that private road had looked overgrown and neglected.

That preliminary survey ended, Travers produced from his pocket a fountain pen and a pad, and wrote a long letter to Helen. He seemed in no hurry. Now and again he would peer round his shelter at the house again, or watch out to sea where the faint smoke trailed from the Channel traffic. Then at last it was ten minutes to twelve by his watch, and he slipped back through the wood to the main road. Twelve o'clock found him at the fork again. A moment or two as of indecision, and he turned back along the track in the direction of Highways.

As he breasted the short rise by the bend, he came full on the man he had planned to meet. He was tallish—three good inches perhaps below Travers's lamp-post length—and was wearing a suit of grey with a double-breasted coat, and a straw hat. Yet the hat was somehow not incongruous, but part of the general Edwardianism that characterized the man; for he twirled a handsome stick, and had a silky moustache with turned-up ends, and his collar looked the old-fashioned kind, with a sort of Gladstonian split.

"Pardon me," said Travers, "but would you tell me if this—er—road will take me to Winchelsea?"

"God bless my soul, no!" Howcrop said heartily. Then he ran a quick eye over the questioner. "You've taken the wrong road, my dear sir. This is—er—a cul-de-sac."

"I should have kept to the main road?"

"That's right." He gave a little twirl to the corner of his moustache. Sixty, Travers guessed his age. Rather like some retired colonel of his boyhood, but Oxford very definitely.

"Thank you very much," Travers said, and turned back.

"I'm going your way," Howcrop said breezily. "I'll put you right."

Before they had gone a dozen yards, Travers was shaking his head.

"What is the time, do you think?"

"Just gone twelve."

"Then I don't think I'll push on to Winchelsea till after lunch. There's a decent hotel in the village here, I believe."

"Two at least," Howcrop said, eyes still surveying the stranger with a kind of furtiveness. "You're not one of these—er—hikers, are you?"

He gave a little laugh at what was apparently a joke. Travers smiled.

"In a sense I suppose I am. You're living here yourself?"

"Well—yes, yes." He had a blustering way of talking, as if it was necessary to create some impression of importance. "Been here some years, as a matter of fact. You—er—know these parts?"

"Yes, and no," said Travers maliciously. "By the way, you won't think me rude, but haven't I run across you somewhere before?"

Howcrop shot him a most curious look, then stopped in his tracks. "Seen me before? Why—what's your name?"

"Travers."

He pursed his lips. "Don't remember you. Must have been somebody else. I've been abroad a lot. I mean, I don't see—"

"I think you're right," Travers said. "I'm awfully sorry, but I remember now the man I took you for." He gave a sheepish shake of the head. "Curious how people do look like other people. Most unpardonable of me, though."

"That's all right, that's all right," Howcrop assured him largely. "A perfectly natural mistake. I leave you here, by the way. Er—good luck to you. You'll find the Magpie as good as any for lunch."

They were at the first houses of the village, and he turned to the right down a narrow lane. Travers moved on towards lunch and in the meanwhile chewed the cud of thought. A gentleman, certainly, as Yardman had said, but a weird survival all the same. Reminded one of an old-time johnny, with his haw-haw and twiddly moustache and Malacca. A tiny bit red and bulbous about the nose, and his suit the least bit threadbare. A tutor—old-fashioned word in itself. A thankless, pitiable job, and undoubtedly a come-down. Which might explain that look—half shame, half alarm—at the mention of having been seen else-where before.

Palmer came to the room as soon as Travers went upstairs. He had nothing to report about Milovitch. There had indeed been a wireless going within earshot of the saloon bar he had chosen at Rye, and he had happened to mention to its other two occupants that a man supposed to be a famous pianist was stay-ing at Seabreak.

"One man said he'd never heard of him, sir," said Palmer apologetically, "and the other one, sir, that wireless ought to be stopped."

Travers smiled. "And how much did the information cost?"

"Three bitters, sir."

"Let's call it eighteen-pence," Travers said, his hand going to his pocket.

"If you'll pardon the liberty, sir, I'd rather not," Palmer said hastily. "I'm taking a great interest in this case, sir, and, if you'll permit me, sir, I'd like the—er—drinks, sir, to be my personal contribution."

Palmer made another personal contribution after lunch, be-ing instructed to walk along the foreshore to beyond Highways and make a report. He said there was hard sand under the cliffs all along to make good going, but at very high tide he thought it would be covered. He also reported that there were two small concrete shelters with steps up to them set in the cliffs just above the beach.

Just before three-fifteen Travers was in one of those shelters that lay nearer to the village; in his hand *The Times* as a possible mask for his face, and in his pocket a pair of field-glasses. The fishy tang of the sea was in his nostrils, and that, he thought, might be a sign of a change of weather, for it was chilly now in that shelter with the sun gone in and a haze over the Channel view. That manageress was probably right about an evening fog, but Travers saw no reason for uneasiness about that. A fog, pro-vided it was little more than a mist, would serve his purpose well.

The tide was coming in, but the little moored boats around him were still high and dry on the beach. Fishing boats were out on the bay's edge, discernible and no more, and a fisherman or two were pottering about on the shore in full view of him if they turned. So he kept the glasses out at the sea, swivelling only when it was safe, and that was why, when at last he saw them, the man and the girl were down the steps three hundred yards away below Highways and already on the beach.

He trained the glasses on them, indifferent now to what the men might think. It was the man Trowte who interested him most. The white hair was visible beneath his soft black hat; his shoulders stooped, and he walked with legs rather wide apart. His clean-shaven face had the sallow paleness of age, his nose looked hooked and predatory, and his eyes immensely dark, while his whole head seemed too large for the body, though that, Travers thought, might be due to some queer focusing and the forward lean of his body as he walked. At a hundred and fifty yards off he seemed to Travers to bear some resemblance to pictures of the Abbé Liszt; at a hundred yards he had something of Svengali.

The queer movements of the girl caught his eye, and he trained the glasses on her. Now he saw that old Trowte, always holding her by the hand, was himself walking on the hard sand and the girl was moving awkwardly on the coarse shingle. Then suddenly they seemed to be playing some kind of game, for she was pulling at him, and then her body was twisting as if she were in fits of laughter. Her face, was pale, too, and she looked a slip of a thing, with dark eyes. And it looked as if she were crying. No, it wasn't. It was laughing—and still pulling at the old man as if to get free. Or was it—

There were voices close by and Travers whipped the glasses down and turned. A young couple—the pair he had seen the previous night—were almost at the steps, and he drew himself into his corner, and was all at once deep in *The Times*.

"There's some one there!"

That was the young woman's voice, and some mumbled answer came from the man. Travers, aware of spoiling the course of love, kept close to his corner. A peep around the edge of his paper showed him the couple making apparently for the next shelter, and in a moment his field-glasses were being trained again. But old Trowte and the child had also turned long since and were almost back at Highways again. They did not mount the steep steps to the house, but went straight on, and now and again the child seemed to be playing that amusing game. Then the far bend of the little bay hid them, and Travers, seeing no point in waiting for their return, pocketed his field-glasses and newspaper and made his way to the hotel again.

Towards half-past six the mist covered the sea and was rolling landwards in good earnest. After the heat of the morning the air was now definitely chill, but there was still a reasonable visibility, and from the bedroom window Travers could see the length of a cricket pitch across the green.

A long night was in front of him and he had ordered a special meal at seven. Then he decided to change out of that thin suit he was wearing, and hurried downstairs again. He put on his overcoat, then discarded it in case it might hamper his movements, only to realize all at once that he looked like being late. But the lounge clock reassured him as he came hastily through and, once clear of the village, he hurried on through the mist.

Now he was making a last rehearsal of the words he would use to old Trowte. "See Colonel Staithe . . . Dead? . . . Come specially . . . suppose you couldn't. . ." But suppose Trowte didn't ask him in? Well, if he didn't, that would be that and there'd be the temporary end of it. But he'd have had a good look at the old boy at close quarters and heard him speak.

He halted for the merest moment at the fork, then went left by the main road. It was dark there by the trees, and even more dark in that narrow avenue that led to the house. Half-way along it, as he judged, he halted for another moment to steady his nerves; and his glasses were damp from the mist. His hand went to his trouser pocket, and at once he was aware of something queer. It went to the other pocket, and then he knew. In that hurry to change his clothes he had forgotten to transfer his belongings from the old suit.

Then he gave a shrug of the shoulders. When Palmer tidied up he would find the note-book and wallet and the rest of the things, and after all there was nothing now that he particularly needed, except perhaps a handkerchief. So he rubbed the glasses on his sleeve, gave a deep breath or two and moved on again. In a minute he was on a gravel stretch, and before him was a door with an ornate Adam porch.

He stared, thinking for a moment he had come to the wrong house. Then it came to him what must have happened. Once, before that wood had grown up, that back road had been a drive, and the door he was now regarding was once the front door. Maybe, he thought, it still was. In that mist and the gloomy dusk he could see nothing that looked like a tradesmen's door, and there was a bell-pull asking to be tugged.

Somewhere in the house to his left he heard the bell tinkle. He bent his head and listened, but there was no sound. For a good half-minute he stood there, ears straining to listen, and then all at once he heard a sound away to the front, like the closing of a door and feet on the path. He moistened his lips at that. Maybe the other door was the front one after all, and Trowte was there.

A path seemed to lead round the west corner, and Travers took it. There was the front of the house as he had seen it from his morning's retreat, and there was the door, with one white stone step before it. But the door was closed, and there was no sign or sound of Trowte.

So he mounted the step and looked for a bell. It was then he saw the door was slightly ajar. His fingers went tentatively out and the door moved inwards. A foot or so it went—then stopped.

Travers drew back, and again he was moistening his lips. There had been a queer soft thud as the door had gently jarred against the thing that stopped it. So again he pushed, then all at once was heaving with his shoulder till the door was wide. All he saw was the pitch dark of the space beyond.

Again he stood for a moment; then his eye fell on the white painted switch, and he turned the light on. He called: "Any one there?" and listened with breath held. A second or two and he stepped inside and drew the door back, and looked down at the thing that sprawled. Even as he looked, the head gave a last movement, and there was a faint sound like a tired moan.

In a flash he was on his knees, arm beneath the head of the dead man. For Quentin Trowte was certainly dead, alive though he might have been but a second before. A jagged rent was in his coat, and blood was now on the sleeve of the arm that was holding him.

Travers got to his feet. He listened, breath held and eyes roving the room. The light shone full on the face of the tall grandfather clock that stood by a far door, and the time was eight minutes to eight.

IV
ENTER THE POLICE

TRAVERS SAID LATER that for some seconds after that discovery of Trowte's body his brain refused to function, and the steps he subsequently took were as ill-considered as those any tyro could possibly have taken. Tempest, on the other hand, thought that Travers had acted with promptitude and the soundest of common sense. George Wharton, always a bit too wise after the event, considered that Travers's first duty should have been to search the house. Travers meekly accepted the reprimand, but could not forbear a somewhat whimsical smile at the thought of himself in that lone house in search of a murderer.

And that murderer was possibly a madman! That was the thought that actually came as he looked down again at Trowte's body. Maybe it was Trowte's custom to let out at night that poor demented soul whom he kept drugged all day; and if so, it was the madman who had done the killing and had rushed out of the house and was abroad somewhere in the misty darkness of the night.

He glanced back apprehensively at that, then suddenly turned and switched off the light. Then he remembered the child, and listened again in the darkness, wondering if she were safe. But there was no sound, and he turned on the light again and went quietly across the room to the far door. He opened it gingerly, listened again for a sound, then felt for the switch. Under his eyes were the stairs in a kind of passage-way.

Once more Travers listened and now he seemed to hear a faint sound. He called quietly:

"Jeanne! Are you there?"

But there was an utter silence. Again he listened, then called, and again there was no sound. His hand went out to the switch, and he backed to that lounge room where the body lay. Then all at once he knew what he must do and how to do it.

The windows of the room, he saw, were heavily curtained, and he backed out to the misty dark, leaving the light on. The door was gently closed and he set off down the path, to make for the track and the bungalow. But the mist obscured his glasses and it was slow work.

"You're earlier than we thought, sir," Lucy said, drawing back from the door to let him through.

Travers stepped inside. "I am a bit early. The fact of the matter is, I want your husband to do a job of work for me."

"I want you to go somewhere with me," he told Yardman, who had come out. "Just something private, that's all." He smiled at Lucy. "We'll be back inside half an hour. You're not afraid of being left alone?"

"I'm not afraid, sir," she said. "And I can always lock the door."

"That's right," said Travers, as if making fun of her. "You lock the door."

A smile and a nod, and he was outside again, and Yardman followed. A few yards along the hedge his hand felt for the other's arm and drew him to a halt.

"I didn't want to frighten your wife," he said, "but Trowte's dead. I found him murdered."

"My God, sir!"

"No panic," Travers said. "But we've got to do various things and do them damn quick. Some one's got to warn the police and fetch a doctor. Then there's that child alone in the house. Which of us is to do what?"

Yardman shook his head and could say nothing.

"Right," said Travers. "I can't go running to the village with my glasses as they are. You warn the police and the doctor—there is a doctor in the village?"

"Doctor Mannin, sir."

"Right," said Travers, and moved on again. "I don't know whether or not the local constable's likely to lose his head, but you remember that the important thing is to get in touch with Seaborough. Off you go, then. Police first, then the—"

His hand gripped Yardman's arm. The mist seemed to have swirled aside for a moment and a something was looming out. Then the mist was obscuring his glasses again, and the some-thing seemed to be a man. Yardman was moving on, and as Travers blinked his eyes and fumbled for his glasses, he heard the two voices.

"Mr. Howcrop, sir, isn't it?" That was Yardman.

"What are you doing here?" That was the blurting, hostile voice of the tutor.

"Mr. Howcrop! It's most urgent. We want you to do some-thing."

That was Travers, seeing nothing as he went forward, and rubbing his glasses on his coat sleeve. He hooked them on again as he blundered full into Howcrop. Everything was happening at once, and in that last lingering of light and the wetting mist it was hard to see at a yard's distance. Howcrop was evidently able to see, for he had recognized Travers.

"I beg your pardon, sir," Travers cut hastily in. "You get off at the double, Yardman. Mr. Howcrop's the one man I should have liked to see."

His tone changed to a quiet earnestness and his fingers dosed gently on Howcrop's arm.

"Don't ask me what I'm doing here. That doesn't matter—just yet. But Trowte's been murdered!"

"Mur-mur—" He got out a spluttering and no more. His eyes were staring, and then he was backing away.

"I'm perfectly sane," Travers said quietly. "I had reason to call at the house here some short time ago, and I found Mr. Trowte murdered. Now let's get on to the house. It's funny work, talking in the dark."

His fingers closed again about the tutor's arm.

"You lead the way," he said. "My glasses are the devil of a nuisance in this mist." And as Howcrop felt for the latch of the gate: "Yardman's an old friend of mine, and I knew he and his wife were here, so I went there first as soon as I'd found—what I found." He kept up a kind of babbling reassurance as they moved along the dark path, for Howcrop was frightened to death, and he knew it.

"That child, Jeanne, is upstairs somewhere. I called to her, but she must have been asleep. She was worrying me, rather. If she'd seen me alone in the house, she'd have been terrified. If she's really awake, you're the one who'd better speak to her. She knows you, and she'll probably answer questions."

They were at the door. Travers shot out a hand and opened it, and the light was suddenly flooding then Howcrop drew back.

"I'm not going in there till I know more about it." He was staring wildly and looking ready to make a bolt "Who are you? And what were you doing this morning?"

"At the moment," Travers told him gravely, "I'm the police. The law, if you prefer it."

"The police!" His mouth gaped foolishly, and he was staring with some new fright.

Travers smiled, then shook a patient head. "We can't talk out here. All your questions can be answered inside. . . . You're coming in? . . . Very well, then; if you prefer it, I'll go first."

He stepped inside and Howcrop slowly followed, but to a yard beyond the threshold, and no more. His eyes followed the eyes of Travers, and he gave a little gasp.

"Who did it?"

Travers shook his head. "That'll be for—for all of us to try to find out."

These all at once his hand was half raised, and he was listening. He gave a quick whisper. "What was that?"

Then suddenly he was running across the room. The door was opened and the light switched on, and he disappeared from

Howcrop's sight. There was a little skirmish, then another, and Travers's voice:

"It's all right, Jeanne. It's only Mr. Howcrop. . . . There now; there now! Nobody's going to hurt you."

He nodded back for Howcrop to come. The child was in her white nightdress, crouching by the stairs; face white and eyes uncannily dark.

"It's me, Jeanne!" Howcrop said, and smiled with head sideways, as a sort of lure. But she still crouched there, head behind her arms, peering frightenedly.

"It's you she's scared of," Howcrop whispered. "Leave her to me and I'll soon have her right."

All his assumptions of bluster and officiousness had gone, and Travers, moving back through the door, was wondering quickly why, for they had seemed part and parcel of the man. And Travers moistened his lips as the queer stillness of the house came over him and he thought of the terrified face of that child. Something had frightened her badly. Perhaps she had heard noises and made her way down and had seen that body. Perhaps she had been in the room and had heard his voice as he talked to Howcrop and had bolted in fright for the stairs again. And yet she had had the presence of mind to turn off the switch, for that sudden click was the sound he had first heard. Now she was crouching there like a little wild animal, eyes staring like a rabbit's when the hand approaches the snare.

There was the sound of quick feet and Travers moved back to the door again. Howcrop went by him, making for an inner door beyond.

"She's fainted! I'm getting some water."

She lay there where he had seen her last, and be tiptoed over as if she was asleep. In that white repose the face had a strange beauty; the eyes closed, the little lips half parted, and the silky blackness of hair. He stooped and his finger touched the soft cheek. Then suddenly his arms went under her.

"I wouldn't take her in there," Howcrop was saying. "Lay her down for a bit and let's see if we can bring her round."

Travers left her to him and moved back once more to the door, ears alert for footsteps down the front path. From the foot of the stairs Howcrop's voice was coming, but as if he were mumbling to himself. Then words came, and again Travers looked through the door. Howcrop was kneeling with his face to the stairs, and in his arms was the child. His cheeks seemed to be on hers, and he was crooning gently like a mother.

"My little Jeanne! . . . There now, everything will be all right now. . . . There now; there now. . . . Everything's going to be all right. . . . You shall come and stay with me. Wouldn't you like that? Won't that be lovely for you?"

"She's better?" Travers was smiling kindly at that amazing revelation of an unexpected side to Howcrop. But Howcrop himself was getting to his feet with a look that had in it something of defiance, for he was glancing back over his shoulder as if about to carry the child upstairs.

"She oughtn't to be worried. I won't stand for her being worried. It's a doctor, that's what she wants. Something to make her sleep."

"The doctor—Mannin, I think his name is—ought to have been along now," Travers told him. "Yardman's—"

"She's not going there," Howcrop told him defiantly. "They're not to touch her." He shot another backward look and gave a sudden shake of the head as if he had said too much. "I'm the one to see after her. I'll wrap her up and take her home with me. The—er—person at the house will look after her. She's had children of her own."

"That we'll discuss later," Travers told him quietly, not liking that return of cheap bluster. "In the meanwhile you'd better take her up to her room again and wrap her up. It doesn't matter where you take her so long as you remain here till the official police come." And, with rather more friendliness: "There's no real need to bother her with questions till she's well enough to understand them."

Howcrop shot him yet another look, then without a word moved up the stairs, the child in his arms. She had neither spoken nor stirred, and, thought Travers, watching him to the landing, that showed a childlike trust and confidence curiously at variance with the Yardmans' story. He turned to the door, then turned quickly back again. Perhaps the child had not recovered after all, and was still in a faint. Curious how Howcrop had kept her hidden from him. And Howcrop himself, and his extraordinary display of affection, almost grotesquely out of keeping with the impressions which he—Travers—had formed. But the most curious thing had been the child herself. When she had fainted, Howcrop must have opened the front of her nightdress to give her air. When Travers had touched the white cheek, he had seen within that open front, not the neck and bosom of the child, but a woollen garment like a jumper, and when he had raised her in his arms he had become aware that beneath the thin nightdress *she was fully clothed.*

Quiet in the house again; a strange, heavy quiet, he thought, that seemed to weigh on one, and set nerves on edge. And there lay that body by the door, and nothing must be touched or moved. Ages, it seemed, since Yardman had disappeared out there. Five-and-twenty past eight, the clock said, which meant over half an hour since he had first stepped inside that door. Yet it seemed more. And twenty minutes since Yardman had set off for the village.

Then he cocked an ear, for there was a sound at last. Feet were trotting up the path, and Travers opened the door in readiness. It was Yardman, panting and perspiring, and the wet dripping from his clothes.

"What's happened?" asked Travers. "Where're the police?"

Yardman managed to get out that the policeman had not been in but his wife had sent some one to look for him, and Yardman had himself used the telephone to notify Seaborough.

"Then I went to the Doctor's," he said, "and he hadn't turned up when I left. No one knows where he is."

Travers gave a click of the tongue. Yardman glanced down, and for the first time became aware of what lay in the shadow by the open door.

"That him, sir?" he said, and licked his lips.

"Yes," Travers said. "Perhaps you'd better get back and set Lucy's mind at rest." Then he shook his head. "Wait a moment, though. She'll know sooner or later. Better tell her the truth, and stay with her till we send for you both."

Yardman made a sudden movement to the door. Travers wondered why he should take him so abruptly at his word, but it was a sound that Yardman had heard.

"Some one's coming, sir! There's the lights. . . . Two cars, sir!"

Travers followed him down the path. A brake squeaked and a car drew up, with another just behind. There were voices, and one at least that Travers recognized. Then a torch was flashed full in his eyes.

"Gawd! if it isn't Mr. Travers!"

"That's you, Carry, isn't it?" asked Travers, blinking in the glare of the Inspector's torch.

"What's that?" another voice was saying, and another torch flashed. "Travers! Good God! what are you doing here?"

"At the moment, wondering when you're going to lower those lights."

Tempest laughed. Travers whispered to Yardman and waved a hand, and Yardman disappeared into the dark.

The Big Three made their way along the path together, and it was not till they were inside the door that Travers would make any report.

"There he is," he said, though far less callously than it sounded. "Nothing's been touched, as far as I know."

A fourth man had come in behind them, and Travers recognized Shinniford, the Seaborough Police Surgeon.

"Lucky you're here," he said. "Our local man hasn't turned up."

Shinniford got to work at once, and the three stood over him and watched while he rolled the body on its back. Carry got to his knees and flashed an additional light, but nothing lay beneath. He was a burly man, Carry; a bull of a man perhaps, who had made a considerable success of bluster. Travers, who had worked with him twice before, knew him as obstinate, opinionated, but thorough in his own pig-headed way. Tempest had a high opinion of him. He had cussednesses of his own, but a sense of proportion; and that trustfulness which valued Carry included also a tremendous respect for Ludovic Travers.

"Knife through the back," announced Shinniford. "I don't know at the moment, but I should say it didn't kill him outright. He's been dead over half an hour."

The statement was made with an inquiring look at Travers. He was to be gratified by the answer.

"Eight minutes to eight it was when he died. And you're right. The stab didn't kill him wherever it was delivered. He'd struggled as far as—as where he was when you came in."

"How do you know it was eight minutes to eight?" asked Tempest.

"By that clock," Travers said, and pointed.

Carry's watch was out in a flash, and Tempest's more slowly.

"I make it practically dead right," Tempest said. "What about you, Travers?"

Travers gave a shrug of the shoulders. "I've no reason to doubt its being right."

"We'll get him on that table," Shinniford said, "then you can get to work."

"Just a moment," Tempest told him. "You've marked the position of the body, Carry? Right, then perhaps Mr. Travers will shed a little more light. Who else is in the house, for instance."

"When he was killed there wasn't a soul in the house, to my knowledge, except a grandchild of ten," Travers said.

"She killed him?" asked Carry, eyes bulging.

"I said, to my certain knowledge," Travers reminded him. "If the murderer was here, and if there was a murderer, I'm unable to say."

"Don't you think you'd better enlarge?" said Tempest.

"By all means," Travers said. "Move the body if you like, and get your print men to work, because nothing I can tell you will make the slightest difference."

So Tempest's men came in, and when things had started Travers told his story. He made no confidence of anything, and, as far as he was aware, he left nothing out.

"Queer," said Tempest. "The Yardmans seem to have seen him alive last." He nodded to Carry. "Better have them here, I think. And about that madman theory. You're in dead earnest? Because if you are, then there's likely to be the very devil to pay if he's loose somewhere outside."

"I gave my own ideas entirely," Travers said. "You've heard the facts, and you should know if the theory tallies." He looked for a moment over at where Shinniford and a man were stripping the body and laying the clothes carefully aside. "He'll probably have his keys on him. Why not go upstairs and look at that locked room? Or you can wait till the Yardmans get here, which shouldn't be more than two or three minutes."

"I've sent a man," Carry said, and went over to search the clothes. Tempest moved across to watch him. He was the quiet unflurried kind, who talked only when he had ideas, whereas Travers generally talked in order to find them.

"Not much of a haul," Carry said ruefully. "Loose change, note-case, handkerchief and a bunch of keys. Never a letter or a piece of paper or anything."

The finger-print men came over to take the prints of the corpse.

"We have Mr. Travers's," Tempest told them. "But what about the man upstairs?"

"Howcrop's?" Travers said. "Hadn't better disturb him if he's getting that child to sleep. But you'll find his prints round a glass on a table in there, by the stairs."

"Most amazing-looking old man," Tempest whispered to Travers, referring to Trowte. "Looks like some old German professor. What was he? You don't happen to know?"

Travers shook his head. He had none of that off-hand indifference in the presence of death that characterized professionals like Carry. The slow, inquisitorial pursuit was his passion; the shedding of blood and the ultimate drop on an early morning were things that still made him wince.

The man at the outer door put his head inside.

"Here's Badger, the local man, sir. Do you want him in?"

Travers shook his head at Tempest, and the questioning was done outside. In two minutes Tempest was back again.

"He was out on regular routine," he said, "and was only picked up a few minutes ago. He's all in a fret about the local doctor—Martin or Mann—or something—"

"Mannin."

"That's it—Mannin. As I told him, if he worries every time a doctor's home late, he'll be in an early grave. You didn't want him in here?"

"No," said Travers. "There's no reason why the village should know anything. The less people know, the more they talk; and, for all we know, we may soon be wanting to hear people talk. The Yardmans here yet?"

"They're outside," Tempest said. "Cover up that body, Shinniford, till she gets through. Get it away if you're dead sure you can't do anything else with it here."

"Perhaps Dr. Shinniford would slip upstairs before he goes and have a look at the girl," Travers said. "If you'd just let us know, Doctor, what you make of her, then we can arrange accordingly. The tutor—he-governess, if you like—is called Howcrop, if you didn't catch his name."

Tempest shepherded the Yardmans past the shrouded body. Lucy cast a frightened glance at Travers, who fell in alongside.

"There's another room we can go to?" he said.

Yardman cut in, only too glad to talk: "This way, sir. I'll switch on the light, sir."

The room was the morning-room. The one from which they had come combined the functions of hall, lounge and dining-room. There was also, Yardman said, a kitchen, pantry, maids' sitting-room, and a large cellar.

"Now," began Tempest, "I don't think we need trouble you much at this stage. Mr. Travers has given us certain information and will doubtless give us more if we need it—about yourselves, I mean. I take it, however, you were the last people to see Mr. Trowte alive?"

"That I don't know, sir," Yardman said. "I cleared away the supper things from the dining-room just before half-past seven."

"You spoke to him?"

"Yes, sir. I said, 'Good-night, sir. Good-night, Miss Jeanne.' "

"And what did he say?"

"He didn't speak to me, sir; he spoke to her, same as he always does—did. He said, 'Say good-night, my little Jeanne.' Then she said, 'Good-night'—just like that—and I closed the door."

"And you, Mrs. Yardman?"

"I didn't clap eyes on him all day, sir, except when he came in with Miss Jeanne at about four. That was the last I saw of him, or heard of him either."

She had spoken with a certain bitterness, and Tempest threw her a quick glance. Travers cut quickly in:

"And you left about when?"

"About five-and-twenty to eight, sir. We'd been home quite a time when you came."

Travers relinquished the witness; Tempest frowned in thought for a moment or two.

"It's no use asking you if you've any ideas who did it?" he said. "Or any one likely to have done it? . . . I see. Well, we'll try Mr. Travers's suggestion of the upstairs room. Fetch the keys, Carry, will you?"

"The locked room," Travers explained.

"Yes," Tempest said. "You can go with us, Yardman, and I'll send two men with you, Mrs. Yardman, to go through the downstairs rooms and the cellar. If anything's different from how you left it, be sure to point it out."

In two minutes the upstairs party was ready to move. Yardman said there was also a service stairway from the maids' sitting-room.

"We'll come back that way," Tempest said. "You ready, Carry? If so, we'll find out for certain what's in that locked room."

"What *was* in," Travers gently reminded him.

V
THE MYSTERY ROOM

"THAT ROOM'S FURNISHED, and that one isn't," Yardman said, and pointed from the head of the stairs.

"Gently, gently!" Tempest told him. "There's no point in waking the child if she's asleep." But he moved over towards one of the doors. "Let's have a look inside."

The rooms were searched and showed no signs of recent occupation. Then Yardman pointed out Trowte's room and switched on the light for them to enter. Carry, rubber gloves on, hastily opened drawers and reported that there seemed to be no private papers.

Out on the landing again, Yardman indicated a door to the far left.

"Miss Jeanne's room," he whispered. And, nodding ominously: "That's the other."

Tempest inserted the key and turned. The door opened a foot and he saw the switch. But the hand which went to it drew back again, and he turned to the three at his elbow.

"There's a light there! A red light!"

"Better switch on the other," Carry said. "We'll stand fast here, and do you push the door wide open, sir."

Tempest shot out his hand and turned on the light, and his foot sent the door wide open. Eight eyes stared—but at what was almost an empty room.

"The electric stove is on," Travers said. "Some one's been in here recently." His hand went out to draw Tempest back. "Let Carry dust the power switch and see whose prints are on it."

Carry set to work, and Travers cast an eye round the room. Its furnishings were few: an easy-chair that had been much used, a corner hanging cupboard at its side, a deal table by the opposite wall and a smaller table near the chair.

"Just a minute, sir," Carry was saying. "I'll slip down and get the old man's prints."

Out he went, and Travers continued his survey of the room. Never a picture on the walls, yet the floor was heavily carpeted. An old-fashioned red Turkey carpet it was, with a pile into which one seemed to sink.

"Just have a look here," Tempest said, and began drawing on his gloves again. "The fireplace behind this stove is absolutely chock-full of burnt paper."

Travers came over, then trod on something.

"What on earth's this?" He picked it up, then smiled. "A toy sausage. The sort of rubber thing you blow up."

He was holding it gingerly by the rubber, with the wooden mouthpiece dangling.

"Red," he said. "The same colour as the carpet. That child must have been in here to-night and dropped it. Trowte must have had her in for a minute or two before she went to bed." He turned to Yardman. "Ever seen the child playing with anything like this?"

Yardman shook his head. "No, sir. It's what they call a dying pig, isn't it, sir?"

"Don't know," said Travers, "but I expect you're right." Then he drew back to make room for Carry, who was comparing prints.

"It's the old boy's, all right," Carry said. "He was the one who turned on the stove." He gave Travers a look of arch reproof. "Looks as if you were a bit wide of the mark, this time, sir. Not much sign of a private madhouse about this little shack."

"You're right," Travers told him. "But it was a good theory—as theories go—and it's only the fools who never make mistakes. Anything unburnt among those papers?"

Tempest had drawn the stove out and was on his knees, peering at the charred heap that filled the original grate. Then he inserted a finger.

"I don't see anything unburnt," he said. "And there isn't a trace of heat, so it looks as if they weren't burnt to-night."

"Doesn't it strike you," said Travers, "that there's no closeness there? If people burn a mass of papers, they get impatient and pile them on. That stops the draught and the papers won't burn, so the next process is to stir them round with a poker.

There's a poker of sorts there, and yet those papers obviously haven't been disturbed."

"You're implying what?"

"That it's been a gradual process," Travers said. "Many letters, were there?"

"Very few, sir." Yardman said. "I never knew a house where there were so few. I should think they didn't average two a week."

"There we are, then," Travers said. "On that table is the *Telegraph*, which was his daily paper. He used to bring it up here and read it during the morning, while lessons were going on downstairs. If there was any correspondence he would deal with it, and burn any letters. Which implies either an admirable memory or a wish for secrecy."

"This locked room shows the secrecy," Tempest told him dryly. "But what's this? Queer-looking thing. Like a pigeon-hole with a glass front."

It was a square of glass with a recess behind it, set in the wall near the corner cupboard. Beneath it was a tiny knob.

"See if it opens, sir," Carry said.

Tempest twiddled the knob—or tried to—then found it moving sideways. He gave a little gasp, then was peering through. For half a minute he stood there with nose against the glass, then he drew back. "Sh!" he went, and, "Have a look in there!"

Carry licked his lips and had a look. It was more of a long stare, and then Travers took his place. Through that foot of recess he could see a room beyond. There was a curtained window; a bed beneath it; white sheets with a spot of black, and a small hand above the sheets. Jeanne's bedroom, and there was Howcrop coming back from somewhere to the chair by the bedside. He was stooping over her—sitting down—fiddling with his moustache—turning to watch her, and sitting there rather like that doctor in Luke Fildes' picture.

"What do you make of it, sir?" Carry was whispering, and Travers drew back.

"Don't know," he said, and shook his head. "Mind if I draw the knob back again?"

The door had been left ajar, and all at once there was a tap and Shinniford entered.

"Just going in to see that child," he said. "Which is the room?"

Travers nodded for Yardman to point out the door, then whispered to Tempest:

"I'm going down for a minute or two. Watch what happens in the bedroom."

It was to that lounge-dining-room that he made his way, and as he walked in he saw a man he recognized, and his hand went out.

"Sergeant Polegate! How is it I haven't seen you before? Just come?"

"You saw me, sir, but I don't think you recognized me," the Sergeant said. "Anything I can do for you, sir?"

"Yes," Travers said. "Let me have a sheet of paper, and then send a message for me to my hotel."

He scribbled a quick chit for Palmer, then moved across to the table where the body of Trowte still lay. He drew back the sheet that covered it and for a long minute schooled himself to a slow, impersonal study of the dead man's face. Predatory was the apt word. No smile in the thin blue lips, no wrinkling at the corners of the eyes as when he fawned before that idolized child. It was an evil face; a repulsive face—and yet what logic was there or contentment of purpose in reading into that chill, sneering mask the qualities that life alone made readable? Give life again, and the face would be transfigured; and yet as he drew back the sheet and turned to the door again Travers was shaking his head. From the first moment of that case, new impressions had come to confound the old. Everything was illogical, and no two facts held together.

He came to the landing as Shinniford was entering the secret room. As he entered, the Doctor was questioning Yardman.

"Yes, but why should the windows be sealed? It's scandalous, I tell you, a child sleeping in a closed bedroom."

Yardman gave a helpless shake of the head.

"It isn't anything to do with me, sir. When I asked about the windows he said the ventilators were there instead."

"Ventilators, are there?"

"Yes, sir, set in the top wall. He said the child was very nervous and might walk in her sleep, and he was afraid she'd climb out and do herself a harm."

Shinniford grunted at that.

"Well, she's got a slight temperature. No great harm, of course, and she's sleeping pretty soundly. Who's your doctor here?"

"Mannin, sir."

"I know Mannin," Shinniford said. "A crusty old stick, but a damn good man. Has he ever attended her before?"

"Yes, sir. Stomach out of order, sir."

"May be that now," Shinniford said. "However, see that Doctor Mannin has a look at her in the morning." He turned to Tempest. "I think I'll get him along to Seaborough. The ambulance is here."

"Give the Doctor any help he wants," Tempest told Carry. "Then take Yardman and go through those top rooms, and come back here."

Travers closed the door after them.

"Well, what happened in the bedroom?"

"Nothing but what you've gathered," Tempest said.

"Could you hear anything?"

"Not a word. Besides, they were talking in whispers so as not to wake the child."

"Shinniford say anything about Howcrop?"

"Said he was making a damn good night nurse."

"Did he," said Travers, and began fumbling at his glasses. "Strange mixture, that chap Howcrop, as you'll notice perhaps when you interview him." He was sliding the knob and squinting through. "There he sits, just as if he were her father."

"Whatever he is, he isn't so curious as the thing you're looking through," said Tempest. "Who made it? What's it there for?"

"Why not see what's the other side?" Travers said. "I'll go in there and you shall manipulate the knob when I tap on the wall."

Howcrop looked round almost startled as Travers quietly entered the bedroom. Travers gave a reassuring smile and tiptoed over. The child was asleep. The face which had been so white now seemed somewhat flushed, yet the cheeks looked pale against the long dark.

"We'll relieve you soon," Travers whispered. "I'll stay here a minute while you go down and find Yardman. Get him to send me a clean handkerchief."

Howcrop shot him a questioning look, but moved off towards the door. Travers watched him to the stairs, then nipped over to the wall. There was a black moulded frame set in the wall itself and enclosing the picture of a mare and foal. He tapped it gently. Eight inches square, like the glass of the other room. But it was moving, sliding into the wall by the frame. An oil sketch, done on panel, it had seemed, and he tapped again. In two seconds the picture was in its place.

Almost at once Howcrop was back and Travers was waiting for him at the door.

"Everything still all right," Travers whispered, and saw him inside.

"What was there?" asked Tempest, and closed the door behind Travers as he entered.

Travers told him, blinking away all the time while he polished his glasses with the handkerchief.

"Two or three other small pictures on the wall," he said. "But for the fact that the frame of that one's attached to the wall, there's nothing peculiar about it."

Carry came in then and asked if Yardman was still needed upstairs. Travers said he would like to ask a question or two, and he had his answers straight away. Mr. Trowte neither smoked nor drank, Yardman said, and he had been absent only two mornings, when he had gone to Seaborough and taken Miss Jeanne with him. They had gone by a private car from Seabreak.

"Now," said Tempest, when he had gone, "let's get this cupboard open and see if there's any more Maskelyne and Devant business. Then we'll try to make sense out of everything."

He tried a key and the door opened. His mouth gaped at the queer collection of objects on the two small shelves.

"What the devil next!"

"Don't touch them," said Travers. "Let's have a look first."

"Two more of them toy balloons," Carry said.

"Balloons are round," Tempest told him severely.

"Well, sausages then, sir, or dying pigs. A dog's chain! My wife bought one just like it at Woolworth's for our terrier. That thing there looks like a little Klaxon horn."

"It's a toy one," Tempest said, "off a child's motor."

"Two telephone receivers," Travers said. "Like the ear-phones of the old days. Wired into the wall, aren't they? And isn't that hanging thing an electric light switch?"

Tempest drew back, shaking his head. Then his gloved hand went forward again and he was drawing out a writing-pad with half-filled envelope, flap inside, and blotting-paper. A pen and a small bottle of ink were behind it.

Carry took them with gloved hands and laid them on the table. The chain followed, and the two rubber sausages, one yellow, one green. Tempest gently tried the plunger of the small Klaxon, then passed that back too.

"Just a moment," said Travers. "Get your hand on that switch thing, but don't move it. I've got an idea."

He went back to the door and turned off the light, but the dull red of the fire still coloured the room. Then he moved the knob of the sliding panel and waved his hand while he peered through. "Back the other way!" he whispered, peered for another moment, then closed the panel again.

"Turn the light on again, Carry," he said. "We may have Howcrop in here any minute, asking what's the matter with it."

"The switch controls the light in there?"

"That's it," Travers said. "From here you can control the bedroom light. It went off there and then on. Howcrop's looking anxiously at it."

"Well, we're getting somewhere," Tempest said, and from his satisfied nod Travers knew he was putting two and two together. "Now let's have a look at these ear-phones."

Each had a little switch at the side, and each had ample flex. They seemed to have been wired, like the switch that Travers had just tested, before the new wallpaper was put up, and then the wires brought through the back of the cupboard. It was also obvious that the seat was so placed that one had only to open the cupboard door, reach for an ear-phone and then hear in comfort whatever there was to hear. Tempest tried one but heard nothing. Then he pushed the tiny switch and all at once his eyes were staring. His hand went up for silence.

Then without a word he handed the receiver to Travers. The eyes of Travers bulged too, and he clapped a hand over.

"It's the Yardmans! . . . Then we're listening to the morning-room!"

"Try the other, sir," Carry said quickly. Tempest tried it with the switch in, and could hear no sound. Travers could hear nothing either.

"Where the devil is it supposed to lead to?" said Tempest, feeling the wall-paper to follow the thin bulge of wire.

"Wait a minute," Travers said. "Carry, you go downstairs to the kitchen and sing or hum a little tune. Then go through to the maids' sitting-room that was and do the same there. Then bolt back here."

Carry did his job and came sprinting back up the stairs.

"Hear anything, sir?"

"From the kitchen," Tempest said.

"Well, if that don't beat the band!" He scowled at the ear-phones as if they could do the explaining. "And what do you make of it, sir?"

"What do you make of it, Travers?" Tempest passed the question on.

"Thy servant is as a dead dog," Travers told him dryly, "In other words, visitors first."

"All right," said Tempest. "But you won't be annoyed if I say just what I think?"

"God forbid," said Travers piously.

"Then I think we've proved very conclusively—or this room has for us—that the Yardmans, and yourself at second hand, have been sitting on a mare's nest. No shrieking by night ever came from here, and there certainly never was any madman or madwoman shut up here. The child did the shrieking. Isn't that so?"

"Maybe," said Travers.

"Well, it was the child who did the shrieking. We've been told that she's highly strung. As I read the evidence, the child did the shrieking, and at two separate times and for two different reasons. She shrieked the first time because she didn't want to go to bed. That's right, isn't it, Carry? You're a father."

"Mine don't, sir," said Carry with a grin.

"That's because you discipline them. Trowte, by all accounts, made a fool of himself with the child. The second time she shrieked was when she woke up and was afraid of the dark. Sometimes that was soon after her first sleep; at other times it was in the middle of the night."

"An excellent theory," said Travers, "and much may be said for it."

"Well, where's the hole in it?"

Travers gave a shrug of the shoulders. "Leave the coat-trailing and get to all these gadgets. What were they for?"

Tempest smiled. "They're easy. I admit that the old man—I don't know that I oughtn't to call him the old fool—had queer ideas about what toys a girl would amuse herself with; but he would bring her in here and try to amuse her—get her in a good mind for going to bed."

"I see, sir," Carry said. "Let her blow up the rubber sausages and play with the horn."

"And what about the chain?" asked Travers in all seriousness. "Did they take turns at being the dog?"

"Why not?" said Tempest. "As for the light switch, that was so that he could see from here—his private den—if she were sleeping all right. The special phone arrangement to the morning-room was so that he could listen to the lessons Howcrop was giving her, in which apparently he took an interest."

"And the one to the kitchen?"

"I'd say he disliked the Yardmans. He thought they would break his injunction about speaking to the child. If he hadn't mistrusted them, he'd never have given that order at the start."

"You realize, of course," Travers said, "that all this elaborate and secret wiring was done before the child arrived here?"

"I didn't know that," Tempest said, "but it doesn't affect the argument. He must have known all the peculiarities of the child before he adopted her."

"Most elaborate hocus-pocus, don't you think? I must insist on that."

"One man's hocus-pocus is another man's hobby," Tempest said. "Trowte was a crank. Even a look at his dead face would tell you that."

"I think the Chief is right." Carry said.

"Suppose I agree," said Travers, "and then, where are we? Our job is to find out who killed Trowte. We've eliminated the supposed madman, which is something. And now—what?"

"Yes," said Tempest. "That's bringing us down to earth with a vengeance." He frowned. "I think we'll shut this room up again and leave the verification of what we were discussing till when we can question the child and get her confirmation."

"The Yardmans say she's a dreadful liar," remarked Travers.

"We shall spot whether she's telling lies or truth," Tempest said, and switched off the stove. "These charred papers can be gone over later."

He drew Travers aside at the head of the stairs. "What about questioning Howcrop?"

"Why not?" Travers told him. "I'll send up Mrs. Yardman to relieve him. Yardman might as well stay here too."

But before Howcrop was admitted, there was a brief conference. Tempest wanted to be dead right about the facts; which were that at about a quarter to eight a man was in the house with Trowte, and probably known to him, since the Yardmans had locked the back door and Trowte himself was accustomed to lock the front.

Just as Travers rang at the back, that man had stabbed Trowte, and since he bungled the job, though striking at his back, it was not unlikely that the very sound of the bell had put him, so to speak, off his stroke. At ten to eight Trowte was stabbed, and he lingered on for two minutes, and was even able to drag himself a yard or two to the door out of which the killer had bolted. The first bloodstain was six feet from the door.

"Let him in now, Carry," Tempest said. "And don't forget that first thing in the morning we must get the telephone people to run us a line out here."

Howcrop came in, with a jauntiness that showed a lack of assurance. Travers introduced him and Tempest recited the usual platitudes about help and duty, and seasoned the mush with vague sympathies and regrets. Then he became official.

"Your name, please?"

"Howcrop. Randolph Howcrop."

"Address?"

"View Cottage. I have a—er—domicile there."

"Rooms?"

"Yes, rooms. With a Mrs. Tadman. A very decent body."

"And, in order that we can strike you wholly off the list of possible suspects, and not have to trouble you any more, Mr. Howcrop, where were you precisely at ten minutes to eight to-night?"

"In my room," Howcrop said promptly. "I was there from soon after seven till just about eight, when I—er—took my—er—usual constitutional."

"Any witness that you were there?"

"The woman of the house saw me there and saw me downstairs," he said.

"There's capital, then," said Tempest. "Now perhaps you'll give us some help. You been here long, by the way?"

"Since last September, when the granddaughter arrived."

"How did you get the appointment?"

"Well"—he waved an expansive hand—"I advertised in the local papers to—er—coach, and so on. Just to eke out my income, of course. The depression hit me like every one else."

"No doubt it did. And if you were asked who did the killing of Mr. Trowte, who—in all confidence—would you be likely to think of first?"

Howcrop pursed his lips. "I'm sorry. I can't think of a soul."

"Your own relationships with the dead man were all that you could wish?"

"Oh, absolutely."

"What'd you think of him?"

"Trowte? Well, he wasn't a bad chap in his way. A bit of a crank. Senile, perhaps, at times. Obstinate; still, I got on very well with him."

"You liked your pupil?"

Howcrop shot him a curious look, then drew himself up with dignity. "Naturally. It's part of my system to—er—gain the—er—confidence and the respect of any pupil."

Travers cut in on the heroics. "Have you ever heard him mention any relations?"

"Er—no," said Howcrop. "I'm afraid we never discussed each other's private affairs."

"Why did you suggest that the child should go with you?"

"Well"—again he waved his hand with a kind of florid indifference—"I—er—was not aware that there mightn't be relatives. I was prepared—I may say I am prepared—to see to the child and continue her studies until such a relative comes forward."

"And why should you resent the Yardmans' seeing her?"

Howcrop looked slowly up from under his eyebrows, He shook his head.

"I'm afraid I'm not at liberty to say that."

Travers glanced at Tempest, then leaned forward, "But if it's decided by Major Tempest that you should appear at the inquest, that question will be put to you in open court. Why not answer it here instead—among friends?"

Howcrop peered at him again, looked down, then finally up.

"Well, gentlemen, I was told by Mr. Trowte—the late Mr. Trowte—that the Yardmans weren't all they should be. He hinted, in fact, that they had a past, and he was keeping them on here out of—er—kindness of heart."

"Did he, by Jove!" said Travers. "And you believed him?"

Howcrop looked surprised. "I had no reason to disbelieve him."

Travers leaned forward again. "And did your pupil have the same impression of the Yardmans?"

Again Howcrop looked surprised. "I believe she did—shouldn't she?"

Travers gave a shrug of the shoulders. "None what ever, except that I can vouch personally for the absolute honesty and integrity of the Yardmans."

He gave Tempest another glance and relinquished the witness.

"I don't think we'll detain you any longer now, Mr. Howcrop," Tempest said. "If you can make it convenient to be here in the morning—"

"At eleven o'clock," cut in Travers.

"At eleven o'clock," echoed Tempest, "then we shall be very grateful. If we need you before, we know where to find you."

Howcrop rose, nervously fingering his hat. "But the child? May I ask what is—er—"

"We're making arrangements for to-night," Travers said. "And I'm sure Major Tempest is deeply grateful—as I am—for all you've done, both for her and ourselves."

There was a finality in his tone that took the incipient wind from Howcrop's sails. Tempest himself conducted him courteously to the door. Carry leaned over to Travers and whispered:

"What about a man on his tail, sir."

"What I was going to suggest myself," whispered Travers in return.

VI
O'RYAN'S BAND

THE DOOR CLOSED on Howcrop, and Tempest came back There was a new springiness in his walk and a complacent smile that lingered at the corners of his mouth, and Travers knew the reasons for both. He halted for a moment to look down at Polegate, who, on hands and knees and with a strong glass, was going over the carpet for stains.

"Got anything else?"

"No, sir," Polegate said, and got to his feet. "You see, he wouldn't bleed at once, so we don't exactly know where he was struck down."

"I don't think it's of any great importance," Tempest said. "Any papers found?"

"Some of the young lady's lesson books and papers in the morning-room," Polegate said. "Nothing belonging to the old man."

"Well, keep on looking," Tempest told him cheerfully. "And what about prints?"

"Only what you'd expect, sir. The Yardmans' all over the kitchen; Howcrop's in the morning-room, and the old man's here. Not a single strange one anywhere."

"Keep on looking," Tempest said, still cheerfully. "Go clean through the house from top to bottom." He gave what might have been a nod of encouragement then came over to Travers and Carry.

"Well, that's the end of Howcrop for a bit. What'd you make of him?"

Travers smiled. "I think he's what might be called a hollow mockery. Once, undoubtedly, he was well off and had a certain position in life; now his main object seems to be trying by that haw-haw bluster to explain away the fact that he's merely a somewhat seedy, second-rate hack." He smiled. "That's not too good as an extempore effect, but you see what I mean? But I rather like him. I like the way he had with that child to-night, and how he refused to take any credit for it."

"What was your idea, Carry?"

"I'd say he's not a bad old gent," Carry said. "One thing about him, sir: he didn't make any fuss about answering questions. He didn't rear up on his hind legs like some we've had."

"That's true," Tempest said. "A pompous old windbag, was how he struck me; rather Micawberish, you might say."

"Not all that old, you know," Travers reminded him. "I'd put him, after to-night's inspection, at just under sixty. Pompous, perhaps, but there's many a kind heart beneath an inflated waistcoat."

"That's right enough, sir," Carry told him. "And, if you ask me, he wouldn't hurt a fly. He's about the last person you'd imagine sticking a knife into anybody's body."

Travers's hand went to his glasses, then fell again.

"In other words, he's the kind who might strike on sudden provocation and make a hash of it."

Carry shot him a look. Tempest smiled tolerantly.

"Well, he's given some details of an alibi. Tomorrow it can be tested, and that'll dispose of him." He frowned. "The one thing that struck me as curious was the way he spoke about possible relatives. I got the idea he knew far more than he was admitting."

Travers nodded. "I agree. Far more, shall we say, than he was prepared at present to admit."

"Well, we'll soon settle that too," Tempest said. "We shall get some information from somewhere and know all there is to know about Trowte. If nothing's forthcoming by the morning, then we'll get out an SOS for relatives along with a Press statement." Then something of the complacency came back. "By the way, Howcrop confirmed certain minor points of that theory of ours." Travers smiled dryly at that inclusion of himself. "Trowte was a crank. Senile, Howcrop called him. Look at that amazing Yardman business."

But there had been a questioning look, and Travers accepted the implied challenge.

"I'll put all my cards on the table. I know Lucy Yardman, and I'll wager my head she had nothing to do with to-night's work. I took her husband at—well, at three values: what my sister said about him, what I judged from personal contact, and the fact that Lucy married him. I also admit that it's possible to manipulate the facts—not unfairly—to make out a case that Yardman had very strong reasons for killing Trowte. He was at his bungalow when I got there to-night, but that doesn't give him an alibi. His wife doesn't count as a witness."

"I see." Tempest nodded heavily. "It might be as well to have them both in."

They talked it over and it was decided that Yardman should be spoken to alone, after which his wife should be relieved from her upstairs watching. But nothing should be said to her. Yardman himself would tell her what had happened, and her reactions might be observed. So as Yardman was waiting in the morning-room, the three moved off.

"Ten past ten," remarked Travers as they went by the clock. "By the way, I don't remember hearing the clock strike?"

"There's a strike and silent movement, and it's set for silent," Carry said. "I asked Yardman, and he said the old man didn't like to hear it striking in the night."

Yardman rose as they came into the room.

"Do sit down," Tempest said. "Very trying, all this waiting, for you, but it'll soon be over."

There followed the usual recital, then the official questions:

"Full name?"

"Frederick Yardman."

"Age?"

Yardman hesitated. "You mean, real age, sir?"

"What else should I mean? You haven't two ages, have you?"

"Perhaps he has," cut in Travers quickly. "Yardman had certain misfortunes which brought him back to service after he thought he'd retired for good. Also, if he'll pardon the personal remark, he found it necessary to dye his hair."

"That's right, sir." said Yardman, and with a quiet dignity. "I gave my age here as fifty, sir. My real age is sixty-seven."

There followed a brief history of Yardman's career, with situations and employers, all of whom Carry noted down. Then came the vital question:

"What would you say if you were told for a fact that Mr. Trowte had informed both Mr. Howcrop and his granddaughter Jeanne that you, Yardman, and your wife had had a past, and he was employing you both out of sympathy?"

Yardman turned his head to one side as if not understanding. "A past, sir?"

"Yes. What he undoubtedly meant was that you'd been in trouble—with the law, shall we say?—and he was aware of it."

"Me, sir, in trouble with the law! And he told that to people?"

"He did. To his granddaughter and to Mr. Howcrop."

"I see, sir." He was preserving his temper extraordinarily well. "Now I begin to understand things, sir, Why Mr. Howcrop looked at me as he did—and the child too." He shook his head bewilderedly, then looked up. "Why did he do such a wicked thing, sir? Mr. Travers knows all about me, sir, and you've got all those people you can ask who've known me off and on all my life."

"It's you who can give the answer," Tempest said. "You seem to me to know the answer. I mean, you're accepting it as a fact that he did it."

Travers leaned forward. "Think of Mr. Trowte as you found him. Now do you find it surprising he should do such a thing?"

Yardman sat bolt upright, lips tightly closed and brow furrowed in thought. Then he nodded.

"You're right, sir. I don't think he was altogether right in the head."

Tempest shot a triumphant look at Travers.

"Now we're getting somewhere," he said. "Tell us any other reasons you have for thinking him—well, not quite normal."

Yardman instanced his behaviour with the child, how he was always fawning and grinning and making a regular fool of himself. Pressed to enlarge on that, he instanced how the old man used extravagant terms of endearment and humoured her with her food.

"I ought to say, though, sir," he said, "that she took some humouring sometimes. She got into her head it was some veal stew that upset her and she wouldn't look at it again. Then she thought it was the porridge, and he had a rare old job to get her to go on with it at breakfast."

Tempest suddenly thought of something, but preferred to let Yardman make a statement in his own way.

"Let me see. What people ever came to the house besides Mr. Howcrop?"

"Never a soul, sir, except the Doctor. He came when she had that trouble with her stomach."

"How many times did he come?"

"How many times?" He pondered for a moment. "I should say four or five, sir. Once he came when he wasn't asked—so to speak—and I have reason to believe Mr. Trowte was very annoyed with him."

"A sort of courtesy visit of inspection?" smiled Travers.

"Yes, sir, that'd be it. I ought also to say, sir, that when Doctor Mannin was examining Miss Jeanne, Mr. Trowte behaved in a most peculiar way, making faces behind his back."

"You don't say so!" Tempest was considerably surprised.

"Well, not exactly faces, sir. You see, sir, my wife and Mr. Trowte put the trouble down to growing pains, and the Doctor rather sniffed when Mr. Trowte suggested it. The Doctor had his ideas what the trouble was, and Mr. Trowte had his, and Mr. Trowte was making faces to show that his ideas were right and not the Doctor's. When the medicine came, sir, Mr. Trowte took a taste of it and then sort of sneered at the Doctor again—to me, that was, sir, not to him. The medicine, I gathered, was not unpleasant to take, sir, and Mr. Trowte sort of hinted it was sugar and water coloured up and then charged for."

"The child got well all right?"

"Yes, sir. In about a week, each time, she was all right. She was in need of humouring about her food, though. The Doctor took an interest in her, sir. Once when he met me out, and once when he met my wife, he asked very nicely after her." Then he thought of something else, "What's going to happen to her, sir?"

"I don't know," Tempest said, "but I gather that Mr. Travers has ideas. There was the little matter of Howcrop not coming in the morning till eleven o'clock."

Travers explained. "I sent word to my man to ring up my sister and have her over here not later than ten to-morrow. I think she's the ideal one to look after the child till some relative or proper guardian appears. That is, of course, if you agree."

"A most excellent temporary home for her," Tempest said. "But one last question, Yardman: Who else—I should say, perfectly frankly, who else besides yourself—had any interest in Trowte's death?"

"You think I wished him dead, sir?" Yardman asked quietly.

Tempest gave a shrug of the shoulders. "You and your wife were most unhappy here."

"Unhappy, sir?" He shook his head. "We were saving money here, sir. Two or three years of it, and we might have been on our feet again. What chance do we stand of another job now, sir, with me at my age, and mixed up in all the talk there'll be over this?"

"Yes," said Tempest. "There is that. And you can't help us, then—in strictest confidence—about who was likely to have done it?"

"I can't, sir."

Tempest left it at that. Then there was some talk about the child. Yardman said he and his wife could sleep near with an ear ready for any sounds in the night. He was also perfectly agreeable to preparing something of a quick meal for the men in the house.

The door closed on him. "Make a note to get him looked into at once," Tempest told Carry. "I though it better, Travers, not to say anything about that listening apparatus in the kitchen. By the way, you wouldn't be too indignant if we sent his prints up to the Yard with the others, just on the off-chance."

"I'd welcome it," Travers told him. "What other did you mean?"

"Trowte's and Howcrop's," Tempest said. "Life's a funny thing, and you never know."

"There's a gardener of sorts to bear in mind," Travers said.

"I've got all his particulars, sir," Carry told him, "We're seeing him first thing in the morning."

Tempest got to his feet and stretched his legs. "Well, I'm taking a busman's breather while Yardman hunts up some food. I think I'll get those prints off and slip along to the station here and find out how Shinniford's getting on, and various other things. You staying here, Travers, or coming with me?"

"As a matter of fact," said Travers, the least bit too indifferently, "I think I'd be more use to you here. Would you mind, for instance, if I tried—with extreme care, of course—to investigate that charred paper in the upstairs room?"

Tempest took the key from the ring and handed it over.

"I might be as long as half an hour," he said. "If any food's going, keep me back my ration."

* * *

Travers loafed round for a minute or two after Tempest's departure in one of the police cars. Then Polegate, who had been puffing white powder from the blower, laid the gadget momentarily aside.

"Funny about the knife not being left sticking in him, sir?" he remarked.

"Yes," said Travers. "Looks as if it must have been some special sort of knife. I suppose, by the way, you've had a look through the kitchen knives?"

"Don't seem much sense in that, sir, does there?" Polegate said, but moved off that way all the same. Travers whipped the blower into his pocket like a flash and turned towards the stairs.

There was a locking catch inside that upstairs room and he slipped it up before the light was switched on. If Carry came nosing round, he thought, he'd tap at the door and take it for granted he was elsewhere. Unless, of course, the light showed beneath the door.

But he made a quick test of that and saw no light. Then he got to work with the blower. Each of the rubber sausages, and the Klaxon, was gone over with meticulous care, and it was the size of the prints with which Travers was concerned and not their conformation. A singular satisfaction showed on his face at what he was finding, and he spent some time in removing every trace of the white powder. Then his eye fell on that folder with its paper and envelopes. A check-book was there, and a receipt from a Seaborough bank for a sealed package.

Travers slipped both into his pocket, switched off the light and moved the knob of the secret panel. The room beyond was in darkness, and he reached over for the switch and turned the light quickly on. The child, he could see, was sleeping soundly, and inside a minute he was out of the room and downstairs again, and replacing Polegate's blower.

Lucy came from the kitchen way with a tray.

"We're making sandwiches and tea, sir," she said. "In the morning-room we're laying it."

"The child's sleeping all right?" he asked, and followed her.

"Sleeping like a log, sir." She shook her head as she set down the tray. "Do you know, sir, I couldn't feel angry with her, seeing her lying there like that? Like a little angel, she looked." A certain bitterness came into her tone. "And him perhaps, who was telling the lies—not her."

"Your husband told you, then?"

"Yes, sir," she said, then shook her head quickly again. "But he's dead and gone now, sir, and maybe it was a judgment on him. Our characters'll bear looking into. I'm not worrying about that, sir."

"Neither am I," smiled Travers, and made his way out again. In the main room he found Carry.

"Hallo, sir!" the Inspector said. "Not gone upstairs yet?"

"I did have a peep," Travers said. "But that charred paper is a job for an expert."

"And how do you think we're coming along, sir?"

"Slow," said Travers. "And, let's hope, sure."

"Mysterious old cove, wasn't he?" Carry said. "This time to-morrow we'll know a damn sight more about him than we do now." He gave a quick and reminiscent gaze at the ceiling. "Things have moved on since I first joined, what with all this science and one thing and another. You might almost say, sir, there's nothing nowadays that we can't do."

Travers smiled. "'Canst thou loose the bands of Orion? Or bind the unicorn with his band?'"

"Bands?" said Carry, who always regarded Travers as a bit of a queer fish. "What bands are they, sir? Dance bands?"

"Well, hardly," said Travers, who liked pulling the Inspector's leg. "In the case of Orion you might be right." He smiled to himself at the quaintness of the ideas. "Orion and his band. The music of the spheres."

Then all at once his hand went to his glasses, and his mouth gaped.

"What's up, sir? Forgotten something?"

"Yes," said Travers. "Something about music. It's pretty late, but I wonder if a man could sprint down to my hotel with a chit for Palmer?"

"You wouldn't call this late for a residential hotel," Carry said. "You write your chit, sir, and I'll see it gets there." He clicked his tongue. "The sooner we get a telephone line run out here, the better."

The chit was sent and immediately Carry began angling for information.

"Funny how you remember things, sir?"

"Yes," said Travers, "And funnier still how you forget them."

Carry simulated a chuckle. "It is that, sir. And something to do with music, wasn't it, sir?"

"Yes," said Travers. "Last night I seem to remember I heard music. Then I seem to think I didn't."

One of Tempest's men came in then and approached Carry, who turned to him impatiently.

"Yes?" Then he recognized him. "Oh, you're the one who was on Howcrop's tail. Find out anything?"

The plain-clothes man pulled out his note-book.

"Still raining, is it?" Carry said, noticing his coat.

"Regular soaker, sir; what these mists turn to half their time. Made it a bit bad tailing him. Still, here it is, sir. First thing he did was to go to a house called Channel View—"

"You're sure it was called that?" broke in Travers.

Carry noted his surprise. "Anything to do with what we're after, sir?"

Travers, already polishing his glasses, gave a slow shake of the head. "I don't know till I get the answer to that chit I sent Palmer. But it rather looks as if we might loose the bands of Orion, after all. Do you mind if we hear the rest?"

The man's eyes had been swivelling from Carry to Travers and back to Carry again.

"He went in there, sir, and I wondered if that was where he lived—and there wasn't a soul about for me to ask. Then he came out again after about ten minutes and went through a kind of passage-way about a hundred yards to a house which turned out to be a Doctor Mannin's. A woman let him in, and he was inside there about ten minutes. The next thing was that a car drew up at the front door, and he came out and a woman with him—I couldn't tell if it was the same one—and off they went. That put me up a gum-tree, sir, so I thought it out for a bit, then I knocked at the door and asked if the Doctor was in—"

The story was interrupted, for the door opened and another plain-clothes man came in.

"Sergeant Polegate about, sir?"

"In the kitchen," Carry said.

"The Chief wants him, sir, urgent. The car's waiting."

"What for?" Carry asked quickly.

"Don't know, sir. The Chief didn't tell me."

"Just a minute," Carry said to Travers, and went off to the kitchen. What he learned there, Travers never knew, but he was soon back with Polegate, and off the Sergeant went. The interrupted story was resumed.

"So I said I wanted to see the Doctor. It was some one like a housekeeper who'd come to the door, and she reckoned word had just come through from Seaborough that the Doctor had had an accident and they'd taken him to hospital. I said I wouldn't leave any name because it wasn't all that urgent."

"And that's the lot?"

"That's the lot, sir. Except that I came back here."

"All right," Carry told him. "There'll be a tot of tea going in a minute. You can get on in there and help Johnson with prints."

"That queers that pitch, then," he said to Travers. "That doctor was one I'd marked down for questioning first thing in the morning. If he couldn't do anything else, he might have given us a tip or two about the old man. And what was that you were saying, sir, about that O'Ryan? You know, sir, the one with the band."

"I can't tell you till I get an answer from Palmer," Travers said, "then I'll put my cards on the table. Here's somebody now."

It was Tempest, much sooner than they expected him. He had met Polegate on the way, he said, and had left Travers's messenger on duty at the station phone. He also handed over a chit from Palmer. Travers read it while Carry regarded him anxiously. Travers heaved a sigh and put the letter in his pocket.

"Now I'll tell you all about it," he said.

"About what?" asked Tempest.

"About something that clean slipped my memory," Travers told him. "Last night when I was interviewing the Yardmans, Palmer saw a man loitering about the grounds here, and this morning he identified him as a certain said-to-be-famous pianist named Milovitch, who's staying at a house called Channel View. That seems to strike you—as it struck me—as highly unlikely. Now, I may say that this chap Milovitch is accustomed to spend his evenings here—he's down for a week or so—either in practice or display, for apparently he plays the piano with the window open from after dinner till ten o'clock at night. Now, last night I seem to remember he was playing when I passed the house. Palmer tells me I was correct, and the manageress of the hotel says he played till ten o'clock again, because she was out on the green listening. Therefore Palmer must have been mistaken. And yet Palmer insisted at the time that he hadn't been mistaken, and he's a shrewd, observant old fellow, as you well know."

Tempest smiled. "Well, what's the odds? You say yourself that you never believed the pianist was the man."

"I know," said Travers. "But the really strange thing is that when Howcrop left here to-night he went straight to Channel View, which is the house the pianist has taken. He was there for ten minutes."

"Oh," said Tempest, and rubbed his chin. "That puts a different complexion on things. But suppose the pianist has a brother."

"Then in the morning," Travers said, "we might get information about that brother."

"You think he has a brother?" asked Carry.

"I'm pretty sure he hasn't," Travers said. "My advice is to leave Milovitch alone and tackle him, if necessary, through Howcrop."

"We'll get it worked out," Tempest said. "Anything been happening here?"

Travers produced the check-book and the bank receipt.

"These turned up," he said, and before Tempest could ask where: "That receipt gives us our first line on Trowte. The bank manager will give some information."

"My own bank!" said Tempest. "I know the manager well enough. As soon as the bank's open, we'll be there." He had been flicking over the counterfoils. "All filled in with initials. Most of them are 'Self.' What we'll do in the morning is have a look at his passbook."

"What's happened at your end?" asked Travers.

"You mean, why did I send for Polegate?"

At that very second Yardman appeared in the door.

"The supper is ready, sir."

"Good," said Tempest. "We'll come and get it." He linked his arm in Travers's. "I sent off Polegate to take charge of a most amazing affair that's just happened near Seaborough. Perfectly inexplicable thing. I'll tell you all about it while we're feeding."

VII
EXIT JEANNE

"It's this Doctor Mannin," Tempest said, and referred to the notes he had made at the station. "You sent for him, didn't you, Travers, just after you'd discovered the body?"

"Yardman went for him," Travers said.

"Well, this is his story," Tempest said, "and there seems no reason to discount it, though it sounds pretty hectic. The Doctor, according to times we can check in the morning, was at the cottage of a certain Mrs. Diddy, an old lady with a young grandson, and was attending the grandson. He left there at soon after eight o'clock. I should say, by the way, that he arrived there at about a quarter to. When he left he asked the old lady to gather a bunch of violets, which he'd admired and she'd offered, and take them to the surgery, where he'd meet her and give her a new bottle of medicine for the boy. She arrived there in due course, but the Doctor didn't turn up, and this is why:

"He was going on to see another patient, just along the cliffs and nearer this way. It was misty, he says, and all at once he ran into a car drawn up by the side of the road. A man—a short, fattish man with a face like a stage publican's—asked him if he could show him the way to a doctor's. Mannin told him he was one, and the man asked him to examine another man in the back of the car, and this man had a knife wound in his forearm. Mannin happened to have some bandages and things in his little black bag and began to see to the injured man, and then the fat man suggested that the Doctor should go on binding him up while the car moved on towards Little Seabreak, where he said they lived.

"The Doctor apparently agreed to this and to take the patient to Little Seabreak, provided the fat man drove him back. It's about two miles, or just less, you may remember; that is, about a mile short of Old Seborough. The Doctor finished his job—it was the devil of a slash, he says—and didn't like the look of the chap, who was remarkably white about the gills. Then all at once the fat man got out of the car and the Doctor, thinking they were at the house, got out too. The fat man pointed at something in the mist, and when the Doctor turned that way hit him the devil of a clout with a spanner or something. The Doctor rolled down the cliffs among some bushes, and when he came to he found he'd broken his leg just above the ankle. Somehow or other he dragged himself up to the road again and hailed a passing car."

"That's a queer story, sir," Carry said. "Any report of a burglary in the neighbourhood?"

"Not to my knowledge," Tempest said. "In any case, householders don't slash burglars with knives."

"From the description, I'd say the fat man and his pal were mixed up with one of the race gangs," Carry said. "There's no closed season for them. And what about the number of the car, sir? Did he get it?"

"He didn't," Tempest told him ruefully. "All he knows is that the car was an Austin Twelve saloon, black in colour, and vintage probably nineteen thirty-four."

"Any possible connection with this affair?" asked Travers. "The times seem to fit, and Trowte may have defended himself with a knife of his own."

"I thought of that," said Tempest, "but I can't fit it in. You heard no struggle, as you would have done if there'd been a set-to between Trowte and the man. Besides, if you work things out, Trowte died at about ten to eight. Mannin saw that car at at least five past. People don't hang about for a quarter of an hour within four hundred yards of the scene of a murder."

"That's true enough," admitted Travers. "It rather looks, then, as if Polegate's handling a separate case. Curious, though, about Howcrop. Almost as soon as he left here he went to Mannin's though it was pretty late. Then he went off with a woman in a car, doubtless to Seaborough, to visit Mannin in the hospital."

"It's a private nursing home run by a friend of his," Tempest said. "But there's nothing suspicious in Howcrop's being a friend of Mannin's. The fact that they'd both had business here with the child would make a point of contact. What Howcrop went round there for to-night was to tell Mannin the news about the murder. He's a garrulous old boy."

As they finished that scratch meal they mapped out the morning's work. The telephone would be in hand at daybreak, and Carry would keep an eye on that.

"I'll call on Howcrop just before eight," Tempest said, "and try to catch him out over last night. He'll probably say he went straight home, or straight to the surgery. I'll test that alibi of his at the same time."

"If you wish," Travers said, "I'll see Mrs. Diddy at about the same time and check the Doctor's times. It'll have to be done sooner or later. Then we can have a rendezvous here just after eight."

"That's capital," Tempest said. "Then I'll call on the bank manager at ten and go from there to the nursing home to see Mannin personally."

"The visit to the bank is likely to be the more important?" asked Travers.

"Undoubtedly," Tempest told him. "We rely on returned checks and the contents of that sealed parcel to give us a line on Trowte."

"Then, if you'll allow me, I'll see Mannin for you, while you're at the bank. You and I can meet at headquarters at eleven or so. That may save considerable time."

Tempest again thought the idea a capital one. But before they left in the morning there was the child to be questioned. Or had a doctor better see her first?

"The Doctor first," Tempest said, "and that puts us in rather a hole. They'll have to get a *locum* to do Mannin's work, but I doubt if that'll all be fixed up. Tell you what; we'll get Shinniford to run over first thing. He can be over and gone in no time, and he knows all the circumstances."

"What questions are you thinking of asking her?"

"Well"—Tempest frowned—"we want to make them as simple as possible. Plain questions to which she can give plain answers. What happened after the Yardmans left? Did she hear anything after she went to bed? That's the sort of thing."

"What I'd like to know," said Travers, "is precisely why she was dressed and had her nightdress over her clothes."

"She slipped it on to come down, sir," said Carry.

"Let's work it out," said Travers patiently. "From all the information we possess, she was accustomed to go to bed at a quarter to eight. There's no reason—unless she tells us to the contrary—to believe the usual procedure varied to-night. Therefore, as soon as she was in the bedroom, the murderer was in the house—or very shortly after. If she heard anything she should have come down then, or at least answered when I called. *Now consider this.* When I returned to the house with Howcrop, she was still not undressed. Yet she had come down, and she had put her nightdress over her clothes! If she was still dressed, why did she need to put the nightdress on?"

"She heard a noise and came down to investigate, and she put the nightdress on so that her grandfather should think she got out of bed."

"That's feasible," Travers said, "but why didn't she answer my call? Yet she came down here all alone. And she's said to be nervous and highly strung!"

"Well, we'll leave it till the morning," Tempest said. "Something may arise out of what she tells us. And you'd better run along to your bed. There's a full day in front of us to-morrow, and you're looking a bit tired."

Carry drove him to the hotel in a police car. As they passed Channel View Travers saw the lights still on, but there was no sound of music.

Next morning Travers woke unusually early. Palmer arranged for a meal and Travers was away in the Rolls before half-past seven. Mrs. Diddy's cottage was the last but two along the road towards Highways, and there was no wonder that she was surprised to see at that early hour the elongated, goggle-eyed Travers. But he soon had her at her ease. Mrs. Diddy, as she afterwards confided to a neighbour, had not spent years in service for nothing, and she knew a gentleman when she saw one.

"I *am* sorry, sir, about the poor Doctor's accident," she said.

Travers, by the way, had given no details, except that the Doctor might have been attacked by a tramp. "And you think you'll catch him, sir?"

"We're hoping to," Travers said. "What we're trying to do is fix the exact time when it happened, then we might trace the movements of the man who did it. What time exactly was he here?"

The old lady plunged into the story with the greatest relish. Her grandson, Will, was in the habit of playing her up over his medicine, and the Doctor had paid a special visit to teach him a lesson. He arrived at about ten minutes to eight, or just before. A quarter to eight, it would be, and Will was in that very room looking at a book the Doctor had lent him. She had then shown the Doctor the violets, and when they came back from the garden she called Will into the kitchen and told him it was time for bed and to take his medicine, which was for his lungs. He took the medicine and it was then eight o'clock, but the Doctor, as arranged, waited for a minute or two downstairs to see if he played any tricks. In two minutes, she thought, she was down again, and spoke to the Doctor at the gate before going back to the garden for the violets. When she had gathered a nice bunch she looked at the clock before she set off to the surgery, and while she listened for a sound from Will, whom she had warned to go straight to sleep. It was almost dark, she said.

"There isn't a clock in here," Travers said. "Where is the clock you're talking about?"

It stood on the kitchen mantelpiece—a cheap metal clock of the alarm kind. It was an excellent timekeeper, she said, and never varied more than a minute a week.

"Well, I'm very grateful," Travers told her. "Now we have the information—thanks to you—we'll soon have our hands on the man who attacked the Doctor."

A uniformed policeman stood at the fork, just along the track, and he held up his hand for the Rolls to stop.

"All right, sir," he said. "You can go through. I thought it was some one come to nose round."

There was another man on duty at the back road, he said. Now the news had got out, the house would be pestered with curiosity-mongers if they weren't kept back. Then Tempest's car drew in behind and the two reached Highways together.

"How'd you get on with Howcrop?" Travers asked.

"Very well indeed," Tempest said. "He said he went straight to the surgery. I put the question, very implicitly, twice. He owned he was a friend of Mannin's, and he went to Seaborough with the Doctor's sister to keep her company. Which reminds me. He confirms that story of the Doctor's—not that it necessarily needed confirmation. He says he happened to be looking out of his bedroom window just a moment before he set off for his walk and he saw the Doctor go by in that car. He can't give any details except about the colour of the car, and he says he caught only a glimpse of the Doctor as it went by."

"That's interesting," Travers said. "I've seen Mrs. Diddy, and the Doctor left there just after eight, which fits in, near as nothing." Then suddenly he was frowning in thought. "But let me see. It couldn't have been more than five past eight when Howcrop was outside the gate there. Do you mind if we jot down some figures?"

Yardman was waiting just inside the door, and the telephone men were there too.

"Mrs. Yardman says will you go upstairs, sir. She's having trouble with Miss Jeanne."

"What sort of trouble?"

"She's been all frightened and shrieking again, sir. Wants to be taken away, she says. We've given her some hot milk, sir, and quieted her, but we don't like the look of things." He gave a little bow. "Mrs. Yardman says you have a rare way with children, sir."

"The devil she does!" said Travers, and blushed. "Tell her I'll be up in a minute or two."

"We'll try those times first," he told Tempest. "A grandfather is the most reliable clock there is, so we'll work by that. Give me a piece of paper, will you, and I'll jot the times down."

There was a considerable amount of cogitation and nodding, and at last Tempest was given the sheet. It had parallel times, as given by Mrs. Diddy and the Doctor himself, and as given by Travers from his own movements at about the same time.

"I'd like you to observe," Travers said, "that I've always been biased against ourselves. I give the events that happened to the Doctor the *quickest* possible time, so as to allow Howcrop to be out of the house as soon as possible. I also make my own movements last the *longest* possible time, so as to delay the appearance of Howcrop."

MRS DIDDY

Boy to bed	8.0
Dr. waits two mins	8.2
Spoke at gate	8.3
Dr. sees car	8.4
Some talk	8.5
First bandaging and car moves on	8.7
Dr. seen by H.	8.7
H. out of house	8.8
Time of walk about 4 mins. H. arrives	8.12

L.T.

Death of Trowte	7.52
Minute's pause	7.53
Out of house	7.56
At bungalow	7.57

| Leave bungalow | 8.4 |
| Howcrop at gate | 8.5 |

"Yes," said Tempest, and checked the times again. "Something's wrong somewhere. By his own statement, fairly well substantiated, Howcrop couldn't have reached here before twelve minutes past eight. By your own statement, well substantiated, he was here seven minutes before."

"Yes," said Travers. "And it may have been ten minutes before. Remember what I said about keeping the calculations biased in his favour."

"That's right," Tempest said. "And ten minutes' difference takes the devil of a lot of explaining away." He shook his head. "Funny, isn't it? Mrs. Diddy, the Doctor and Howcrop himself all confirm one time, and everything you did confirms the other." He rubbed his chin. "We'll just pigeon-hole this paper of yours. Something may arise out of the Doctor's statement this morning."

Travers made his way up the stairs, and Lucy met him just outside the bedroom door.

"I'm glad you've come, sir. I've had a rare bother with her."

Before Travers could speak there was a cry from the room; an agonizing, frightened cry.

"Don't go away! Don't go away!"

"Drat the child!" Lucy flew back to the room and Travers was at her heels. Jeanne was sitting up in bed, her face puckered up as in pain. Her cheeks had an intense pallor, against which her eyes and hair had the blackness of jet. Travers had not thought her so frail.

"Do lie quiet, there's a good girl," Lucy said. "And look! Here's a gentleman come to see you."

Travers smiled. "Jeanne knows me. We've met each other before."

But Jeanne was cowering beneath the bedclothes. Lucy drew the blanket over her and was frowning at Travers and shaking her head. Then she tiptoed back to where he was standing by the door.

"I can't make her out, sir. She's simply terrified. You know how she dislikes me, and now she can't bear to let me out of her sight. I wish that doctor would hurry up and come."

"She's unwell," Travers said. "It can't be natural for a healthy child to be like that." He cocked an ear to listen. "There's some one coming now. Perhaps it's the Doctor."

Shinniford it was. Lucy flew back to the room with, "Here's the Doctor come to see you." Travers lost the adjurations as he went towards the landing. Tempest was coming up the stairs too.

"I've given Shinniford a list of the questions," he said. "They'll come better from him than from us."

They waited outside the door while Shinniford went in. The child had evidently expected Mannin, for Shinniford was at once making explanations.

"And this is the patient, is it, Mrs. Yardman? Oh, no. I'm not Doctor Mannin. He isn't well, and he sent me instead."

"I want to go away! Take me away!"

Travers shook his head.

"Something's radically wrong with that child. It makes my blood curdle the way she calls out like that. Can't something be done?"

"Shinniford will handle her," Tempest told him quietly. And, sure enough, the frightened cries had ceased. Shinniford's voice could be heard as a soothing murmur. Travers caught the name of Mannin, and, "Of course you're going away!" A minute, and he heard distinctly the words of the question. "Tell me what it was that frightened you. . . . What was it, now? . . . Was it something you heard last night?"

There was a whimpering, then the sound of sobbing. Shinniford's voice was soothing again, and a murmur in which they could hear no word. Another minute or two and he seemed to be preparing to go.

"Give her anything in reason she likes to eat, Mrs. Yardman, and more hot milk if she wishes it. Perhaps, if she lies quiet like a good little girl, Doctor Mannin may come after all."

He came out of the room, nodded to the waiting pair and passed on down the stairs.

"That child mustn't be questioned yet," he said. "She's had a pretty bad shock, and she has a slight temperature. Undernourished too, and I can't quite make that out." He called over to Yardman, who was coining from the kitchen: "Why is that child so thin? Doctor Mannin say anything about it?"

"Not to me, sir." Yardman shook his head. "And if she's thin, sir, it's her own fault. Good food was always coming away from the table."

Shinniford made an explosive sound. "Food's nothing to do with it. The child's a bundle of nerves. She's been living on her nerves."

"She may be moved?" asked Travers.

"Sooner she's out of this house, the better. But where's she going? Found any relatives yet?"

Travers explained about Helen. Shinniford pursed his lips and said Pulvery was a goodish way off. Travers said that as far as he was concerned he'd be happy for Shinniford still to attend the child, and he'd foot all the bills.

"I admit I'd like to keep an eye on her," Shinniford said, "but it isn't that only. She must have absolute rest, and the right sort of sympathy. It's a mother she wants—"

Steps were on the path and there was a voice that Travers recognized. He had the door open in a flash.

"Helen! Why, we didn't expect you for an hour or more."

She smiled. Tempest shook hands and introduced Shinniford.

"Glad you've come," Shinniford said, appraising her.

"About the child, is it?"

"Yes," he said. "About the child."

Helen's nod was like a rolling-up of mental sleeves.

"I couldn't sleep last night for thinking of her, after what Palmer told me. This morning I was up at six. Where is she? Upstairs?"

Shinniford led the way with much explanation of the case. Helen was nodding entirely without concern, like a woman who has had three babies, two of them girls, and knows the precise limitations of men. She marched into the room like a conqueror. Lucy gave a little curtsey. Jeanne stared, her small mouth gaping.

Helen smiled, and all the love in the world and all its pity sat for a moment on her face.

"And this is Jeanne. . . . Oh, you poor darling!"

She came slowly towards the bed. Jeanne watched her, moistening her lips. Then as Helen stooped over her she gave a little sob, and all at once was weeping in her arms. Helen's check was bent to hers, and she was rocking the child and crooning gently as over a small baby.

"Pack all Jeanne's things at once," whispered Travers, and, like the others, tiptoed from the room.

"Well, that trouble's over," said Shinniford with a strange sheepishness when they got downstairs.

"That reminds me," Tempest said. "Howcrop was very anxious about the child—how she'd slept and so on. It'll be a shock to him to get here and find she's gone."

"I think I'll be going too," Shinniford said. "Inquest on Monday morning, but it won't affect you, Mr. Travers."

"Discover anything at the post-mortem?" Travers asked.

"Not a lot," Shinniford said. "It was a long, thin knife that did it. Blade about seven inches. It hit a rib, touched the heart and skewed round to the base of the lung. Haemorrhage was the actual cause of death. He lived for about a minute or a minute and a half, and of course he couldn't call out."

"That makes it ten to eight when he was actually struck," Travers said. "And the knife seems to have been a peculiar one, which explains why it was taken away."

"Why not because there were prints on it?" That was Carry joining them. The telephone was all in order, he reported, and Travers made a note of the special number. Shinniford noted it too.

"How'd you get on, Carry?" Tempest asked. "Carry's been searching the beach," he explained to Travers.

"Nothing doing," Carry said. "The tide's in again now, though, so we might have another look when it goes out, in case the knife should happen to get washed up."

"I hadn't thought of that," Travers said. "But, of course, if the man ran out of the front door, the sea would be the best place to throw the knife to."

"I'll have another look during the morning, sir," Carry said. "Wouldn't be a bad idea, either, to barricade off some of the foreshore down there, or we'll be pestered with people dodging round that way. There was one fellow pestering me down there just now. Reckoned he'd lost a boat he'd tethered down there. I sent him off with a flea in his ear to see the local man. Some pressman or photographer, I shouldn't be surprised, making out he'd lost a boat."

Lucy came down and reported that the packing was done. Jeanne had gone to her bath as good as gold, and they'd be ready to go in a quarter of an hour.

"That gives an excellent opening," Travers said to Tempest. "Helen's got a way with her. A few days down there and Jeanne will be a different person. My two nieces will be home, for one thing, and they'll make a difference. What I'm getting at is that if we supply a list of questions, Helen can very tactfully and patiently extract the answers."

"If it's going to be a question of days, sir," Carry said, "we may have our own answers long before then."

"As soon as the coast is clear, I think I'll have a bath," Tempest said. "I feel a bit grubby after hanging about all night. Call for you at your hotel at about half-past nine, Travers?"

"Suit me splendidly," Travers told him. "I'll see Helen off and then make a move. That gardener been seen, by the way?"

"He's all right, sir," Carry said. "And his alibi, too." "Anything arise out of the check-book?"

"I don't know that there is," Tempest said. "Just one little thing perhaps. Most of the counterfoils are to 'Self.' One's made out to Zq. That's a curious combination."

"Zq?" said Travers. "You're right. Still, the check itself and the pass-book may elucidate that. Anything else before you go?"

"Only the wires from that room upstairs," Tempest said. "They run down to what look like ventilators in the upper walls of the morning-room and kitchen. A most ingenious listening apparatus, and evidently installed by the old man as soon as he got here. Carry's consulting local builders about that. The gardener doesn't know who did the job, though he says men were in and out of the house for over a week."

Yardman came down with the luggage and reported the bathroom clear. Tempest went up at once, and Carry said he would christen the new phone by beginning that systematic check of neighbouring builders.

"Before you go," Travers said, "tell me about that man who pretended to you that he'd lost a boat. He wasn't a fisherman, was he, disguised as a civilian; or the other way round?"

"Oh, him, sir," said Carry, and gave a little snort. "He ain't a disguised murderer come back to the scene of the crime. He reckons he's staying at the Royal Oak and keeps his boat for fishing." He still had to labour the joke. "He hadn't got any false whiskers or anything, sir."

"Only false intentions," said Travers dryly. "Which reminds me. If the way to hell is paved with good ones, why not counter by saying the way to heaven is paved with the false?"

"And what's heaven got to do with it, sir?"

"A metaphorical expression," Travers told him. "Heaven, the ultimate good and final climax, and the single aim. Our single aim is the solving of this case."

"And you think that Nosey Parker's going to help?" asked Carry, highly amused.

"I think nothing," Travers told him piously. "I merely hope."

He turned towards the stairs. Helen was coming down, with Jeanne in her arms and Lucy at her heels.

VIII
NEWS OF TROWTE

THE UNIFORMED NURSE read the card.

"Mr. Travers? This way, sir, please. The Doctor's expecting you."

"Better, is he?"

"Much easier," she said, and at once was opening a door on the ground floor and showing him in.

It was an airy little room, all windows and light, and the old doctor lay with his head propped up on pillows as if he had been enjoying the view. He looked a general practitioner of the fine old country type; the kind of man who kept himself abreast of the times and had the knowledge of immense and varied experience. From his straggly white moustache Travers pictured him as one indifferent to appearances and conventions. A bit obstinate, perhaps, but just the kind of man to fall into the trap of the previous night.

"Come and sit down, Mr. Travers," he said, his eyes wrinkling pleasurably at their corners.

"Glad to hear you're feeling easier," Travers said. "But I shall not be worrying you more than two minutes."

"Why not?" the old doctor asked him gruffly. "I've had a crack on the skull"—he rubbed it ruefully—"and a perfectly simple fracture. Otherwise I'm utterly normal."

Travers smiled. "Except, of course, that that leg of yours is hurting like the very devil."

"That's nothing," he said. "If a doctor can't bear a bit of an ache, who can?"

But he had been casting curious, if polite, glances at his caller, and Travers answered the unspoken questions.

"I imagine you were rather expecting some one of the accepted type. I'm not a policeman, exactly. Merely connected at times in what they are pleased to call an advisory capacity. This happens to be one of the times."

"You're not by any chance Ludovic Travers, the author?"

"Well, yes—I am."

The Doctor shot out a hand, and winced as he did so.

"You're one of the few men I've always wanted to meet, Mr. Travers. I consider your *Economics of a Spendthrift* the best bedside book after *Copperfield*"

"That's very nice of you," Travers said blushingly. "But, I fear, grossly flattering. Still, it does rather help as a certificate of respectability, so to speak. But about yourself, Doctor. I hope the statement won't sound too callous, but what I want to question you briefly about is not your own unfortunate experience, but about that other affair of last night—the murder of Trowte."

"Yes," he said reflectively, and pursed his lips. "Howcrop told me all about Trowte." He shook his head. "It may surprise you, Mr. Travers, but I wasn't surprised to hear it. I may say, in fact, he was one of the numerous people I'd have liked to murder myself."

Travers smiled. "The irritating type?"

"Perversely so," the Doctor said dryly. "Not that I ever had anything else but a few words with him. They were about a patient, and words to which I was entitled."

"I wonder if you'd mind telling me about it," Travers said.

"There's nothing to tell," the Doctor said. "His granddaughter's whole digestive system was generally upset, and he was prating about growing pains. Growing pains!" and he snorted.

"And what was wrong with her?"

"What's that?" The Doctor was having a sudden deafness, and Travers knew he had been committing the unpardonable offense of asking for the divulging of professional secrets. And yet apparently he had not, for the Doctor was going on: "Atmosphere of the place all wrong. Nobody but the Yardmans and Howcrop; all very nice people, but not the company—the sole company—for a young child."

There had been a quick questioning glance at the mention of the Yardmans' name, and Travers guessed he had heard that story of their supposed unfortunate past.

"What did you think of the child herself, as a child?"

"I rather liked the child," he said, and with what seemed a deliberate gruffness. "Wouldn't have minded if she were my own. Well, you know what I mean. An old fool like me is apt to talk nonsense, Mr. Travers." Then, before Travers could speak: "How is she, by the way? Not—er—distressed at all over the unfortunate—er—"

"As a matter of fact," Travers cut in, "she left about an hour ago with my sister, for Pulvery Manor."

He gave a brief, and highly edited account, and cautiously mentioned Shinniford.

"Capital for her, capital," the Doctor said. "The very best thing. Shinniford was right about the questioning. I'd go easy on that for a few days."

"I think you can rely on that being done," Travers said. "And between ourselves I don't mind admitting that I've rather taken a fancy to the child too. Which is curious. From all the accounts given of her, I'd judged that she was a most unpleasant sort of child—undisciplined, crafty, lying, tale-bearing, and heaven knows what else."

"You gathered that from the Yardmans?" the Doctor said, with a quick look from under his bushy eyebrows.

"General impressions," said Travers vaguely. "But about Trowte. What were your ideas about him?—in strictest confidence, of course."

The Doctor made a wry face. "I don't know that I have any. I didn't like the man, and that's all."

"But just why?" persisted Travers.

Now Mannin's smile had a deliberate malice. "Acromegalic in type," he said airily.

Travers smiled. "So that's what you call it. I'd noticed his head too big for his body, but my layman's explanation would have been something like elephantiasis. It's a disease of the pituitary gland, isn't it?"

Mannin begged that particular question. He gave a contemplative rub of the mouth. "Affects the mentality, of course, and makes for stupidity—so they say. My own experience—which isn't worth much—doesn't agree—altogether. I've known cases where it made for cunning."

"Yes," said Travers thoughtfully; but at that moment a nurse peeped anxiously in, and by the time the Doctor had waved her humorously away, the precise thread had been lost. Travers got to his feet.

"Well, I don't think I'll do any more worrying. Except, of course, to ask the old routine question, which is if you have any ideas as to who might have done it?"

The Doctor shook his head. "I've not the least idea. I might have done it myself, as I've told you—except that if we murdered every one we disliked, this would be a bloody world."

Travers laughed. "Well, I'll be pushing off. When do you expect to be home again?"

"Two or three days, perhaps," the Doctor said. "Must stay here under observation. We insist on it with others, and the least we can do is make a pretence of it ourselves."

Travers laughed again, and out went his hand.

"Good-by, and hurry up and get home. I'm going to harass your convalescence by coming round for a yarn."

"Now, if anything would get me there, that's the very thing," the old doctor told him heartily, and Travers, fearing more compliments, hastily made for the door.

But he was smiling to himself as he came out to the corridor. The old doctor was a man after his own heart, and maybe—

"Mr. Travers, sir? You're wanted on the phone."

It was an attendant who had come up unawares. And it was Tempest on the phone. Would Travers come at once to the Blue Anchor teashop next door to the bank in Royal Square.

"Something turned up?" Travers asked eagerly.

"Not too much," Tempest said, "but it looks like providing a job of work for you."

The Rolls drew up with almost a jerk before the Blue Anchor, and Travers nipped out, and collided with Tempest just inside the door.

"I've ordered coffee for you," Tempest said. "Over there's my pew."

Travers told him about Mannin, and when the coffee had come and the waitress gone Tempest produced a pass-book and a sheet of paper which seemed to be covered with notes.

"What about that Zq?" Travers asked impatiently.

"Oh, that," Tempest said. "That's very interesting. I'll give you a hundred guesses and lay you a fiver you don't get near it. This is it. Zooquariums Limited, of 35 Pladgett Street, which is just off Regent Street. He paid them a sum of twenty-five shillings, you'll remember."

"How'd you get the address?"

"Had a brainwave," Tempest said, "and looked at the London Directory. I gather it's a place where they sell animals and live fish."

"Creeping things innumerable; small and great beasts," quoted Travers in high good-humour. "Looks as if he bought the child some sort of a pet. I don't suppose it matters, but we might do worse than ring up the Yardmans and ask."

"Here are the really important things," Tempest said, pointing to the sheet of notes. "The sealed package contained the agreement for the house, which was a seven-year lease; the insurance certificate for the current year, and insurance certificates for the two indoor and the one outdoor servant. It contained exactly £10,000 of 3 ½ per cent Conversion Loan, and 34,000 Ordinary Shares in Parker, Boyle, Limited. Does that convey anything to you?"

"Parker, Boyle." He frowned. "Electrical engineers with works at Slough. Ordinary shares round about thirty shillings."

Tempest grinned. "Not far out. They're in this morning's quotations at thirty and six. But tell me. Am I right in saying that since he apparently got in on the ground floor and holds a biggish block of the shares, he must have been an original director or something?"

"Not unlikely," Travers said. "The practical certainty is that we can get information about him from Parker, Boyle at their offices at Slough." He frowned again. "Boyle . . . let me see. That'd be Geoffrey Boyle. . . . Yes, I think I could put my hands on Geoffrey Boyle."

"But here's the absolute winner," Tempest said. "I've left all the originals of everything at the bank, but this is the main gist of it. An agreement concluded a year ago between Trowte and Lorette Trowte, whereby she relinquishes all control and authority whatever over Jeanne Trowte in perpetuity to the said Quentin Trowte, in consideration of the sum of one thousand pounds. All very legal and, I'd judge, watertight."

Travers let out a whistle. "But weren't we given to understand the mother was dead? I take it the Lorette Trowte was the mother?"

"I think we were," said Tempest, "and that's one reason why it wants inquiring into."

"Any will?"

"Yes, and the bank the sole executor. The will was drawn as soon as he got to Seabreak, and it leaves everything to charity except a hundred a year to his beloved granddaughter—those are the exact words—his beloved granddaughter Jeanne Trowte, for her maintenance during her lifetime, with the usual reversion. The bank is sole guardian."

Travers was all at once polishing his glasses.

"Strange wording that—*for her maintenance*. Sure you've got the wording right?"

"Dead sure."

Travers shook his head. "And at the child's ultimate death the annuity capital reverts to charity. Well"—and he gave a shrug of the shoulders—"I can only repeat that it's most damnably queer, and I very much doubt if it's legally watertight. Anything else?"

"Plenty," Tempest said. "Quentin Trowte is described as of Oxley Lodge, Maidenhead. Lorette is of the Stevenson Hotel, London, widow."

Travers nodded. "Well, we might say we've gulped down a quick meal that needs time for digesting. And what about the job of work you mentioned? Want me to go to Slough and Maidenhead?"

"That's it," said Tempest. "To-day's Saturday, which may affect all sorts of people you may want to see. You've got the main facts, so why not push off straight away? I'll notify Palmer and everybody. With luck, you might be back early this evening."

"Yes," said Travers, "I think I'll push off, as you say. Just a minute or two to take a few notes. And while I'm doing it you might tell me precisely what you want to find out."

"I think you know," Tempest said. "Get what's known as the inside dope on Trowte as people knew him at Slough and Maidenhead. Find out about Lorette Trowte and why she should give up her daughter to the old man."

"Right," said Travers, still scribbling. "Meanwhile you ring up Lucy Yardman and ask about that pet from Zooquariums."

He was waiting in the Rolls when Tempest came.

"No pet the Yardmans know of, but a box came and Trowte handled it himself. Yardman has an idea it was an animal of some kind."

"Vague," said Travers with a shake of the head.

"Not to a brain like yours," Tempest told him ironically. "Besides, you'll want some occupation to cheer your road."

"Very thoughtful of you," said Travers. "And now a job of work I'd like you to do. It needs a brain of rather more subtlety than your own, but perhaps you won't bungle it beyond redemption." His voice lowered. "Get a handkerchief and mark the corner E. M. Then call on that pianist—Ephraim Milovitch—and say it was picked up in the Highways grounds. That's all. Just watch his reactions. If necessary, say definitely he was seen there on Thursday night, and you can prove it. All that may be lying, but you can reconcile your conscience and call it bluff."

But Travers had not the least intention of winding an intricate way through the outer suburbs. A short cut to information was in his mind, and when he saw on a Bromley placard—

THE SEABREAK MURDER

and on another:

MYSTERIOUS MURDER

he thought the short cut would be forthcoming. So he looked up Geoffrey Boyle in the Telephone Directory and found a private address at Lancaster Gate. There he was told that Mr. Boyle was playing golf at Crews Hill, which meant the crossing of London. But he cut through towards Kensington and out at Camden Town and, with traffic easing on a Saturday, was at the club-house shortly before one.

A peep in the dining-room showed him Geoffrey Boyle and three others at a corner table, and a message brought Boyle out.

"Mr. Travers?" he said. "Of course. I remember you now."

Travers did some explaining.

"Murdered?" said Boyle. "That's the first I've heard of it. Wasn't in the morning papers." He nodded. "Old Trowte murdered, eh? Extraordinary. And who did it, do you think? That daughter-in-law of his mixed up in it?"

Travers's heart gave a little leap, but at the moment he was disposed to go carefully.

"You're a bit out of my depth," he said. "Perhaps I'd better wait till after your meal; then we can talk about things."

"You've lunched?"

"I haven't," Travers told him.

"Come in with us, then," Boyle said. "There's just a four of us. Harry Parsley's one—you know him. We've only just begun."

So over an unexpected lunch Travers heard the story of Quentin Trowte, and imparted in exchange certain information which later the papers would in any case publish. Parsley had also known Trowte, and as he was mixed up with the theatrical business, gaps were filled in and the whole made coherent.

Trowte's father-in-law, Joshua Parker, was the founder of the firm of electrical engineers, and on his death Trowte was for a time a director. But just before the war he retired to live at Maidenhead. He had been queer in his manner for some time, Boyle said; had the gift for getting people's backs up, interfered with the executive and took a decision or two that nearly landed the firm in Queer Street. At the time of his death he had nothing whatever to do with the firm, though he had resolutely refused to part with his shares.

Trowte's son, Edward, was—said Boyle—a most unusual sort of bird. He was very arty, very high-strung, and most temperamental, and was by profession a costume designer; a job which apparently made him largely dependent on his father. But the old man worshipped him, and allowed him to make a fool of himself to his heart's content. Then Edward married a Lorette Cowan—Letty Cohen off the stage, according to Parsley—who had a small part in Martin Warbag's futuristic revue at the Odeon, for which Edward Trowte designed some of the costumes.

The rest of the story Boyle left largely to Travers's imagination. Edward Trowte had been infatuated with his wife, but she grew to hate him like the devil. So bitter was the hatred that she refused to divorce him, or let herself be divorced, though—still according to Boyle—old Trowte bid a pretty high price.

"Everybody knew she was unfaithful to him," Boyle said. "I believe she used to flaunt it in his face and dare him to prove it. But she was always just a bit too clever for him, or for his father. Edward was mad about her. She could have had a dozen men and he'd have come crawling.

"Then there was some sort of reconciliation. I believe old Trowte stumped up heavily, but whatever it was, they lived together for a bit and the child was born. Then it began all over again. The kid must have had the very hell of a life. Lorette was pretty frequently on tour—she was pally with—well, a certain manager I won't name—and used to take the kid with her. Edward used to follow her about, and there were scenes. My God, there were scenes! Then Edward was carted off to a private mental home and there he stayed. He died about fifteen months ago."

"I see," said Travers. "And then old Trowte managed to get the child."

"That I couldn't say," said Boyle. "Didn't she marry Solly Lakin, Harry?"

"Not Solly," Parsley said. "You're confusing him with Benny. She married Benny. That'd be about a year ago. It was a year ago. You remember, there was that deal with Universal Motions, and Benny went to Hollywood."

"I remember now," Boyle said. "But she didn't marry Benny. Benny married her, which is quite a different thing. If you remember, she had the very hell of a row with—with her other pal, not long before her husband died, and I know for a fact she hadn't a sou."

Parsley turned for more confirmation to another of the party.

"You remember one night at the Pied Piper, Tom, asking who a certain woman was? You remember—a rather smart-looking dame in red, and I told you she was Lorette? She was doing thrice-nightlies and cadging drinks. That's what she'd come to before Benny fell for her."

"Tell me, then," said Travers, "if I should be pretty near right if I assumed this: she only parted with the child for two probable reasons—she was so hard up that she couldn't refuse old Trowte's offer—"

"Did he offer?" cut in Boyle.

"I have reason to believe he did," Travers said. "He made a bid and she accepted. She renounced the child entirely, and he adopted her. The other reason that made her accept was the likelihood of her marriage. I mean, the man might have been put off if the child had been there."

"I didn't even know Trowte had adopted the child," Boyle said. "I admit I hadn't even thought of Lorette for months, and I sort of took it for granted that the kid was in America too. But I'd say you're right. I'd say, considering what you know, that you certainly are right."

"You're not going to worry about Lorette, I hope," Parsley said. "I'm not loose-mouthed about women, but if ever there was a bitch, she was one. Had the face of a saint, as they say, but vulgar as they make 'em. And foul-mouthed? It takes a bit to turn my stomach, but she was the absolute limit."

Travers shook his head. "Must have been pretty awful. I suppose it's a foolish question to ask if old Trowte hated her?"

"I'll tell you something that sounds preposterous," Boyle said. "I saw him between Edward's death and the funeral, and he told me in cold blood that if she turned up at the funeral he was going to do her in. What's more, I believe he'd have done it." He sneered. "She didn't go—which was a pity."

"You knew he'd gone to Seabreak?" Travers asked.

Boyle opened wide eyes. "My dear fellow, you could have knocked me down with a feather when you told me he'd been murdered down there. To tell the truth, I imagined he was still at Maidenhead. You see, we've got nothing in common nowadays. I never did cotton to him much, and I didn't like the look of him latterly. Weird-looking old bird. Damn great head and hooked beak, like an old vulture." He laughed. "Funny way to speak of the dead, but there you are. No good saying what you don't think."

The meal and the disclosures came to an end at the same time. The party rose, and Travers knew himself somewhat in the way. Boyle confirmed the fact.

"You won't think us rude, but we're booked off at two-ten. Devil of a rush here on a Saturday afternoon."

Travers rendered profuse thanks, shook hands all round as seemed to be expected, and gracefully retired. In ten minutes he was through Enfield and heading for town, and with a considerable deal to think about. It was nearly three when he came down Charing Cross Road, and there he remembered something and turned the car right for Shaftesbury Avenue. Tebbitt, the agent, happened to be in, and he remembered Travers from a previous visit.

"Well, sir, how are you?" he said. "And what can I do for you this time?"

"An absolutely confidential matter," Travers said. "Can you tell me anything about a pianist named Milovitch? Ephraim Milovitch?"

"Milovitch! Can I tell you anything about Ephraim Milovitch!" He spread his palms contemptuously. "My dear sir, I got him his first job at a little cinema down in Hoxton, long before the war, when he was Eph Cohen."

"Cohen?" said Travers, extraordinarily quietly. "Any relation to a woman known as Lorette Cowan?"

"Letty's brother," Tebbitt said, and with something of the same contempt. "Jack Cohen, the father, did a juggling act on the halls and drank himself to death. Three children he had. Ephraim was the eldest, and he won a scholarship and took up music—the sort that don't pay. Jake was a boxer, and he died of consumption, and Lorette's now in America. Friend of yours?"

Travers shook his head.

"Then I can say what I was going to. Best thing she ever did, and it'll be a damn good job if she stops there." He rubbed his hands. "And now what can I tell you about Ephraim?"

Travers rose. "Nothing, thanks. In fact, you've told me more than I ever expected to know. Anything I can do to thank you?"

Tebbitt waved at the hospital box. Travers contributed and hurried down to the car.

At the end of Shaftesbury Avenue he turned into Regent Street, on the look-out for the Pladgett Street opening. Then he overshot it and left his car at the Regent Street curb and walked back. Zooquariums Limited lay within a cricket pitch of the main street. In the shop window were the usual puppies and the usual highly coloured birds. There was also a tank in which assorted creatures appeared at intervals out of the most depressing looking vegetation and greyish mud.

His hand went to the door-knob and his nose against the glass, for the door was shut. There was a blind down it too, and it was plain that Zooquariums Limited closed on a Saturday afternoon. Yet there must be some one to feed the animals, and he rapped at the door. But nothing happened. Whoever it was that did the feeding would apparently be coming at some later time. And after all, it was perfectly easy to ring up the firm on Monday, if the matter were important; and after due consideration Travers decided that it was not.

He circled round and so back to Charing Cross Road again, and into St. Martin's to make the distance call from the flat. It was Carry who answered, and Travers was not disposed at the moment to tell him very much.

"You're coming down at once, sir?" Carry asked.

"I hope to be with you in a couple of hours or under," Travers said. "Anything been happening at your end?"

"Happening, sir?" Carry paid Travers back in his own coin. "You wait till you get here, sir—and the Chief's back too. You'll have the surprise of your life."

"Of what sort?" asked Travers warily.

"About a certain party, sir. The one who made the accusations against other certain parties. It turns out he's been inside himself."

Travers hung up bemusedly. What he gathered was that Howcrop, who had claimed that the Yardmans had a past, had himself spent some time in jail.

IX
HOWCROP TALKS

In *Kensington Gore; or, Murder for High-Brows*, which was Ludovic Travers's somewhat whimsical contribution to the literature of crime, there is a chapter on "Coincidence," wherein its author argues that its absence is infinitely more surprising than its supposedly rare occurrence. Consider our daily lives, says Travers. X walks down a street and may or may not pause to look into a shop window. Again, he may look long, or the look may be only a glance; but upon those simple timings may depend various happenings. He may or may not happen to meet Y, whom he has not seen for twenty years. He may step absent-mindedly off the curb and be knocked down by his own wife's car. All our lives, in fact, are series of coincidences, and the paradox is that coincidence itself should be endowed with any capability of surprise.

That Saturday afternoon Travers came to one of those timings, as he terms them. He left the Rolls at the Seabreak hotel, where he had a polish up, a quick tea and a word with Palmer, then set off towards Highways on foot. Then it occurred to him that he had never walked by the beach all the way to the steps that led to the house, and there was also in his mind the missing knife which the murderer might have thrown into the sea. Yet so little was the urge to go the beach way that he afterwards attributed the taking of that actual route to a kind of absent-mindedness, so that he found himself there before he was hardly aware.

He hugged the cliffs where the sand was hard, and found the going good. The fine promise of that earlier April was fast disappearing, for the sky was overcast and the wind had shifted from the east. Once he had left the immediate confines of the village there was never a soul in sight, but as he neared the Highways steps a boat was coming in, and the rower beached it almost under his nose.

"Nice state of affairs," he said to Travers. "And a nice lot of police we've got about here. Reckoned this boat had broken away even when I showed them the rope had been cut. Then I get word she's found at Old Sea borough and I have to go and fetch her myself."

Travers recognized the man from Carry's description; a grizzled man of middle age, and most likely a visitor.

"You think she was stolen?"

"Think?" He snorted contemptuously. "Here's where she was made fast with the oars shipped inside. Here's the end of the rope that was left. Now I ask you, sir. Is that a break or a cut?"

Travers polished his glasses and had a look.

"Well," he said, "I'd say it was slashed with a knife, then pulled at. Looks as if the one who did it thought the knife had gone clean through, but it hadn't, but when he pulled, the rest frayed away."

The man gave him a quick look. "Do you know, sir, I reckon you're about right. But have a look at this. See that caulking? That hole was made to sink her, and she did sink, only the tide beached her. That's how she got found. Practically full of water, she was. One oar alongside her and the other one gone altogether."

"Extraordinary," said Travers. "But who on earth should want to do that? One hears of stolen cars being found abandoned, but this is something quite new. More like boys' mischief, don't you think?"

Then suddenly he stopped and his fingers went to his glasses again.

"Have you a knife on you? I wonder if you'd let me take about an inch off the end of that rope. It strikes me as most interesting."

The man began stropping the knife on his boot. "You mean you think you can prove it was cut, and not what the police said?"

"I think it's extremely likely," Travers said. "If anything happens, then I'll let you know."

Carry was in the house when Travers walked in. Tempest, he said, was up in the secret room examining the charred papers. But while they were talking Tempest came down, and before he could open his mouth Travers was motioning for silence.

"You've got hold of something good," Tempest said, when he had heard about the boat. "We'll rush that piece of rope off to Shinniford and get him to test it for blood. You send it straight away, Carry, and I'll warn Shinniford on the phone."

"I didn't like going too much into detail," Travers said when the Inspector had gone. "Carry had other ideas about that man and his missing boat and I didn't like to hurt his feelings. But the theory's feasible, don't you think? The murderer had to go somewhere after he left through that door. Why shouldn't he have gone down to the beach and taken the nearest boat? If he walked or ran along the beach he might have bumped into some one who would recognize him, whereas if he went by the boat he'd run no risk at all. Then he got lost out in the mist, and ultimately he holed the boat and set her adrift to cover up the theft."

"A cool customer," Tempest said, "to cut that rope with the knife he'd just used. Still, I'll get hold of Shinniford."

By the time Carry was back they were ready for a quick conference. Travers gave an account of the afternoon's happenings, and no sooner did he mention Edward Trowte and the mental home, and the subsequent death there, than Carry was bursting to propound a theory.

"Suppose you were right after all, sir!" he said at last to Travers. "That first theory of yours about somebody gone cuckoo being locked up in that room upstairs!"

Tempest stared. "You imply that Trowte's son didn't die?"

"How could he have died if he was up there?" asked Carry, with a most plausible illogic. "Only a theory of mine, sir, but take those private mental homes. I believe they're under supervision nowadays, but what sort of supervision would it be? A little graft here and little faking there, and anything might go on. Mr. Travers says old Trowte was absolutely potty about him, so why shouldn't the death have been faked, and him brought here?"

"Pretty desperate doings, surely?" said Tempest. "Trowte and the proprietor of the home and the doctor who gave the certificate—"

"Probably one and the same person, sir."

"Maybe," said Tempest, "but that doesn't much lessen the gravity of the deception. And if Trowte knew of the likely marriage of his daughter-in-law, then he was deliberately inciting to bigamy."

"And why not, sir?" said Carry, whose ducks were always prize swans. "Why shouldn't Trowte have got even with her like that? From what Mr. Travers has been telling us, he'd have done pretty nearly anything to get his own back. Once she'd married the other man he could have held it over her so as to get custody of the child."

"You're forgetting that when he did that he'd have given her a very powerful counter weapon," Travers said. "He'd have been presenting her with a magnificent chance of blackmail. Not that I don't agree that your theory, Carry, is most clever and convincing. Trowte might have kept his son—his partially recovered son—in this house, and that son may have murdered him in a mad fit."

"It was your original theory, sir," Carry told him generously.

"I know," said Travers. "And since it's only the fools who never make mistakes, I hastened to renounce it as soon as it became untenable. For, don't you see, we can prove beyond all doubt whether or not Edward Trowte died and was buried. We can prove it from information with which Boyle will supply us. But to me there's here under our noses a proof equally satisfying, and it's this: *we did not set foot in that upstairs room as expected guests*. Nothing was camouflaged or obscured. We broke in, so to speak, and yet there was no trace of any person's having been there other than old Trowte himself."

"To me that's final," Tempest said. "And what else happened, Travers?"

Travers came to his grand climax and the real identity of Ephraim Milovitch.

"Good God!" said Tempest. "Then Palmer was right after all."

"More or less," said Travers. "Either our pianist friend or his double was prowling round the grounds here on the night before the murder. By the way, did you adopt my handkerchief suggestion?"

"Carry and I rather improved on it," Tempest said. "We faked an envelope addressed to him at Seabreak, and I took good care not to let it go out of my hands. I'll tell you just what happened.

"I went to the house and asked to see Mr. Milovitch, and gave the maid my private card. I waited in a sort of hall under the room upstairs, which is the one he uses for music, so I afterwards calculated There was a most peculiar sound coming from up there, by the way, like a lot of lumbering noises, and something being moved over the floor, then the maid came down and I was shown up. Very affable, he was, and I congratulated him on his perfect English, whereupon he told me be was English—-on the mother's side. Then I put on the heavy stuff and told him who I was, and produced the envelope. It hit him clean in the wind; there wasn't a penn'orth of doubt about that. I told him the letter was addressed to him, and murder was a damnably important thing, and we had to explore every avenue. No thought in our minds, I said, about connecting him, but we wanted to know who was likely to have the envelope in his or her possession.

"You can guess what happened. He simply disclaimed any knowledge, so I fired my second shot. It was most peculiar, I said, but we'd already had a mention of his name in connection with the affair. In fact, we had a witness who would swear that he had been seen in the actual grounds of Highways on the Thursday night."

"What'd he say to that?"

"He got up with what I can only call the most impeccable dignity; stalked over to a bell and pushed it without saying a word. In came one of the most highly decorated works of female art I've ever seen. His secretary—name I've forgotten. 'Miss So-and-So,' he says, 'this gentleman has the impression that I was out of this house between seven o'clock and ten o'clock on Thursday night. Will you be so good as to disillusion him?' Which she did. Swore blind he was never out of the house and that he was playing the piano in that very room from just before eight till nearly ten."

"A perfect secretary," said Travers dryly. "And what did you do then?"

"I rose in all the majesty of the law," said Tempest with a wink. "While fully accepting the alibi, I ventured, however, to point out that what the secretary said was not perfect evidence. It might have been she who was playing the piano."

Travers laughed. "Good for you. And then what?"

"He bowed most urbanely and said that the lady might be capable of playing the simplest of nursery exercises, but as he was playing—he recited the devil of a list, including Bax and Sibelius—he didn't think my own argument had much force. Any musical person in the village who happened to be listening would, he said, bear him out. That entirely settled my hash, and I grovelled suitably and departed."

"And your impressions of him?"

Tempest made a face. "To tell the truth, I thought him a bit of a bounder. He was posing all the time too. I don't say that he hadn't a very good layer of veneer."

"If only I dared do it," said Travers, smiling wryly, "I believe I could smash his alibi."

"How, sir?" said Carry like a flash.

"Wait till he's out with his secretary on his morning constitutional and then have a man with a peaked cap call and tell the maid he's from the Electric or something. I'll wager that if he got his nose inside the music-room he'd find something interesting. I'm a long way off sure, mind you, but why shouldn't those noises you heard have been the removing out of sight of some automatic player apparatus which could be attached to the piano?"

"By jove! you're right."

"Perhaps I am," said Travers. "The lady might find Bax and Sibelius beyond her capacity, but not when they were on perforated sheets. While she was manipulating the apparatus, Milo might be playing the very devil elsewhere." A gravity came into his tone. "Indeed, the more I think it over, the more uneasy I am. For instance, doesn't all that evening playing of his appear now in a new light? Not practice or display, but the deliberate attempt to create an alibi?"

"Yes," said Tempest, and gave a shake of the head. "As you say, it all looks a bit different. To be absolutely frank, Milo may be our man."

"Leave it for a bit," said Travers. "My own experience has always been—and Carry doubtless will bear me out—that clues and evidences and theories, once they become the least degree puzzling or less clear, are best left for a bit. They're just like the old arrows. Shoot one into the blind and hunt for it, and ten to one you'd find the ones you'd lost. I think, for instance, we can still get at Milo another way." He remembered something. "What was that great discovery about Howcrop?"

"Hasn't Carry told you?" Tempest said. "Tell him, Carry. You got the information."

"It came from the Yard just after you left, sir," Carry said. "I called them up as a matter of routine to give them the number here, and I was told to hang on. Then they said: About those prints sent in, Yardman's was unknown and so was Trowte's. And what do you think about Howcrop's, sir?" He was asking the question while he felt for his note-book and found the entry. "Here it is, sir, and just you listen to this:

"John Randolph Cropford: obtaining money under false pretences, twelve months, 1912. Forgery, three years, hard, 1914.

"They gave me that to go on with," said Carry with a grin, "and the official packet came along later. Like to see it, sir?"

Travers said he most certainly would. J. R. Cropford, it appeared, had taken a degree at Oxford and then got mixed up with a fast set and was bought out of trouble once or twice by his people. Then he embarked on hotel swindles, posing as a man of wealth and moving on when bills came due. It was for that that he received his first term. When he came out his people disowned him and he adopted the name of Howison and took a job as private tutor. There he forged a check for a considerable sum. When he came out after his second term in jail, he joined the Army under his own name, served in France and was wounded in the shoulder at Givenchy. Shortly after that his father died and left him the bare pittance of seventy-five pounds a year on the condition that he went to some nominated place and stayed there, and that he kept out of further trouble. Where or not the war had made him pull himself together, or he knew his chance the last one, the fact remained that there had been no further trouble. The name Randolph Howcrop had probably been adopted to avoid recognition by any acquaintances of his old days.

"Trustful people about in those days," said Tempest. "Got a job as tutor and nobody apparently inquired into his references."

"Carelessness is the rogue's safeguard," Travers said. "Their stock-in-trade is their face value. Still, I don't know what you're thinking about Howcrop, but I'm rather disposed to be of the opinion of the preacher—there, but for the grace of God, goes Ludovic Travers."

"Yes," said Tempest. "A wild youth and a heavy punishment; and now a kind of beachcomber. Served the war and has gone straight since. All the same, we can't be sentimental in our game. For all we know, may still be the most slippery old humbug and liar. And we must use what we know to get the last ounce of information out of him. I don't think he's kept anything back about the house—"

"Just a minute, sir," cut in Carry. "What about the lies he told about the Yardmans? Reckoned they had a dirty past, and it was himself he might have been talking about all the time."

"I still think he was speaking the truth about that," Travers said. "He claimed that his source of information was Trowte."

"Well, let's see what information we want from him," Tempest said. "Why he went to see Milo, why he told lies about it; anything else?"

"You'll pardon my suggesting it," Travers said, "but I think George Wharton's method will be as good as any with Howcrop. Take the wind completely out of his sails and then ask for the truth. Many's the time George has heard things he'd never even suspected. For instance, when that poor devil Howcrop's gasping, and wondering how you found him out, just hint that you know heaps more, but you'd rather hear his version. About Milovitch, we'll say."

"You're right," Tempest said. "That's the technique to use with a man like him. You remember, by the way, how we noticed last night that he mentioned possible relatives. That sheds quite a lot of light on Milovitch and their relationship." He rose from the chair. "What's better to do? See him here and make him all alarmed? Or go and see him at his rooms?"

"Here, I think," Travers said. "That will set him wondering."

"You ought to have seen his face this morning, sir" Carry said, "when he came round here at eleven and the Chief and you were away. I made out I didn't know what he'd come for, then he started asking about the little girl. You ought to have seen him when I told him she'd gone. I said I wasn't at liberty to tell him where. Do you know, sir, I thought the old boy was going to shed a tear."

Travers nodded, not relishing over much the baiting of Howcrop.

"What about your taking a car and bringing him here? Don't go doing any funny business. Just be reserved and secretive. What do you think, Tempest?"

So Carry left to bring Howcrop in. Tempest remembered Zooquariums Limited, and Travers told what had happened.

"I had a word with Yardman about that parcel he mentioned," Tempest said. "According to him, it was brought by the railway van and the man who handed it over to Yardman tried a joke about something being alive inside and mind he didn't get bitten. Old Trowte heard the talk and came rushing out furiously and took the box himself, and that's the last Yardman saw of it. He says there was a big red label on it which he hadn't time to read because he was signing for the box."

"Where are the Yardmans now?"

"At their bungalow," Tempest said. "I said I shouldn't want them except to get a scratch meal later."

"Find anything among that charred paper?"

"Nothing at all. The only thing I did manage to get against the light was an old check or two. The bank people said they had instructions to return every check as soon as cleared."

Travers took out his pipe and prepared for a restful five minutes before the arrival of Howcrop. The five minutes became ten and then fifteen. Tempest was a bit anxious.

"He may have been out somewhere," Travers said. "Carry may have had to go and pick him up."

Five more minutes passed and then all at once the telephone bell shrilled. It was Carry, speaking from the railway station, which lay about a quarter of a mile from the village.

"Where's Howcrop then?" Tempest asked, thinking in a moment of panic he had bolted by train.

"I haven't been there yet, sir," Carry said, and went on to explain.

As he passed Channel View he noticed a van drawn up and two men carrying something from the house. Purely on spec, as he put it, he kept an eye on them and followed the van which was making for the station. There the large wooden case was unloaded and ultimately put on the platform ready for a train. Carry managed to note down the address, which was to a house in Hendon and to Milovitch himself.

"I'll lay you a fiver, sir," he told Tempest over the, phone, "that it's that pianola apparatus Mr. Travers guessed at. He got the wind up about that alibi and shipped it back home."

"One of the brainiest things I've known Carry do," Tempest told Travers. "The thing is, can we make use of it?"

"Howcrop's my ace," Travers said. "When we've finished with him we can have a quick pow-wow over Milo."

"You handle Howcrop," Tempest suddenly said. "I'd much rather you did. You're a literary gent, and I think he's a bit terrified of me."

But there was nothing that seemed the least terrified about Howcrop when Carry brought him in. His "Evening, gentlemen" had all his old aplomb and complacency.

"Take a seat," Travers said, smiling. "Cigarette? Or would you prefer a pipe?"

"Cigarette, I think," Howcrop said. "I never did take to a pipe. Cigars!"—he waved his hand—"Wish I had a fiver for all I've smoked."

But a silence was settling on the room, and at once he could discern a vague uneasiness. Carry took a seat, and Tempest, and Howcrop was shifting his gaze to three pairs of eyes.

"I fear this must be a painful interview for you, Mr Howcrop," Travers began in his best Whartonian manner. "If it is any amelioration, I may assure you that it is a confidential interview—for the moment. Whether facts which have come into our possession will have to go beyond this room will depend largely on yourself. If, for instance, you tell us what is known as the truth, the whole truth, and nothing but the truth, then I think you need not be afraid of exposure."

"Exposure?" He licked his lips.

"We have your finger-prints and your record," Travers told him bluntly, and picked up the sheet of paper. "Do you wish us to address you by your present name, or as Cropford?"

Then the unexpected and the extremely painful was suddenly happening. Howcrop had stared feebly and shaken his head, and then all at once his head was in his hands and he was sobbing his heart out. Tempest looked down and Carry looked away. Travers waited for a moment, then walked quietly across, and his hand fell on Howcrop's shoulder.

"Forget it, Howcrop. Pull yourself together. . . . That's all over and done with."

He stood there shaking his head, and gradually Howcrop ceased his sobbing and began wiping his eyes.

"You'll tell us you've been going straight," Travers told him in a friendly way. "We believe you have. And none of us can afford to cast stones."

He left him to gain his self-possession and had a word with Tempest about a cup of tea, for Yardman could be heard in the kitchen.

"You'd like a cup with us, Howcrop," he said. "Would you mind seeing to it, Carry?"

The brief interlude made a difference. Howcrop, like a pricked balloon, flopped limply in his chair, but his eyes were dry and his hand more steady. Travers offered another cigarette.

"Glad you're feeling better," he said. "And now you must tell us things. There's an enormous deal that we know, but we'd rather hear your own account."

"There's nothing I haven't told you already," Howcrop said.

"Oh, yes, there is," said Travers, and a sternness crept into his tone. "You've told us nothing. You've even concealed things."

Howcrop shot a timid look. "You know about—about what happened after I came here?"

"It's your version we're waiting for," Travers reminded him.

"Well, he found me out as soon as I got here," Howcrop said, and at once was gaining confidence as he talked. "I wanted the money to eke out things and I gave everything correct—my credentials and so on." He shook a mournful head. "But he verified them, and then he found out. The change of name it was. Then he treated me like dirt and threatened to expose me."

"If you did what?" added Travers quietly.

Then Howcrop hesitated. Travers could almost see his brain hunting for some uncompromising answer, and the trouble was that for the life of him Travers himself could never have hazarded a guess at what it was that he was concealing.

"He cut the salary down," Howcrop suddenly said. "Do you know what he paid me, gentlemen? You know the work I put in here. Half a crown a day! And he cut that off if there were no lessons, whether it was my fault or not."

"Fifteen shillings a week," said Travers. "Damnable, as you say. But don't let me interrupt you."

Howcrop shook his head. "That's all there was—except the way he treated me." He suddenly remembered something else. "He used to annoy me by making me wait. Once he paid me all in coppers. Then he used to sneer at me and class me with the Yardmans. 'All jail-birds together,' was what he called us."

Travers nodded. "I understand. But let's leave that for a while. It must be very painful to you. Tell us precisely what happened after you left here last night. Shall I say, the truth?"

Again Howcrop shot him a look. Once more he was thinking quickly.

"You won't bear any malice?"

Travers shrugged his shoulders.

"Well, I called to see a man who'd asked me some questions about my pupil. Just formal questions, so I thought as a matter of courtesy I'd tell him her grandfather was dead."

"And what did Milovitch say to that?"

Howcrop's hand shook and Travers thought he was about to blubber again. With a look of humorous despair he handed him over to Tempest.

"I'm afraid we can't go on like this," Tempest said. "I think we must ask you to go along to the local police station and make a formal statement there."

"All right, gentlemen." Howcrop raised his hand. "He told me, in strict confidence, that he was her uncle and he'd called to see Mr. Trowte and Mr. Trowte wouldn't let him see her and had slammed the door in his face. That was on Thursday—yes, Thursday. I met him near his house and he asked me in. I think he wanted to—to see the child, and speak to her. It was necessary to do it behind Mr. Trowte's back."

"And you were to help," said Travers.

"What was he paying you?" asked Tempest bluntly.

"Nothing, I assure you. Nothing. There was not a word said about pay."

"What did you tell him?"

"Nothing. Nothing at all. Merely where she slept. That was all."

"You informed your employer?"

"No, sir, no," said Howcrop hastily. "I was trapped into saying what I did. I didn't want to be mixed up in it. I told him so. I assure you I did."

Tempest got to his feet. "Well, we're seeing Milovitch at once. Anything you'd like to add first."

Howcrop shook his head. Words were stammering at his tongue's end, then he caught Travers's eye and Travers was gently nodding.

"He offered me five pounds. I pretended to—to fall in with him. I was leading him on, gentlemen. That's all I was doing—leading him on. Then I intended to inform Mr. Trowte." His eyes were suddenly opening as he spoke and Travers knew he had hit on some happy idea. "Why, that's why I was coming here last night! When I met you, sir."

"Leading him on," said Tempest grimly. "That seems rather a specialty of yours. You're staying in this room till we get back. Inspector Carry, you keep an eye on him. If he gives any trouble, take him away."

Carry accompanied the two to the door.

"Suppose he wants to go on talking, sir?"

"What of it?" asked Tempest curtly. "What do you think we left him here with you for?"

X
THE LAST WORD

THE DOOR CLOSED, and no sooner was his foot on the path than Tempest was unconsciously explaining that curtness he had shown with Carry.

"Snivelling old humbug!" he said. "He made me so damned infuriated I could have shaken the life out of him."

"Howcrop's of a different generation from our own," Travers said as he followed Tempest into the car. "Tears were not so uncommon then." Then he shook his head, and his fingers fumbled at his glasses. "I'm afraid I'm a poor cross-examiner. I doubt if I've the ruthlessness or the effrontery."

"You're too kind-hearted," Tempest told him, still ruffled after that last half-hour. "There he was; fast as we disposed of one lie he had another ready." He sniffed. "A pretty horrible specimen altogether. Frowsty, shifty—the sort that smells."

"Crumbs round the mouth and egg on the waistcoat," said Travers. "But that doesn't constitute a *crime*. As for lying, I'm a believer in Wharton's dictum. A liar's the law's best friend. Trap a witness in a lie and you'll soon arrive at the truth."

Tempest grunted. "You can produce what optimisms you like, but there's no denying he's holding up."

"This is a game where you have to earn your money," Travers told him amiably. "And it's still less than twenty-four hours since Trowte was knifed."

Tempest slowed down the car. "Well, I hope you'll agree, but I'm not going to be put off with lies a second time. This fellow Milovitch is going to get it straight from the shoulder. I'm after him from the word 'Go!'"

He left the car with lights on drawn in on the grass verge that lay between the road and the small houses along the cliffs. A maid answered his knock, and at the same moment there was a burst of music from the room above. Tempest smiled grimly as he pencilled something on the back of the card.

"Let Mr. Milovitch have that, will you? We'll wait."

He whispered to Travers. "I've addressed him by his proper name and simply said that Howcrop has owned up."

Travers nodded, then cocked an ear. The trills and runs had come to a sudden stop, and there was the faint sound of voices. A door was shut; feet moved quickly, and a door shut again. Through the door at the passage end Travers caught a quick glimpse of the maid with a tray.

"They were having coffee," he whispered to Tempest. "He's just cleared that secretary out."

But there was no panic apparent on the pianist's face when the two stepped into the room. His attitude was one of reproving dignity, and he gave the curtest of nods to Tempest's "Good evening" and his introduction of Travers. Then he flourished Tempest's card.

"Very bad taste, sir, if I may say so?"

Tempest flushed. "You mean, the name?"

"Yes, the name." With one hand tucked under the back of his velvet coat, he still flourished the card. "What right have you to inquire into my private circumstances? My professional name is Ephraim Milovitch, and I'll thank you to remember the fact."

Tempest shrugged his shoulders. "By all means. And you've no objection to my alluding to your friend Howcrop?"

Milovitch drew back from the fire. "There's no point in standing, gentlemen. Sit down, please." He nodded as if in approval. "And what precisely is it you've come about?"

"You're going to do the talking," Tempest told him. "We have Howcrop's statement. Unless you can explain various matters to our satisfaction, a serious charge may be—"

"Oh, no," he said. "I'm not being intimidated. If you have questions to ask, then ask them."

"Very well," said Tempest airily. "Why did you tell me lies?"

There was a smile of amused contempt. "Haven't you ever been told, my dear sir, that those who ask no questions hear no lies?" He cocked his head on one side. "I take it, by the way, you've made yourself acquainted with the whole of my private affairs?"

Tempest was uneasy. The man was putting up more than a good show. Where he had expected a cringing defence he was meeting with a somewhat contemptuous attack.

"Not the whole," he said blandly. "A good deal, but not the whole."

Milovitch shook his head, and Travers watched almost fascinated the wobbling of his mass of greying hair, like the swaying of a hedge in a gale. Then he pursed his thick lips.

"My sister wrote to me from America. She was anxious to know how her daughter was, and I promised to—to ascertain. I had intended originally to come down here, or near, for a brief holiday. I called on Quentin Trowte, and he shut the door in my face. Thereupon I made inquiries, and then had a word with the man Howcrop. I was determined to speak with the child, and if it couldn't be done openly, then it should be done the other way." He gave a shrug of the shoulders. "My methods may seem highly suspicious to you, but I found out from Howcrop where the child slept. I had a look round the place on the Thursday night, and on the night of the murder I had the intention of rapping at her window with the end of a fishing-rod. I set out with that purpose in view, but saw the cars at the house, and the lights. Later Howcrop told me what had happened."

He raised his eyebrows as if announcing that it was Tempest's turn. Tempest was smiling ironically.

"You wanted to speak to the child. You called on Trowte, and therefore you expected to speak with the child. Yet you had already made arrangements to fake an alibi!" He gave a contemptuous wave of the hand. "I don't want to go into the contents of that heavy box that was sent a short time ago to the station for return to your house. In other words, I'm still asking questions and you're still telling lies."

"There's my story," Milovitch said. "Take it or leave it."

"I may do neither," Tempest said calmly. "But I put it to you that the least charge that may be brought against you is one of attempted kidnapping." He turned to Travers. "I think, with Howcrop's statement, we have more than a case."

"I wonder if Mr. Milovitch would answer a simple question?" Travers said. "Howcrop reported to you that Trowte had been murdered. Why didn't you come to the house at once—"

"It was late; very late."

"Well, why didn't you come in the morning? You could have stated you were the child's uncle, and I'm certain every facility would have been given you to talk with the child."

"There was time; ample time."

"But you've still not come," Travers said. "Doesn't it look, on the open face of it, as if you had a certain purpose in mind—shall we say, kidnapping?—and that having failed, you ceased to be interested?"

"I don't mind how it looks," he said.

"Very well," said Travers. "Why aren't you claiming some kind of temporary guardianship?"

The other gave him a long, wary look, then his lip twisted to a smile.

"You don't catch me out like that. My sister re—"

"Yes," broke in Tempest provocatively. "You certainly had no rights. But you and your sister were carrying on that vendetta against Trowte. You were to get possession of the child. How-crop was to assist till you could get her clean away. You paid him how much, exactly? I'd like to know if his account tallies with yours?"

"I gave him five pounds," Milovitch said, with a humorous raising of eyebrows. "I had to do that before he would talk at all. Also, I think you'll admit that after Trowte shut the door on me I had to keep Howcrop's mouth shut."

Tempest rose from the chair. "Well, we've dealt fairly with you, and I'm afraid you'll be hearing considerably more. But about the night of the murder. That's something we'll settle at once in my own way. Unless I'm satisfied that your alibi is per-fect, I shall have to ask you to accompany me to Seaborough and make an official statement there."

His tone had so much cold menace that Milovitch was chang-ing his look and his attitude, and at once.

"Check what you call my alibi by all means," he said. "I was delayed for dinner—" He broke off. "At what time do you want to know just where I was?"

"From a quarter to eight till eight o'clock will do," Tempest told him.

"Then allow me."

He pushed the bell and in a minute the maid was in the room. Travers knew from the unhesitating way he spoke that he must have rehearsed the scene, at least in his mind.

"Minna, what time was it exactly last night when you took the coffee cups out?"

"About eight, sir. . . . About ten to, sir. I got out by eight."

"I was in this room?"

She smiled. "Why, yes, sir."

"Do you know if I went out at all?"

She smiled again. "I wouldn't know that, sir. You were here when I left, sir, because I heard you talking upstairs."

"Thank you, Minna." He nodded away, even at the closing door, then turned to Tempest.

"Well?"

"I'm satisfied—so far," Tempest told him. "You're staying here for some days yet?"

"Perhaps."

"There's no 'perhaps,'" Tempest said. "Take this from me as an order. If you wish to leave it must be by my express permission. Meanwhile, take good care that when we want you we know where to find you."

He made for the door with considerable dignity. But Milovitch, with a kind of provocative courtesy, was ringing the bell. Tempest turned for a last word.

"I don't know what engagements you've got, but I may be able to allow you to fulfill them. But you'll have to let me know."

He gave a curt "Good night," and, with the maid leading and Travers at his heels, moved majestically downstairs.

It was pitch dark in the road, and they halted for a moment to get their bearings.

"Well, that's that," said Travers cheerfully.

"Yes," said Tempest. "Twice in one night I've allowed myself to be put off my stroke. And by that greasy lump of smugness . . ."

Travers clapped him gently on the shoulder. "No hard names. Let's own up he's been one too many for us, and leave it at that. After all, we ought to be pleased. He's eliminated as a murderer. He ceases to clutter up the case."

"Eliminated!" Tempest grunted. "So is Howcrop; so are the Yardmans; so's the madman. The trouble is, there's nobody left. The only one who might have committed the murder is yourself."

A car came round the bend and they slipped across the road and over the verge.

"By the way, which is Howcrop's house?" Travers asked.

"I think it's that one there," Tempest said, pointing to a light well back from the verge.

"Handy enough for the house we've come from," Travers said, and got in alongside. "And something else. If that maid Minna came out at eight she might have seen Mannin meet that car. It was drawn up somewhere near here."

"Just a minute," Tempest said, and began getting out again. "No time like the present. Howcrop's alibi hangs on it too."

He disappeared in the direction of the house, and Travers smiled to himself, guessing he was going back there chiefly to trail his coat and hope for another meeting with the pianist. Then Travers turned his look towards the house where Howcrop lived, and all at once remembered something.

Those few hours ago—days they almost seemed—when he had walked with Howcrop towards the village; Howcrop stopping and turning to the *right*, and hinting that he lived that way. But he lived *there*, which was to his left. Why the lie? To avoid an unwelcome or too inquiring companion? Or because after all his bluster he was ashamed of the tiny house? Or was it that he had gone to the surgery, which lay at the end of the tiny lane he had taken? No importance in that, of course, though every act of a suspect was important for that vital day.

Handy rooms, those of Howcrop's; handy for Highways, that is. A nip down to the beach, a short cut along by the cliffs and then up the steps. Three minutes at the most for a man in a hurry, and even Howcrop could do it on his head. All that, of course, if he had no alibi. But he had an alibi.

Then, all unawares, just as he came to that stage in his reasoning, Travers was Lack at the night itself. He was staring away into the darkness, lips parted and breath held. Then his fingers went to his glasses and he shook his head. *Howcrop had no alibi.* He might have committed the murder and then, hearing voices at the gate, have bluffed a kind of innocence. But one thing was sure. *He was claiming an alibi which he had never had.*

Tempest's feet were heard on the road and Travers turned again.

"It's all right," Tempest said, ducking his way in. "She went the other way. Even if there had been anything, she says she wouldn't have seen it. It was too misty. Which leaves Howcrop's alibi in order." He got the car moving. "What about him, by the way? Shall we throw just one last scare into him and then let him go?"

"Yes," said Travers, much to the other's surprise. "I'm experiencing a slight change of heart towards Howcrop. Just one more scare, as you say. But you've got to do the scaring."

Carry heard them coining down the path and met them outside the door. Polegate had been along, he said, and had just gone. The S O S description of the Austin saloon and the two men had so far brought nothing in. Carry was suggesting an appeal to all doctors who might have been called in to attend a man suffering from a gash in the arm.

"Howcrop say anything to you?" asked Tempest.

"Not a thing, sir," Carry said. "I had one or two goes at him, but he wasn't giving anything away."

"Right," said Tempest. "We'll talk a bit loud at the door, and you follow my cues."

So there was a certain amount of argument. Tempest said Howcrop ought to be taken to Seaborough for an official statement. Carry said he was sure he was going to talk, especially in view of what had been learned from Milovitch.

The three came in again. Howcrop was sitting in his chair with a look of dogged resignation. Tempest was at him at once.

"So you took money from Milovitch, did you? Agreed to be assistant to a kidnapper. In the States that might mean twenty years. What it means here I don't know, but it'll be a pretty good stretch. Then there're the terms of your father's will, whereby the trustees pay you only on condition of good behaviour. One word from us and you'll have sold everything you have for a dirty five pounds. . . . Well, got anything to say?"

Howcrop shook his head and remained with eyes looking blankly across the room. Tempest made an angry gesture, but Travers's hand fell on his arm.

"Tell me something, Howcrop," he said. "I believe you were genuinely fond of that pupil of yours. Why should you wish to see her taken away from you?"

Howcrop shook his head. "You're wrong, sir. I never thought of any such things. I never suspected it."

Travers let out a breath and turned to Tempest with a grimace of despair. Tempest gave him a nod and jerked his head at Carry, and the three retired to the far corner of the room.

"We've got nothing against him," he said. "Bluffing any farther would only make fools of us."

"Better let him go, sir," Carry said. "Pity I haven't got a man to put on his tail."

"Wait a minute," said Travers. "There is a man we can use. Take him outside and keep him hanging about for a minute or two while I get on the phone to Palmer. He's absolutely unknown to Howcrop."

So Tempest and Carry went back to Howcrop.

"You'd better come with us," Tempest said curtly, and hoping that the last bluff of a visit to Seaborough might make him speak. But Howcrop merely shot him a look, then with the same dumb resignation put on his overcoat and picked up his hat.

But Travers, even while speaking to Palmer, had still as a kind of oppression on his mind that new manifestation of the queer illogicalities which the case had shown from the first beginnings. A child, described as with every repulsive characteristic, but to whom he had felt himself drawn and whom Helen had hugged and consoled. Trowte, fawning on the child and almost besotted, and yet with no quality capable of demanding respect. Howcrop, garrulous to a degree, and now with lips closed like the shell of an oyster. Howcrop in his entirety, a paradox on two legs; likeable at one moment and repulsive the next; and yet, if a balance were cast, Travers knew that in his deepest heart he had a queer affection for the man.

So when Tempest and Carry came back he spoke to them about those strange disturbing feelings that were in his mind.

"All the time," he said, "I seem to have the idea that we're on the verge of something. It's just as if we're in a maze, and the more hopeless things look, the nearer we are to getting out." He shook his head. "There's just one thing lacking. One little clue, or some little revelation, and everything's going to become sense."

"I don't know that you aren't right, sir," Carry said. "It's got me regular up a gum-tree. Let's go and get something to eat, sir, then we may have an idea or two. There's some sandwiches in the morning-room, and Yardman's making some coffee."

"You come and have a spot of food with me," Travers said to Tempest. "Carry can hold the fort here. And if I don't see you again to-night, Carry, I shan't be seeing you till some time on Monday. First thing in the morning I must run down to Pulvery, and Monday morning I must be in town on business."

"Good-by, then, sir," Carry said, and held out his hand. But he was smiling suggestively. "Going to get that girl to answer a question or two, sir?"

Travers shook his head. "Depends on what the doctor has said. But one thing I am going to do on Monday morning if I have time. I'm going to consult my own solicitor on the terms of that agreement between Trowte and his daughter-in-law. I think it's only fair to my sister that she should continue to look after the child at least until she's what any doctor expects her to be."

"I don't think there'll be any relatives turning up," Tempest said. "Milovitch might get some power of attorney from his sister, but that'd take some time."

So Carry remained behind in charge, and the two left for Travers's hotel. Palmer had gone, and it was just as the late meal was ending that there was a surprise, for who should walk in but Carry.

"My man's just back from Shinniford," he said, "so thought I'd better leave him in charge and come along myself. You were plumb right about that rope, sir. Shinniford says there's blood—mammalian blood—on the cut."

Tempest nodded. "Do you know, I've rather been expecting it. And I've been thinking about it at odd times all this evening. What must be done first thing in the morning is to get two or three of the local experts to have a look at the boat and examine the hole in her, and try to calculate how long it would have taken her to fill. By that means, and from the particular tides, we might work out just where she was abandoned and set adrift. The fact that she was found where she was may have no relation whatever to where the murderer stepped on shore. My own idea is that she was abandoned near the village. Still, we'll know more tomorrow."

"You'd like me to go round a pub or two and collect some fishermen for the morning?" Carry asked.

"Just as well," Tempest said. "Then get another relief man and take the night off. At seven in the morning I'll meet you at the house."

A waitress came up. Mr. Travers was wanted on the phone. Travers raised his eyebrows.

"Might be Palmer. You didn't see him hanging about round Howcrop's place when you passed, Carry?"

Palmer it was, ringing from a public call-box at Seaborough. Howcrop had taken the bus from Seabreak green—there was a service every twenty minutes—and Palmer had followed him to Seaborough. He had gone straight to a place which Palmer had discovered to be a private nursing home, and Palmer himself now awaited instructions.

"Any prominent landmark near? A pillar-box or anything?"

"A pillar-box," Palmer said, "just where I am."

"Then stay there till relieved," Travers said. "A man will come up and relieve you in a few minutes."

Tempest was told and he took over the phone to make the arrangements.

"Of course there may be nothing whatever in it," he said when he came back to the table. "I expect he promised to spend an hour with Mannin and we kept him late."

"Wonder why he didn't phone the nursing home," Travers said.

"He may have done, for all we know," Tempest said, "but Palmer didn't think it worth repeating. Still, it isn't what he's doing there with old Mannin that need worry us. It's where he goes when he gets back here. If he calls on that damn musician, for instance."

Carry left for the quick tour of the pubs. Tempest finished a cigarette and then said he would be pushing off home. Travers went out with him to the car, and the last thing Tempest did was to shake his head and make a remark about Howcrop.

"I can't get away from the idea that we're wasting our time over him. We're looking for the man who killed Trowte, not trying to work up a kidnapping case. Howcrop doesn't fit the gap."

"What precisely did his landlady say about his alibi?" Travers asked, though with none too great a show of interest.

"She said she saw him go out. About eight o'clock she believed, though I had the idea she thought it was a bit before." He shrugged his shoulders. "It's not even worth worrying over whether or not Howcrop's nobbled her. He saw the Austin saloon, and his story is linked up with Mannin's."

Travers had hooked off his horn-rims and was blinking away into the darkness.

"Howcrop may be our man after all."

Tempest whipped round on him. "What do you mean?"

"That he hasn't got that alibi," Travers said. "He saw Mannin on the night of the murder and heard his story, and out of it he faked what should have passed full muster for an alibi for himself. He claimed to have seen the very car that the Doctor was in, and the Doctor himself in it. Therefore, since Mannin's times are correct, he could not have been out of the house till after eight o'clock. *But Howcrop never saw that car.*"

"Why didn't he? How do you know?"

Travers hooked the horn-rims on again.

"You know his house. You and I were right against it not so very long ago to-night. I don't know which window is his bedroom, but the fact remains that *any* window of that house is over thirty yards from the road. That night there was a heavy mist. I know what the visibility was like, for I came that way myself. The maid at Channel View said she couldn't have seen a car if there'd been one. But I'm prepared to swear that Howcrop couldn't have seen that car, or more than half-way to it, even with Sam Weller's magnifying glasses."

"You're right," said Tempest, and clicked his tongue. "What a thing to miss! Right under my nose and didn't think of it. And Howcrop may be our man." His eyes opened wide. "I'll lay a fiver he *is* our man!"

XI
ONE GRASS SNAKE

ON THE SUNDAY MORNING Tempest and Carry were at Highways as arranged, and about to go down to the beach for the discussion with the local experts, when who should appear but Travers.

"Hallo!" said Tempest. "Thought you were going to Pulvery."

"So I am," Travers said. "I thought I'd run along here first and hear what happens about the boat. And about Howcrop. What'd he do last night?"

"He left the nursing home five minutes after Palmer was relieved," Tempest said. "He waited for a bus on the pavement outside, and came back here and went straight home. There was a light upstairs as if he was going straight to bed, and then it went out. The man waited half an hour and nothing happened."

Carry reported that the experts were assembling and it was time to move off.

"Funny thing, sir," he said to Travers, "but one of 'em is Powell, the gardener here. They reckon he knows as much as any one about boats."

"Well, you push on and do the preliminaries," Travers said. "I'd like a private word with the Yardmans; then I'll join you." He answered the inquiring look. "Only in case Lucy wishes to send any message to my sister."

He found the two at breakfast in the kitchen, and both rose rather confusedly as he walked in.

"Don't let me disturb you," he told them quickly. "I shan't keep you a minute. Just wanted to see you both to hear how you are. I don't seem to have had a moment this last day or two."

"It's like being in a different place now, sir," Yardman said. "I don't mean because there isn't much to do, but it's different, sir."

"As if some one had opened the windows and let the sun in?"

"That's it, sir," Lucy said for him, and then shook her head. "The trouble is, sir, it can't last."

"When are we likely to have to go, sir?" Yardman asked anxiously.

"Can't say," said Travers, but with no sign of alarm. "It might be in a week or two. Some one's got to be here to look after the place. But tell me." He smiled. "I don't say it's a certainty, but I have hopes, and if they materialize, then things will depend on you. Would you be prepared to take over the charge of some quiet little country inn or hotel, even if it meant leaving this part of the world?"

"Oh, sir, would we!" Lucy said, and her eyes shone. Yardman was shaking his head as if it was too good to be true. Travers was moving to the door, afraid of the thanks.

"Don't count on it too much," he said, "but I think it's going to happen. By Monday night we'll know for sure."

Then he was away and gone. Voices came from the beach, and he made his way down the steep steps to the party that was gathered round the boat. The arguments were in full swing and he stood apart for a time and tried to catch their thread. On one thing only were the experts in agreement. If the hole had not been enlarged or scraped open to admit of the caulking, then the boat would have filled in twenty minutes.

Of the three, two—including Powell—said no boat could drift round to Old Seaborough except from beyond Seabreak Point. Travers, listening to the hot debating, wondered just where the outcome would lead. If Howcrop had done the murder and taken to the boat, he could have had no time to abandon it even at the village and then return to Highways. And since he did return to Highways, why go to all the trouble of rowing to the village in a boat? The mist alone that night would have afforded ample protection if he wished merely to hide for a time and then return to the house to make that gesture of ignorance and innocence.

"Not much nearer than we were before, sir," Carry told him gloomily when the conference began to break up.

"All the better," said Travers. "You'll get a day's rest."

Once more he said good-by to Tempest and then mounted the steps to where he had drawn up the Rolls. Powell was examining her with interest.

"Can I give you a lift?" Travers said.

"Thank you kindly, sir," the old fellow said, and gave a grin. "I never reckoned as how I should ever ride in one o' them Rollses, sir."

He got in a back seat with a touch of his hat, and another to the stately Palmer, who in his unofficial black might well have been the Travers chaplain.

"You've lost a good master, I expect," Travers called back to him.

"I wouldn't say that, sir. Me and the old gentleman always got on all right together."

"What'd you think of him?" asked Travers, letting the car dawdle along the track.

"I don't know as I thought anything of him," he said. "He paid up regular. Never wouldn't let me have no one to help, though. Everywhere might have gone to rack and ruin for all he cared."

"You think he was a bit queer in the head?"

He chuckled at that. "I reckon he was, sir. I know he once or twice asked me for worms to go fishing with. Big worms, he reckoned he wanted. 'What do you reckon you're going fishing for then, sir?' I say, and didn't he shut me up for that all of a hurry?" He chuckled again. "Never did an hour's fishing in his life, from what I made out. And asking me for worms—and big 'uns!"

He was getting out at the green, he said, so there was no more time for talk, and Travers had to move the car along to give the old fellow some satisfaction out of the ride. But he made a mental note to have a longer yarn with old Powell. Asking for worms, big worms, and never going fishing after all. Very curious indeed. And yet, why should big worms be banned? And why could Trowte not have fished unknown to Seabreak village? But by the time Travers had thought of those simple problems it was too late to question the gardener, for the Rolls had long since set him down, and was heading inland away from the coast.

Helen had been warned over the phone that Travers would come, and she stayed home from church. The Major, whom Travers was accustomed to partner, was playing his Sunday morning round with the club pro.—a surreptitious attempt, as Travers duly noted, to improve his game. Peter was staying with a friend, Helen said, and Ann was spending a fortnight with the Cloudsleys in Cornwall. Ruth had gone to church with one of the maids.

"I'm hoping great things from Ruth," Helen said. "She's Jeanne's age and they should be great company for each other when Jeanne gets about."

"How is she?" Travers asked.

"Shockingly worn and tired. It was dreadful in the car. I couldn't hold her, of course, so she just rested against me while I drove. I had her to bed at once and sent for Nanny—"

"Nanny's here, is she?"

"She came at once," Helen said, "and she's staying a few days, much to Ruth's delight, as you can imagine. Then I sent for the doctor—"

"Banham?"

"Of course. He's wonderful with children. He was absolutely shocked at her." she shrugged her shoulders. "I had to make some sort of explanation, so I said she was a relative of a friend, and she'd been living with her grandfather who'd died very suddenly. I'm sure he didn't believe me. You know how he looks at you."

Travers nodded. "And what did he actually say?"

"Oh, that she was under-nourished and a bundle of nerves. She was to have rest and quiet. He was most inquisitive about the shock. I hinted that she'd had a shock. He said that anything that reminded her of it was to be kept away."

Travers raised his eyebrows. "That rules me out—not that he need know. He needn't even know I'm here."

"But he's coming to lunch!" Helen said. "I asked him special-ly. He doesn't know it, of course, but I thought you might like to have a word with him."

Travers shook his head dubiously. "That'll mean some thinking beforehand. But tell me. How's Jeanne been with you yourself?"

Helen gave a far-away smile. "I think she—well, she trusts me. It's pathetic how she looks at me, just like that poor old Bingo when he got his paw in a trap and I used to dress it for him. She was frightened when she woke up late in the afternoon, but she soon quieted down. I think she's taken to Nanny, too." Her eyes narrowed and she gave him the strangest look. "Ludo, was it true what Lucy hinted to me, that she was a very deceitful child?"

"I don't know," said Travers bluntly. "It's a mystery to me. My brief experience is that she's all sorts of things: excitable, quick, timid—maybe even cunning. Why'd you ask?"

"She told me an untruth, and Nanny. Nanny put her medicine in some milk as Banham ordered, and Nanny didn't deceive her at all. She saw her drink some and imagined she was drinking the rest. She told Nanny she'd drunk it. Then we discovered she'd poured it away. I taxed her with it and she denied it, and then she began to cry."

Travers shook his head. "Give her time," he said. "She's unbalanced and ill. Yet there's something about her you can't help liking. Don't you think so?"

"Yes," said Helen slowly, "I do."

"And what did Tom say to it all?"

She smiled. "Tom's always amenable. He never makes trouble. Besides, I said you'd explain."

Travers smiled dryly. "You seem to have committed me to a deal of explanation. Still, I'll spin the whole yarn at lunch—in the strictest confidence, of course. Banham's all right. He might as well know just where we all stand."

So Ruth, after ten minutes with her uncle, was sent up to Nanny, and over the lunch Travers told the whole story.

"And so you see," he ended, "why it is that I say I don't know. She had a shock, and it may have been the finding of the old man's body. Or—and I put it most diffidently—her condition may be due to the confined, unsuitable life she's been leading at the house and after that terrible time she must have had."

"Poor little devil!" Tom said.

"It's a bad business," said Banham, shaking his head.

"But you make it a good business," Travers said; and at the doctor's look of surprise: "Now you know the facts, you can, if you wish, make a stand against her being questioned. Anything that reminds her of Seabreak would set her back. That would be unfair to Helen and to the child herself."

Banham smiled grimly. "You needn't worry about me. I absolutely refuse to have her upset. In fact, I here and now say she's certainly not to be questioned until I give the word—if ever."

"But you'll make an exception in my case," Travers said earnestly. "It's essential that I should gain her confidence. Everything's a riddle—you must have felt that, if I made any hand at all at telling the facts—and she's the only key. I don't want to question her. All I want to do is to gain her confidence and her trust. And that far you've got to trust me."

Banham pursed his lips. "Well, I think I can do that. Perhaps you'd like to go up with me before she takes her afternoon sleep."

"I'm Aunt Helen, and Tom's an uncle, and you shall be Uncle Ludo," Helen said, all enthusiasm. "Why shouldn't we all go up?"

Travers shook his head. "You'll think me obstinate and most cocksure, but I'd like to do it my own way. At what time is her tea?"

"At four," said Helen. "Why?"

"I've got to work out a plan of campaign," Travers told her. "Perhaps I might be allowed to take up tea myself."

But as he came that afternoon to think out his methods of approach, a curious idea came to him. He had not wished the more official representatives of the law to question the child. Banham had been in agreement that the child was ill bodily and mentally, and yet, Travers now asked himself, were those the only reasons that had prompted his own solicitude for the child's freedom from worry? Was he not in fact a contradiction in terms? Were not all his interests in finding a murderer and solving a problem? And yet he had gone out of his way to place the child where she could not be questioned, though one simple answer might mean the vindication of the law.

And yet, when Travers found some sort of answer to the question of his own solicitude for the child, he saw it all as a kind of inevitability. From the beginning he had adopted an attitude which events, in the opinion of Banham, had justified. The first moment when he had seen her had been when she scurried like a frightened elf to the dark corner by the stairs. Then there was Howcrop, holding her and rocking her in his arms, and calling her his little Jeanne. Those were the first glimpses of the child, and out of them had grown his first quick appraisal. Then there had been the lonely house and the darkness, and how she had come down to the room where Trowte lay. Everything about her had been evocative of sympathy. "Something about her has appealed to me," said Travers to himself, "and analysis is no more than waste of time. It is myself I should analyse; why did I want her to trust me, and why did I want her to be fond of me."

But though the moment might be delayed, it also would inevitably come, and sooner or later the questions would have to be put. And, if he himself were given the framing of them, what would they be? Not perhaps those stereotyped ones that Tempest had mentioned as to what she had heard or seen that night. "In fact," said Travers, again arguing with himself, "I might content myself with one question only—why she came downstairs fully dressed but for her slippers, and with a nightdress over her clothes. That would be my one question, and that would be no answer to the thing that keeps teasing at my mind—the strange paradox which is called Jeanne Trowte. From Lucy's description I should have hated her, yet, much though I trust to Lucy's judgment, I was wholly unable to be prejudiced. I liked the child from the first. I saw her, as it were, through Howcrop's eyes. And perhaps," thought Travers with some whimsical twist, "I am exhibiting the qualities that make people spoil their off-spring and refuse to see their faults. Some trick of shadow on her face that night; the white face, perhaps, and the tragic black eyes, or associating her with those shrieks in the night; and that strangely emotional climax when Helen soothed her and crooned over her; those are the things which I associate with Jeanne Trowte,"

Though Helen carried up the tray that afternoon, he was close at her heels. She whispered to him on the landing that she would go in first, and he stood listening by the partly opened door.

"Well, how is she, Nanny? . . . How are you, darling? Had a lovely sleep? And Nanny has washed you and made you ever so wide awake. . . . And who do you think is coming to see you? Not Uncle Tom or Doctor Banham, but a new uncle. Uncle Ludo!"

Ruth clapped her hands. "Oh, yes, Uncle Ludo!"

"Not so noisy, Miss Ruth," came Nanny's reprimand.

Travers came quietly in, with: "How are you, Nanny? And how's the patient?"

Helen's arm was gently round her as she sat up in the bed, and at the first sight of Travers she cringed away. But Ruth had sidled up to her uncle, and Travers's hand was on her shoulder while he watched Helen and the child.

"This is Uncle Ludo, darling. Ruth's Uncle Ludo, and now your Uncle Ludo. . . . Come and watch us, Uncle, while we have tea." She made a quick motion to Nanny to take Ruth away, and as she spread a wafer of bread-and-butter with the jam, she was soothing the child with her talk. "This will be a lovely sandwich, strawberry jam, and here's a whole baby strawberry. What jam do you like, Uncle Ludo?"

"I like all jam," he said. "Not rhubarb jam as much as other jam, because my Nanny used to say it was specially good for us and we had such a lot of it."

"I know," said Helen. "Like rice puddings and porridge."

"Oh, but rice pudding makes your hair curl."

"There's a lovely bite," said Helen, holding the sandwich. "And does rice pudding make *your* hair curl, Uncle Ludo?"

Jeanne's eyes turned solemnly to him, and he smiled.

"I expect it did, but it's a dreadful long time ago."

"Jeanne mustn't have rice puddings unless they're very milky ones," Helen said. "Her hair mustn't curl. It's lovely smooth hair, just like black silk."

"Jeanne's a lucky girl," Travers said, and now he was at the bedside and smiling down. "A lovely warm bed, and a nice Nanny, and Ruth. Nothing to do but get strong and well. . . . Not even any lessons."

132 | CHRISTOPHER BUSH

He had said the word with deliberate intent, and it seemed to him that her hand shook suddenly and she nestled against Helen, who held her with cheek on her hair.

"I think I'll be going now," he said.

Helen looked up astonished. "But you've only just come!"

"Perhaps I'll come again," he said. "Good-by, little Jeanne."

"Say good-by to Uncle Ludo," Helen told her.

She gave him a quick look. His eyes, as he smiled, held her own for a moment, then she was nestling to Helen again.

"Why did you run away so quickly as that?" Helen asked him when she came down.

"She hasn't even begun to get used to me yet," he said. "She still connects me with things that frighten her. In the morning perhaps, after breakfast, we'll have another try."

That night he had a confidential word with Ruth, who said that a toy-shop with real things to sell was the thing she would most like to have. Next morning Travers was away and at the county town by nine. At half-past Ruth was in ecstasies over a new present.

"You simply spoil her," Helen said. "And what's the other parcel, Ludo?"

He smiled and shook his head. "That's for upstairs."

Nanny looked at him questioningly when he came in, and then together they began undoing the long parcel at the side table in full view of the bed. There was rustling of thin paper, and almost all the mystery of birth, and then with a flourish Travers lifted the doll out.

"Oh, how lovely!" said Nanny. "What a beautiful doll! And look at her clothes. Beautifully made, just like a real little girl's. I don't think I ever saw such a lovely doll."

"But she's not for you, Nanny," Travers said, and was all at once turning towards the bed. Jeanne's eyes were on the doll, and then as he halted within an arm's length of her, the eyes lifted to his own. He smiled, and held the doll out. The fingers took it gently, and then all at once she was hugging it to herself.

"And now what are we going to call her?" Travers said. "What do you think, Nanny?"

"I'd have to think about that, Mr. Ludovic," Nanny said. "She's too grand to name all of a hurry. And it's Jeanne who'll have to give her her name."

"Why, of course!" Travers said. "And what's Jeanne going to call her?"

She looked up at him, and then was hugging the doll.

"I know," said Travers. "We'll call her Sylvia. Sylvia's a lovely name."

"Sylvia." Solemn eyes regarded him and for a moment a little smile hovered about her lips; then she once more was hugging the doll to herself.

"That's all settled, then," Travers said, and his hand went gently out and fell on the thin shoulder. It rested there, and he felt the faint trembling. "Two lunches to-day, Nanny," he said. "One for Jeanne and one for Sylvia."

"I'll see to it, Mr. Ludovic," Nanny assured him.

"And now I'll be going." He straightened himself and watched, smiling, till again she looked up at him. "I shall be coming back, Nanny, but not to-day. Some time soon. . . . Good-by, Nanny."

"Good-by, Mr. Ludovic."

"Good-by, little Jeanne."

Her lips trembled as if the words were there but would not come. His hand fell gently on her hair, and then with a smile and a nod to Nanny he was gone.

"And how was she?" asked Helen.

"Much better," he told her. "I think she may be talking to me next time I come. And by the way, when that will be I can't say, but I'll ring you up in good time." He looked away for a moment. "Oh, and, Helen, you won't let any one ask her any questions?"

"Not on any account," she said. "Not even Ruth."

"And if she should tell any little untruths, you'll let me know?"

"Why, of course," she said. "But she won't now; I'm sure she won't. And if she should, why do you want to know?"

"No particular reason," he said, "except to try to get at the back of her mind. The medicine, for instance. Have you any idea why she should avoid taking it?"

"I don't know at all," she said. "It wasn't at all disagreeable. In fact it was rather nice."

"Then some time or other she must have had some nasty medicine," he told her. "It was the name she was afraid of, not the milk and what was in it." He nodded. "I must remember to see Mannin, the Seabreak doctor, and try to find out."

It was nearly midday when he reached town, and his first objective was Oxford Street, and the headquarters of Service Hotels, whose general manager he knew pretty well. It took him half an hour to put the case for the Yardmans and fill in a form for them, and when he left he was very well satisfied.

He had breakfasted early and was wondering about lunch, and a certain little restaurant just off Old Bond Street came to his mind. So he circled round and came in by the south end, and as he waited in a momentary jam of the traffic was aware that the narrow street on his right was Pladgett Street. On a sudden impulse he flicked out the indicator and drew across, and when the Rolls slipped through, found himself almost at once approaching the shop of Zooquariums Limited.

"We're in no special hurry," be said to Palmer. "You take the car home and have some lunch. I shall be along later, and may want to phone. Or, better still, you do it for me. Ring up Highways and ask if there's any news."

He paused for a minute to look in the windows, then entered the shop.

"Might I speak to one of the principals or proprietors?" he said to the man in the baize apron who came up.

"Better try the office, sir," the man said, and led the way towards the stairs. On the first landing he stopped at a door, tapped, and put his head inside.

"Gentleman wishes to see you, sir."

Travers walked in. In a room that looked far too small for the work done in it a man in shirtsleeves sat at a desk, with a gas fire full on within a yard of him. He gave a peering glance.

"You want to see me, sir?"

"Yes," said Travers diffidently. "I'm connected with the Seaborough police and I'm making inquiries concerning one of your customers. A certain Mr. Quentin Trowte, who was murdered last Friday night at Seabreak."

"You don't say so!" He got to his feet, glasses in his hand. "I remember that. I read it in the papers. One of our customers, was he?" He nodded. "And what did you say was his name?"

"Trowte. Quentin Trowte."

"Yes, of course."

He began rummaging among the piles of papers of the desk; frowned; paused with head aside like a listening sparrow, then made for a filing cabinet—a tin island in a mass of more papers.

"Trowte," he kept saying to himself. "Trowte. Quentin Trowte." Then he drew himself erect again. "Any idea of the date?"

Travers told him, and he dived into the drawer again. Then at last there was the long-drawn, "Ah!"

"Here we have it," he said. "A Quentin Trowte of Highways, Seabreak." He paused exasperatingly. "Most of our business is done on the premises, so we don't keep much of an office." Then he returned to the invoice copy or whatever it was he held in his hand. "Quentin Trowte, of Highways, Seabreak. One grass snake and one toad, common—twenty-five bob."

XII
TRAVERS TELLS THE TRUTH

TRAVERS HAD no lunch that day. As he left the shop he was mechanically aware of a tea-shop just across the road, and found a quiet corner there and ordered coffee and a roll. But it was not from any desire to eat. It was thought that he needed; solid, concentrated thought, and the slow piecing together of facts to make an unanswerable whole.

And as he put fact to fact and reared new facts from old deduction, he was feeling like a man who comes in the dark upon some unimaginable horror and recoils, then nears again, and at last forces his nerves to steadiness and marks remorselessly the workings of the foul, unspeakable thing. Sometimes, too, a tremendous anger came over him so that his fingers crooked as if to set themselves round a man's throat and squeeze and squeeze till the bulging eyes ceased to stare and the head drooped in his hands. Then there would be moments of incredible pity, when he would shake his head and blink away in the silence of that little room while his fingers fumbled at his glasses.

Then at last he drank his cold coffee and paid his bill, but with thoughts not yet wholly clear wandered for a time across the park, till at last he found himself in the Mall and heading for home. Then he suddenly knew what he must do, and his course of action was daylight plain.

"Get Pulvery for me," he said to Palmer when he came in; then while he waited he sluiced his head and neck with cold water till he felt braced and more like himself again.

"That you, Helen?" he said. "I've discovered something very interesting, and it's essential that we should all talk it over. . . . Yes, it's to do with Jeanne. . . . No, nothing derogatory, just the contrary. Your instincts and mine were for once absolutely right. . . . About half-past seven, but it may be later. And Banham must be there. His surgery will be over. . . . Ask him to dinner by all means, but I'd rather not talk as we eat. . . . Did she, by Jove! Said it was Uncle Ludo who did the christening. . . . Splendid! . . . Right. Good-by. See you somewhere round about eight."

He went back to the bathroom to finish his dressing while Palmer got Highways on the phone. Tempest was not there, and it was Carry who answered.

"Hallo, Carry!" said Travers cheerfully. "Nothing been happening at your end, so Palmer tells me. . . . Really? Came back from the nursing home about an hour ago. Got that leg of his in plaster, I expect. And now listen carefully. I expect to be at Seaborough soon after five o'clock, and I want you and Major Tempest both to be there. Also there must be a stenographer to take down a statement. . . . Whose statement? Well, my own. Certain facts I've run across up here. . . . Oh, just so that you can have them all in document form, so to speak. . . . That's right. Good-by."

He rang off then to give Palmer his orders.

"Repack a bag quickly," he said, "suitable for three or four days. I'm going down to Seaborough, now, alone. After that I don't know, but I'll keep you informed."

It was a highly intrigued Tempest who was waiting for him in the Chief Constable's office with Carry.

"Well, what's the mighty brain been unearthing now?" was his greeting.

Travers shook his head. "You'll hear in a minute. Stenographer and everything all set? I'm in rather a hurry, and it's going to be a long tale."

The three settled themselves comfortably in their chairs, Travers with his long legs outstretched, fingertips together, and face wrinkled in beneficent thought. A glance at the stenographer, and he was off. He spoke slowly and with a strange gravity, and only at rare emphases did his voice rise above the gentlest pitch.

"I'm going to propound a thesis," he said. "I'm mentioning nothing of which you are not perfectly aware, and I would rather not be interrupted unless you definitely find me obscure. Before I begin I would like you to inspect this note which I obtained from Zooquariums Limited, which is evidence of the purchase by Trowte of an ordinary, harmless, English grass snake and an ordinary garden toad." He passed the paper over. "Then when I refer to it, you'll know precisely what I mean. And now, if you'll allow me, I'll begin all over again.

"I'm propounding a thesis, under two main heads: firstly, that Trowte was definitely mad, and secondly, that he was a sadist of the most horrible kind. You both have doubtless formed your own opinions as to his sanity, and you know far better, perhaps, than I do that sanity and insanity are very relative terms. In everything but the one kink—shall we say?—a person may be normal. Trowte may have had his normalities, but in one thing he was most certainly insane.

"You know his family affairs: his doting on his son, his hatred of his daughter-in-law, and the culmination of that hatred when the son died in the mental home to which her treatment of him had undoubtedly driven him. He was himself acromegalic in type—if that's what you call it—and Mannin, who knew him at close quarters, mentioned or hinted to me that the stupidity which generally accompanies that particular disorder of the pituitary gland manifested itself in his case by a morbid kind of cunning.

"As to the sadistic form his insanity took, that is what immediately concerns us, because it must have led to his murder. What he, in fact, determined to do by way of revenge for his son and as a final, unspeakable gloating over his daughter-in-law was to obtain control over the granddaughter, Jeanne, and by a deliberate series of subtle tortures to drive the child insane. She was, in short, to end as her father ended.

"I can see that you begin to remember things. Well, let's take a few of his actions and see how they fit. He was proposing to have the child under his entire care and supervision both by day and night. To face the horrible facts calmly, I think we might say that he visualized days of intense ironical amusement and nights of sporadic gloating. Now I'll try to enlarge on them both.

"Let's take what used to happen by day. The child was expressly forbidden to speak to the Yardmans, as they were to her. He took good care, in fact, that there should be no tale-telling to them, and unhappily the child must have always been the shy, timid sort, and it was easy to enforce the rule. The law demanded some education, so he had a tutor. While lessons were going on he sat in that spider's den of his listening to every word. Howcrop didn't tell us so, but I should say that Trowte was overjoyed when he wrote to the university registrar for Howcrop's credentials and made the discoveries which put Howcrop completely in his power. I'd say he warned Howcrop to confine all talk to the lessons. I'd say that at least once he heard Howcrop break that order and he warned him, and one warning would be enough. There were occasions, you remember, when he warned the Yardmans in precisely the same way. He also set Jeanne against the Yardmans and Howcrop against the Yardmans. Remember what the Yardmans said, how that the whole house was quiet and full of suspicion, and it was like living on a volcano edge, where even a careless thought might start an eruption?

"Now, take that supposed doting on the child. When any one was in the room he would speak to the child, leering and fawning, and gloating to himself over the delightful irony of it all. 'Dear little Jeanne,' it would be, and, 'Won't my dear little Jeanne do this?' and, 'Say good-night, my little Jeanne.' Can't you see that ghastly face of his? And the terrified child, not daring to do more than look. A suspicious, crafty look, the Yardmans thought it. I'd call it a helpless look; the look of frightened hopelessness that wonders what will happen next and is too tired to care.

"And, you see, he would create endearments and occasions for that damnable, hypocritical sympathy out of the very tortures themselves. Take the food, and how he'd try to wheedle his little Jeanne into eating. The child's stomach was out of order, and why? Mannin may never have guessed half-way to the truth, but what was that truth?"

"He'd tampered with the food," cut in Carry, whose eyes had never left Travers's face.

"Yes," said Travers. "He doped the food. A mild poisoning perhaps. Then the same food—porridge or harmless rice pudding—would be specially ordered, and think how he could gloat when she turned against it and retched at the thought of it and how, when the Yardmans were listening, he would wheedle his little Jeanne and coax her into eating the good food.

"What else he did in the daytime we can only guess at, but there's one thing which has only just come to me, and it's this. Each afternoon, whenever suitable, he used to take her for a walk, as you both know. He held her in the most affectionate manner by the hand. I saw her tugging to get away from him, and doubling up with laughter at some game they were playing. But it wasn't laughter and it wasn't a game. I'd say he would grind the bones of that tiny hand of hers till the pain was unbearable. He would do it unexpectedly—the best tortures are unexpected. And there were other little delightful tortures—

making her stumble along on the rough shingle while he walked on firm sand.

"And one other very subtle one. He had listened to the Yardmans in the kitchen, and in the child's presence he accused them of loose talk, so giving the impression that the child had done the tale-bearing. That would make a new timidity when she met the Yardmans on the stairs or in a corridor, and the Yardmans took it for more cunning. I dare say if you think for yourselves you'll find a score more cases of what we might call torture by day. But night was different. Night was his own peculiar time; night—when the house was dark and utterly quiet, and he had the child all to himself."

He gave his glasses a polish and took a peep at his notes.

"I want you to imagine that house through the winter months, when the Yardmans had gone. You can imagine him spreading his hands and fawning on the child and leering, and telling her it was time for bed. She had been taught to undress herself and do her small toilet, and he would doubtless see her safely inside the room and then he might even turn the key. No open windows there and no chance of escape or calling for help. Then he would settle himself in that room of his with the fire on and an easy-chair. But the tortures would always be unexpected. If we hear a noise at night it doesn't keep us awake unless it's irregular in its occurrence. A curtain may flap or a door jar, but it's the waiting and listening that's trying to the nerves and makes us get out of bed to stop the rattling window or whatever makes the unrhythmic noise.

"And again, you see, he had to go to work steadily and by degrees. What he was counting on was a slow accumulation; not a sudden, desperate fright that should have a drastic, immediate effect. She had to sleep sometimes, or she would have been bodily ill, and that would have meant calling in a doctor, and the risk of awkward questions. Lucy Yardman said that the child would sometimes be seen shuddering and making queer faces, so we may take it that the child's nervous system was gradually being undermined.

"No," said Travers, and shook his head. "Trowte's method was one of exciting fear and keeping the child in the most harrowing of suspense. For nights, perhaps, she would be allowed a fitful or restless sleep, then things would happen. The light would go off and she would be left to undress in the dark. The light would go erratically off and on while she lay awake. There would be weird moans when he blew up those damnable rubber toys and let the sounds of the dying pigs go through that opening into her room. There would be noises—clankings of that chain and gurgles from the Klaxon horn. Always unexpected, they'd be; sometimes to wake her up from or before she had gone to sleep, or even in the middle of the night."

He shook his head again and gave another polish to his glasses.

"As to the other things, they're so fantastically horrible that they hardly bear thinking about. That comatose snake put in the bed, and, later on, the toad. Then something more simple and to hand—big worms which he got from his gardener on the pretence of using them for fishing. What else, we don't know. There may have been spiders, or mice. And she shrieked. 'Shrieked like a person who is being tortured or is going mad'—that's how the Yardmans put it. Shrieked so madly and frantically that, though the windows were sealed, the Yardmans heard her in their bungalow all that distance away."

"My God!" said Carry. "I'd give a hundred quid to have him alive again, and here."

"Yes," said Travers quietly. "I think perhaps I would, too. But the horrible things are not what I've told you; they're what we each imagine. We're here in this room, in each other's company, in daylight. Jeanne was in that house, in that bedroom, alone, in the dark. In her eyes it must have been an immense house and huge rooms with monstrous shadows, and each normal noise of the night must have made her cower. That's the background we have to bear in mind; that, and Trowte himself as one huge, omnipresent shadow; Trowte, with his monstrous head, hooked beak and terrifying eyes.

"In any case," he said, and looked at his notes again, "even if we can never quite get her fear into our own bones, we can make sense out of a considerable number of things which we never previously understood. I ought to tell you, I think, that, ill though the child is, my sister has caught her out in a subterfuge. She calls it a lie, or untruth, because she doesn't know the facts. The child said, in fact, that she had drunk her medicine, and she hadn't. I think we know why. You may not agree with me, but I'd be prepared to swear that Trowte made capital even out of the medicine which Mannin gave her. He'd set her against Mannin and the medicine. He'd make out by some devilish cunning that the medicine was responsible for the sickness, if only to give himself the pleasure of watching her retch as she took it.

"But even if the child became lying and cunning—which I'm not prepared to admit—I am prepared not only to condone it but even to applaud it. It shows that, small though she was, there was some stuff of resistance and bravery in her. If she was cunning, it was a pitiful cunning of defence. It was her one small pitiable weapon."

"And everything was under our noses and we couldn't see it," said Tempest.

"There's no blame to us in that," Travers told him. "We saw nothing at first hand. Yardman had no children of his own, and his account to me, and his wife's, were embittered accounts which only just missed the truth. Yet even she took to the child when Trowte was dead."

"Lucky that we didn't question the child," Tempest said. "No wonder she screamed and wanted to be taken away." He nodded determinedly. "From now on you can take it that I'm on your side in that particular matter. How is she, by the way?"

"The fear's just beginning to seep slowly out of her," Travers said. "How long it'll be before she can look calmly back, I don't know. Maybe never. At the moment she's in a wholly new environment. What care and rest may do, I don't know." He shook his head, then all at once was whipping off his glasses. "But there're two things I might as well say here and now. I want you to see the bank and back me up in obtaining at least a temporary guardianship. Failing that I warn all concerned that I'll go to any lengths and spend every penny I possess to stop that child being reminded—"

"That's all right," Tempest told him. "I don't think you need worry about either."

The strange bellicosity had suddenly gone, and Travers was shaking his head again.

"That's good of you, Tempest, and you, too, Carry. But just one other thing, and it's the foulest of all. We've got to round off everything by visualizing the climax as Trowte saw it. The time would have come when that child's brain gave way. And, for his own protection, he'd have made a thorough job of it. What would he have done then? I think he'd have sent for the child's mother. I don't think I need say more.

"And just one last thing. Remember the queer wording of that will he made as soon as he went to Seabreak? How he left a hundred a year for the child's maintenance? Maintenance—in a mental home, to the end of her days. Then a final end, like her father's."

He got to his feet. "Anything you'd like to ask further?"

Tempest shook his head.

"If there is, sir," said Carry, "we can always ask you later."

"I'm afraid not," said Travers. "You see, I'm no longer available."

Tempest stared. "You've got to go away?"

"Yes and no." He shook his head. "I won't prevaricate with you or beat about the bush. If you'll understand that I'm not being rude, I'll say perfectly rudely that I'm resigning from the case."

"But, my dear fellow, just when—"

"I know," said Travers, shaking his head again. "I'm sorry, but all this is peculiarly personal to me in some ways. I simply can't go on. That was why I came down here and told you everything I knew. Every card I have I've put on the table. You've taken a statement from me and I've also started you off on certain trains of thought. Where those trains of thought may lead you, I don't know, and I wish to God I could say I didn't care." He waved a helpless hand. "Still, there we are. Anything arising out of this statement I'm prepared at any time to elaborate—over the phone. Otherwise I'm definitely out of the case." He held out his hand. "Good-by. And let me know occasionally how you're getting on. Good-by, Carry, and best thanks to both of you."

Tempest pursued him to the outer door.

"But you're not going now! Just wait and check the statement. Stay and have some sort of a meal."

"Sorry—no," said Travers. "It's good of you, but—" A last shake of the head and he was making for the car.

But Travers had not run away from the case. It was himself he was trying to evade, and the thoughts that would still persist in taking up the story where he had left it. That was why he had hurried away before Tempest could put the inevitable questions—where did the story lead to? and was Trowte's murder in any way connected with his treatment of the child? And to each of those questions Travers could have given plain answers.

"Let us look at all the suspects in the most dispassioned way," he might have said. "I might have killed him myself, but the main arguments against that are insufficiency of motive, and my general record. I thought for one moment that the child might have done it herself, but that was based on a temporary and wholly false appreciation of the child; moreover. I doubt if she could possibly have driven home the knife, have effectively concealed it afterwards, or have gone out of the front door and come round to the back without dirtying her slippers. If either of the Yardmans killed him, then it was not on account of the child, but in some sudden flare of temper.

"But if you take the torturing of the child as something which the murderer considered he was unable to stop by means less drastic than actual killing, then either Howcrop or Milovitch is the man. Milovitch could never be touched, since he has an alibi which, whether cooked or faked, could not be upset in any court of law. Howcrop has no alibi."

"And," Travers might have added, "that is why I am withdrawing from the case. Howcrop the wrong 'un; Howcrop the *poseur*, and Howcrop the beachcomber have nothing to do with me. But

I remember Howcrop as he held that child in his arms and tried to fight in his own way for her. And that's the Howcrop whose side I'm on, and since no man can serve two masters, then the law can go hang rather than any word of mine should get Howcrop hanged."

But Travers could not wholly evade those issues or conceal them from himself. After that long talk with Helen and Tom and Doctor Banham, it was they who saw the clear issues and reminded him of them.

He used much the same words as at Seaborough, warning them of the urgency for absolute secrecy, and warning Helen in particular that it might be better perhaps if she heard the talk at second hand from Tom. But Helen insisted on being there, and though she more than once wiped her eyes, it was Banham who was most openly moved and indignant.

"And that's the law!" he said. "People like you are now sweating blood to hunt out the man who wiped scum like Trowte off the face of the earth. A knife in the back—my God! I'd have liked to have him alive on a dissecting table."

"If the police ever get the murderer on the run, and he comes this way and wants a bed and a bob, he can count on me for both," Tom said.

"You're not going to do any more interfering, surely, Ludo," Helen said indignantly. "It makes my blood boil to think of it. I'd have killed him myself."

"As a matter of fact," Travers said, "I've already resigned from the case, though I don't want to take any credit for that. But we've all got to preserve a sense of proportion. The law entitles us to keep our mouths closed, but it doesn't stand for being deliberately hindered. Sooner or later Jeanne may be taken out of Banham's hands by some doctor or doctors ordered by the court to make a report. Jeanne may know the one vital thing that may send Trowte's murderer to execution."

"I'll see she's not questioned for months yet," Banham said. "I may get a specialist's opinion to back me to the lengths of smuggling Jeanne to some place where the law can never find her, or what?"

"That will be for the future to decide," Banham said. "We can deal with that when the situation arises. In the meanwhile there's not the slightest danger of her being questioned, or—if you ask me—of her answering any questions."

"The child's our first consideration," Helen said.

"It all comes to the same thing," said Tom in his blunt way. "We're all agin the Government, except possibly Ludo here."

Travers smiled. "There's no reason even to except me. Though for appearance' sake you'd better write me down as one who loves his fellow man."

Helen was going up for a last look at the children. Travers went with her, past Nanny's open door and to Jeanne's room. The night-light shone on two figures in one bed—Jeanne herself and the doll, discarded unwittingly in sleep. The two grown-ups looked down for a moment or two, and then Helen suddenly stooped and lightly kissed the sleeping child.

"Isn't she pretty?" she whispered. "Such a sweet face, and so sad." She squeezed his arm. "I'm glad Nanny and I were wrong about the lies."

Travers nodded, eyes still on the placid face.

"To-morrow, if it's sunny, she shall come down to the back summer-house with Nanny and Ruth—" She broke off. "Wasn't that the telephone?"

Travers followed her to the door. Tom was craning up the stairs and signalling that it was Travers who was wanted.

"It's Superintendent Wharton," he said, when Travers came down. "I told him I thought you'd gone to bed, so you needn't speak to him unless you like."

"Mightn't be anything to do with this affair at all," Travers said. "I'd better hear what he's got to say."

George Wharton was most genial and jocular. The Seaborough authorities, he said, had asked the Yard to take over the Seabreak case. Chief-Inspector Norris was already on the way there, and Wharton hoped Travers, already familiar with the case, would see his way clear to lend a helping hand.

"It's a bit irregular," he said, "but I may be down there myself. Tempest specially mentioned it."

"Tempest tell you anything else?" Travers asked.

"Nothing in particular," Wharton said airily. "He did happen to mention that you were a trifle upset about things and you'd thought of taking a little holiday."

"Well, I'm sorry, George," Travers said, "but I've got to take a longer one than I thought. But I'd love to look you up if I happen to be that way."

At that moment some one mercifully cut in on the line, and in the brief confusion Travers hung up. Tom was still in the drawing-room with his night-cap, and Travers was back there at once.

"There's the very devil of a complication, Tom. Wharton's virtually taking over the Seabreak case. You know what that means? If the truth's to be found, he'll find it, even if he stays there a lifetime."

"No panic," said Tom. "Besides, he's a friend of yours—ours too, for that matter. You can keep yourself informed on how much he knows. You can even do a bit of heading off if you think fit."

"Yes," said Travers thoughtfully. "I won't lie downright to George Wharton or any man, but, as you say, I can keep abreast of what he finds out."

"Just a minute, young feller," Tom said, and lowered his voice. Then he got up, tiptoed to the door, and carefully shut it. "There's a question I've been wanting to put to you for the last half-hour," he said, when he came tiptoeing back. "I don't want to know all the answer, but just how much do you know?"

"Know?" said Travers, with an assumption of ignorance.

"Yes—know. Aren't there things you could tell Wharton?"

"I don't think so," said Travers blandly. "Tempest will have handed over my statement."

"Statement, my eye!" said Tom, then whipped round on him again. "I'd bet a fiver you know who did it."

"Yes," said Travers slowly. "I think I do. I know who did it and how it was done. I know who *must* have done it." Then he smiled ruefully. "The only snag is that he couldn't have done it. If he did do it, then he not only committed a murder, he also committed a miracle."

"Then what's wrong?" asked Tom triumphantly. "Wharton can't explain miracles."

Travers was still shaking his head. "I know. That's the very thing that worries me. Wharton may not be able to explain them, but he's got an uncommonly awkward habit of proving that the age of miracles is over."

XIII
IN SEARCH OF TRUTH

BUT THOUGH Ludovic Travers, in his capacity of unpaid expert, had seen fit to withdraw from the case, there was no reason whatever, as he assured himself, why he should not arrive at the truth. The killer of Quentin Trowte might in his opinion be more of a public benefactor than a murderer, yet there was no reason why the private citizen, Ludovic Travers, should not, for the satisfying of his own curiosity, discover who that benefactor was.

So when the following morning he woke so early that an hour must elapse before the arrival of tea, he began with paper and pencil to summarize the known facts, and at once he was aware that he had spoken too hastily to Tom in his claim that, but for the existence of a miracle, he himself could name the killer. Howcrop had been his fancy; Howcrop, who somehow had got to know the horrible obsession of old Trowte's days and nights; Howcrop, whom old Trowte may actually have sounded—with a hint of exposure—with a view to making him an accomplice, by perverting the mind of the child through her lessons or carrying out some new and subtle torturings of his own devising.

Assume that Howcrop had killed Trowte, then from 7.52 till 8.5 was an interval of thirteen minutes, during which he had to get back to the village to scuttle that boat, make himself visible to his landlady for the purpose of an alibi, and find out by questioning whether or not she had noticed his absence. Then he had to walk to Highways—and he *had* walked, for he had not been in the least out of breath—and show himself at the house or bungalow. And when Travers worked out the times taken from the moment that Howcrop had left Highways, he could not for the life of him find it within human possibility to fit the series of actions within the thirteen minutes or anywhere near it.

Besides, there were other complications. As Travers saw it, the killer of Trowte was one who had committed the deed only when sure of an unbreakable alibi. Howcrop's alibi depended too much on the evidence—or co-operation—of his landlady. And was Howcrop the man of steady nerve and shrewd calculation whom the deed demanded? Would he have had the wit, even if he were a skilful rower, to take the boat through the mist, to bring it, still through the mist, to the one essential spot near the village, and then to scuttle it and set it adrift? Travers shook his head. If Howcrop did the killing, then he performed two miracles: he made time stand still and he made himself a wholly different person.

"Very well," said Travers to himself, "we will dismiss Howcrop as sole killer, but that does not rule out the fact that he may have been a confederate. But let's leave out that possibility, too. Let's try to make a synthetic murderer. Let's take every circumstance that accompanied the killing, and from those circumstances try to create the actual man."

The first obvious thing, as Travers saw it, was that the killer was aware of the habits of the house. He must therefore have learned of them either by hearsay or by experience. The latter was the more probable, since Trowte knew him and admitted him. Then there had to be a motive for the killing—curious, thought Travers, how Howcrop still fits!—and two motives suggested themselves. If Howcrop did the killing, it might have been to remove the man who had discovered his past and was threatening to expose him. If another than Howcrop did it, then the motive most likely—the only one, in fact, that could possibly be surmised—was the protection of the child.

But could the child have been protected any other way? There Milovitch entered. He had undoubtedly thought of kidnapping the child, as agent, as it were, for her mother's spite, and had definitely secured the help of Howcrop as accomplice. Milovitch might have forced his way through the door when Trowte opened it that night, and have killed him in a quarrel. Then Travers shook his head. A special knife meant preparation, and the intentions of Milovitch could never have been murder. And he was the last man to have got away by the boat. One could never imagine him hurtling down those steep steps to the beach. In the first place he'd probably have slipped and broken a limb—

And there Travers stopped. As though by a flash of lightning in the pitch dark of night, he suddenly saw as in broad daylight the things that darkness had securely hidden. It was Mannin; Mannin, that lovable old doctor, who had killed Trowte!

He nervously moistened his lips, and his brow furrowed as he began to work things out. That story of a wounded man and the chance car had been a fantastic one, and even though Howcrop's evidence had bolstered it up, it should never have been accepted without suspicion. And yet, who could possibly have connected Mannin with a murder? A kindly old country doctor to kill a man whom he hardly knew; and again, there was the question of an alibi.

But Travers set the alibi temporarily aside and began to consider the probable facts. Mannin had rushed out of the house by the front door. He had originally intended to make his way out by the back and so home through the woods, but the ringing of the back bell had closed that way of escape. So he had fled frantically down those steps and had fallen, cracking his skull and breaking his leg. But with grim determination he had continued that way of escape. The knife had fallen from his hand, but he picked it up, and was about to hurl it out to sea when he saw the moored boat. In a flash he hopped his way to it—the sea had later obscured the marks—cut the rope, and then threw away the knife.

Then the fog had defeated him. The boat had drifted round Seabreak Point and it was only when he heard from the nearing main road the sounds of people and traffic again, that he could get his bearings and row for the land. Then under cover of the mist he had scuttled the boat and had dragged his way up the low cliffs to the main road and hailed a car.

Then, at the nursing home, Howcrop had heard the story, and had at once volunteered corroboration. Howcrop himself may have been out that night on business for Milovitch, and it was to his interest to create an alibi for himself. Or perhaps Howcrop, that garrulous old windbag, had wished a little limelight. He had been looking out from his bedroom window and might have seen a car, and therefore in his own imagination he did see the car, and the Doctor in it. Mannin must have smiled dourly at that unexpected confirmation of his fantastic tale.

Then, with those facts clear, Travers began thinking back. What of Mannin's alibi? And the more he thought, the more his own brave theory became a fantastic thing. Mannin could establish on unshakable evidence that he had been in Mrs. Diddy's house not only before and during the vital time, but he had also not left it till after eight o'clock. And no matter how Travers tried to fake an alibi, he found it beyond his powers. Mannin must have done the murder, and yet no human brain could conceive a way whereby he could have been in the house at anything near the vital time.

And then Travers had a quick and hazy glimpse of a way out. Had there been collusion between Howcrop and Mannin? Could that cold, quiet brain of the Doctor have worked out some unshakable alibi, and a scheme whereby his own acts and times and those of his confederate were so interwoven as to be inseparables. Collusion?—there was evidence everywhere. Howcrop had headed for the surgery on the night of the murder. On the Saturday he had gone straight to the hospital, and he and the Doctor made no denial of acquaintanceship.

But by the time Travers had hunted for the main co-ordinating events of the murder night, his brain was beginning to go giddy, and he laid his paper and pencil aside. Another method must be tried. Concentrated thought was useless. Better, perhaps, to register the problem and leave it at the back of the mind till from time to time new ideas presented themselves of their own accord. And, he told himself, Nature had endowed him with a nimbler imagination than George Wharton's. Wharton's method was the slow accumulation of facts, and the remorseless and final elimination of suspects till concentration was demanded on one alone. And, thought Travers, Wharton was unfamiliar with the case. In two days, perhaps, he might find the flaws in Mannin's tale of assault and abduction, but even then he would boggle at the idea of formal checking of the alibi.

So Travers was in no immediate panic. That morning he accepted Tom's special invitation to a round, and the case was more or less dismissed from his mind. But it was a sunny day, and from his bedroom window after lunch he caught sight of Helen and Ruth, with Nanny, who was carrying Jeanne, making their way round by the beech-tree to the old back lawn that faced southwest. Then an idea came to him and he made up his mind to test it out.

But he waited for a time till the party should be settled down. Helen was coming back to the house as he came out.

"Not going to sun yourself?" he said.

"I'm going out to tea," she told him, "and I've heaps of things to do. You're going to the children?"

He smiled. "Hercules among the women. What are they all doing?"

"Ruth and Nanny are playing shops, and Nanny's trying to make a nightdress for Sylvia. Jeanne is watching."

"Still very shy?"

"Very," Helen said. "She just sits and watches, all solemn-eyed. Now and again she says a word or two to me or Nanny. Nanny persevered this morning in getting her to say, 'Good morning, Uncle Ludo,' and was very disappointed when you didn't arrive."

"Plenty of time," he said. "By the way, isn't Jeanne rather old for dolls? I've been thinking, and ten seems a pretty big age."

"Nonsense," she said. "I loved dolls long after I was ten. Besides, Jeanne's never been used to children of her own age, or any play at all, if you ask me. That doll's the first real playmate she's had."

There was a small table outside the potting shed as he passed, and he carried it with him to the chair where Jeanne was sitting, smiling quietly at her as she watched him.

"Now you stay here, Miss Ruth," Nanny said. "Your uncle will play shops only if he wants to,"

"Will you come and buy something, Uncle?"

"Heaps of things," Travers said. "That sugar of yours, by the way, looks to me remarkably like sand."

"It is sand, Uncle," she laughed. "It's real rice, though; isn't it, Nanny?"

"You get on with your weighing," she told her. "Your uncle wants to be quiet for a bit."

Travers looked at Jeanne, and the two smiled at each other, and shyly as she smiled, her cheeks seemed almost to be plumping, and there was a faint colour in her face. His hand fell for a moment on hers and patted it; then with the table between them making a rest for his arm, he sat for a while watching the weighing of the sand. It was deliciously quiet there, so that a robin hopped unconcernedly within a yard of Nanny's chair.

Travers took a piece of paper from his pocket, and two pencils. One pencil he laid within reach of Jeanne, and with the other he wrote:

"What bird is that by Nanny's chair?"

He smiled as he put the paper under her hand, then looked away again. A moment, and she picked up the pencil. She wrote, then looked timidly at him. His fingers closed on the paper and he drew it away.

"A robin."

He nodded gravely as if a discovery of due importance had been made, frowned in tremendous thought, then wrote again:

"Do you like me? I like you."

"Yes," she wrote, and so the correspondence went on, like a lovely secret game:

"Did you sleep well? I did."

"Yes, I did."

"Is Sylvia a good girl?"

"Ever so good."

"Isn't it lovely that you and Sylvia are going to stay here always?"

"It is very nice here."

"Nobody is to know we write each other little letters. Shall we keep it a secret?"

"Yes."

He was watching her while she wrote that last word, and he smiled confidingly when she looked up and their eyes met. Then as he drew the paper carefully towards him, Ruth suddenly called:

"What are you doing, Uncle Ludo? I believe you're playing something."

"Jeanne and I have got a game of our own," he said. "It's a secret. Now we're both going to do our shopping. We're going to write a list and then I'm coming to the shop."

He put that first paper in his pocket, and began writing on a second. Then he pushed it across for Jeanne to add a contribution, and so it went on till the list was complete. But long before tea Ruth tired of shops.

"Will you tell us a story, Uncle Ludo?"

"Your uncle's got a bone in his arm," Nanny said.

"Oh, but just a little story," Ruth said. "A fairy story."

"You're too old for fairy stories," Travers told her. "Besides, fairy stories aren't true,"

"That's right, Uncle Ludovic," Nanny said. "I know a little girl I had to speak to this morning for telling fibs."

"Not Ruth, surely!"

"It was me, Uncle," Ruth told him unblushingly.

"That's dreadful," said Travers, and shook his head. "When I was a little boy I once told a fib, and my Nanny told me to try telling the truth for a bit—"

"A bit of what, Uncle?"

"Listen and don't interrupt," Nanny told her severely. "Jeanne is ever so much better mannered than you. She's listening."

"Ah, well," said Travers. "And where was I? Oh, yes. So when my Nanny said I was to try and always tell the truth, I said to myself I would. And soon after that I did something I shouldn't have done, and my Nanny said, 'Did you do that, Master Ludo?' and I said I did. And what do you think happened?"

Ruth shook her head. Jeanne, listening intently, gave no answer to his smiling, questioning look.

"I'll tell you," he said mysteriously. "I had ever such a funny feeling. A good feeling. It came all over me, right down to my toes, just like a tingling. And after that for ever such a long while I was ever so good."

"There you are!" said Nanny. "And that just shows you. When you tell the truth you always know it, just as when you tell fibs and it makes you all ashamed."

Ruth licked her lips; the story was taking an unexpected and moralizing twist.

"And now will you tell us a story, Uncle? A made-up story?"

"A little one, then," said Travers resignedly. "Any you particularly want?"

"Oh, yes!" said Ruth delightedly. "The one about Ali, the porter, and the carpet, and how they all climbed on and—"

"Who's telling this story, Miss Ruth?" said Nanny ironically. "You or your uncle?"

It was Travers's custom to save his serious problems for the half-hour before sleep, and not infrequently he would wake to find the problems solved. But that night it was rather a satisfied review that he made. He felt nearer to Jeanne and knew her nearer to himself, and above all he had confirmed a theory that affected the case.

If old Trowte, in that spider's den of his, had listened to the morning-room lessons, and if Trowte had seriously warned Howcrop of the danger of questioning the child or exceeding the bare duties for which he was paid, then—Travers had thought—Howcrop must have hit upon some silent and safe method of communicating with the child, once he had discovered that something was radically wrong and had set himself obstinately and determinedly to get at the heart of it. That very afternoon, Jeanne had unknowingly disclosed that method. For a brief moment he had seemed to discern a hesitation and a gesture of recallment, but it had gone as quickly, and at once she had taken the pencil and had written.

And now—what? A visit to Seabreak and a call on Mannin Pointed talk and subtle allusion which a man of the Doctor's penetration could not fail to see. Later, perhaps, a secret call on Howcrop, and more allusion. After lunch might be the best time, and the Rolls must not be taken, for Wharton would spot it at once. Helen's little car would do admirably, and he would draw up outside the surgery and be in the house in a flash. And after that—what? Useless, perhaps, to plan. But maybe a friendly call on George Wharton.

It was about half-past three when Travers actually arrived, and he was at once shown into the small drawing-room, where the Doctor was taking his ease on what looked like some special kind of couch.

"Well, this is a pleasure," he said, and held out his hand. "I wondered if you were serious when you said you might call."

"Serious enough," Travers told him. "And how are you? Leg finished giving pain?"

"Oh, yes." He waved to the chair which Travers was already drawing up. "Nothing to do but eat and sleep. Which reminds me. You'll have some tea?"

"Well—if it's just you and me."

The Doctor tinkled the bell on the table at his elbow. He had changed very much, Travers thought. A greyish look about him, and dark under the eyes.

"Well, that's arranged for," he said, as the door closed behind the maid. "You're not at the hotel now, so they tell me."

"I'm not," Travers said.

The Doctor's eyes twinkled. "You mean, how do I know? The fact is there's precious little that every one doesn't know in a place like this."

"Milovitch still here?"

"Milovitch? Oh, yes—the pianist. He went yesterday, so they tell me. But we've got newcomers in the village; gentlemen from

Scotland Yard, so I'm told. The principal one is staying at your old hotel."

"Really? It's possible I may know him. I'm staying at Pulvery myself. Little Jeanne Trowte's there with my sister. We thought it better to get her right away."

The old doctor nodded. "And how is Jeanne?"

"Slowly getting better. She had a shock of some sort, you know. But the police are not going to be allowed to question her for a long time yet."

"Hm! Very sensible. . . . But you're coming back here?"

"Afraid not," said Travers, and his hand went to his glasses. "I'm merely an ordinary citizen. By the way, you're a doctor, and accustomed to confidences?"

"Yes?"

"Then tell me." He gave a queer shake of the head before looking up to make the unusual question. "Do you trust me?"

"Trust you?" He had plainly expected the question to be framed the other way about. "Yes, I think I can say I do."

"And I'm going to trust you too," Travers said. "I've resigned from the case, and I'll tell you, in the very strictest confidence, why."

"That's a terrible story," Mannin said, when Travers had finished. "Terrible—if it's true."

Travers shook his head. "Let's remember what we said to each other about trust. What we're talking about will never to go outside this room. That's why I say you ought to know whether or not the story is true. Didn't you have suspicions? Am I entirely wide of the mark in suggesting that when you attended the child you weren't altogether satisfied as to the cause of the sickness?"

The Doctor spread his hands. "Well, I didn't think things were normal. They weren't normal."

"You didn't think the child was suffering from a mild form of poisoning?"

The Doctor smiled dryly. "All disorders of that kind are a form of poisoning."

"Ah, well," said Travers, "where doctors' terms are concerned I'm a mere layman. And in the other sense too; I mean, that I'm no longer connected with the police in this particular case."

Early tea came in then, and the talk was stayed till tea was poured and the toast passed across.

"What was your precise job with the police?" Mannin then asked.

"I'm merely an amateur," Travers said, "with what they're pleased to call ideas. I do a lot of chattering which they listen to in the hope of finding an occasional word or two of sense."

The Doctor shook his head. "I'm not swallowing that. Just what ideas do you specialize in?"

"Well, if you must know—in alibis."

Mannin shot him a look. "Alibis? You mean, testing people's alibis?"

"That's it. Trying to prove that no gentleman, however ingenious, can be in two places at once."

"Most interesting," Mannin said. "No, I won't have any more toast. I'll try a piece of that cake. . . . And about the alibis. People fake them, do they?"

"They try to," Travers said. "Clock manipulation, most of the times. Of course the best dodge is to convince some impartial witness that you were not where the police claimed you were." He smiled. "But why talk shop? As I said, I'm now a private citizen."

"And what are your views as such?"

"My views?" He frowned. "Well, I'll say to you what I'd probably say to no other soul. I resigned because in this particular case I'm not on the side of the law. I think you feel that way too."

"I?"

"Why not? Whatever the medical profession may say, you and I know that doctors take life—to end useless suffering, for instance. I regard the killing of Trowte as something in the same category. Whoever killed Trowte ended the sufferings of that child. The killer saw no other way. He knew, but he couldn't prove. He knew it was useless to complain to the police or the societies, because Trowte was too diabolically clever. So he did things his own way. Isn't that so? And aren't you on his side?"

Mannin shook his head. "Perhaps I am—speaking like yourself as a private citizen. Do try some of this cake, by the way. It's rather good."

"Thanks," said Travers, "I think I will. Any news yet about that attack on you?"

"Nothing. Inquiries are going on, I believe."

"Now there's an illustration of something I've always claimed," Travers said. "It may be trite, but truth beats Action all the time. Which reminds me. Looking at that leg of yours brings beck to mind how I nearly broke my own the other night. I was in a bit of a hurry coming out of the gate at Highways, and I was sprinting down those steps to the beach, intending to go that way, when I nearly came a cropper—"

"Steps to the beach?" He pursed his lips. "Oh, yes, I remember. They are a bit on the steep side." He smiled. "But let's talk about something more cheerful. What are you writing now? Anything at all?"

For a quarter of an hour they talked about books. The Doctor had not read *Kensington Gore*, and Travers promised to send him an autographed copy. Then suddenly Travers rose to go.

"No idea it was so late till I saw that clock."

"You'll come in again some time?" Mannin asked anxiously.

"I hope so," Travers said. "I hope to bring you that book. By the way, isn't Howcrop a friend of yours?"

The Doctor shot him a look. "Well, he is—in a way. A queer fellow, Howcrop, but a heart of gold, as they say."

"Yes," said Travers. "I rather like Howcrop. What I was going to ask was if you knew whether or not he might be at his rooms."

"You're calling on him?"

"Just a courtesy visit," Travers said airily. His hand went out. "Good-by, then. And take care of that leg of yours. You're not so young as you were."

Mannin gave him a strange look. "How old do you think I am?"

"Well, not a long way from seventy."

"Too long away," he said. "Next July, if I live that long, I shall be seventy-nine."

"Then you don't look it," Travers told him smilingly. "Next July I hope to congratulate you. Don't shake your head like that. You're good for ninety, and I wouldn't mind a small wager on it."

A smile still lingered as he entered the car. There was something enormously likeable about the old doctor: sturdy, reticent, dour, and obstinate in purpose. Never a word or sign had he given, though every word must have pierced like a knife—if indeed it was he who had been the killer. Nothing but a quick look was all he had given when a question or remark had struck near home. "And yet," thought Travers with a shake of the head, "how much nearer to the truth am I? Has there been a single word or gesture to confirm what I still believe to be the truth?"

He took the narrow lane that led to the main road, intending to come out by Channel View and to leave the car there while he slipped across the road in search of Howcrop. But just as he neared the end of the lane and the road was in sight, he was all at once treading hard on the brake. There at Mrs. Diddy's gate, and saying an unctuous if hasty farewell to the old woman herself, was George Wharton.

Travers ducked his head as the old general hurried by not twenty yards away. When he sidled the car out to the main road, Wharton was still in sight, making for the green. Travers's fingers fumbled at his glasses. Wharton, and Mrs. Diddy. Wharton the plausible, who always had a way with women. And there had been a jauntiness about Wharton's steps as he had hurried away. Mannin's alibi for the murder night—that had been Wharton's business, and his cause of elation. *Whatever there had been to know, Wharton now knew.*

XIV
HELD AT BAY

WHARTON ENTERED the hotel and Travers brought the car round by the back and went in by the side door, and there happened to run into the manageress.

"If it isn't Mr. Travers!" she began.

"Sh!" went Travers. "A friend of mine is here—a Mr. Wharton—and I want to surprise him. Would you mind if I waited in the drawing-room?"

So from the drawing-room Travers watched Wharton at his tea. Beside him he had his note-book, and between the intervals of buttered toast he would make notes, frown at them, grunt in the best Whartonian manner, or consider with head cocked sideways whatever it was that he had just written. Wharton's antics were always a source of joy to Travers: his subterfuges and showmanship; his playing to the gallery and his unctuousness.

Then at last he finished his meal, and with a handkerchief of flaring design wiped the huge moustache that gave him the look of a harassed paterfamilias. Then he nodded at the note-book as if in commendation, but just as he went to stow it away, a voice came from near by.

"So here you are, then. Doing yourself pretty well?"

"Well, well, well!" said Wharton, and his face beamed. His hand attached itself to that of Travers and worked it pump-handle-wise. "Come down to lend us a hand? Had tea yet, or shall I order some?"

"No to both, George," Travers said, but took a seat all the same. "This is merely a friendly call. The fact is I might be called away at any minute."

"Not tonight, surely?"

"I'm afraid so," Travers said resignedly. "Much as I should have liked—"

"You can spare an hour?"

"Well, since it's you, George—"

Wharton hopped up at once. "We'll go up to my room. This way. Number 14—first floor. Been up to Highways yet? Norris is there, or was when I left."

He showed Travers in and drew the easier of the chairs towards the window. "Make yourself at home. Cigarettes are there. Excuse me a second and I'll get my notes."

"Case not finished yet, then?" said Travers.

"You always were a one for a joke," Wharton chuckled. "But it isn't finished—yet. Ask me tomorrow at about this time and I may be giving a different answer."

Travers raised his eyebrows. "Like that, is it?"

Wharton waved his hand. "Well, perhaps I exaggerate. When you hear what I've got to tell you, then you'll know as much as I do. By the way, I read that statement of yours about that—that beast, Trowte, l must say I never read anything so concisely put. Masterly, as I said to Norris—"

"What particular favour is it that you're preparing to ask?"

"My dear Mr. Travers"—Wharton was highly indignant—"you surely don't think I should say what I do if it wasn't true. I have faults, but hypocrisy isn't one of them. I'm saying the same about you as I said to Tempest. I never knew a case where the facts were placed so clearly in our hands."

"That's very generous of you, George," Travers said. "And what have you done so far?"

"That long-haired pianist—we've cleared him out," Wharton said. "I've also had a return cable from the States about his sister, that little girl's mother, and she denies ever having given him any commission to see the girl. A pretty good liar, by all accounts."

"And who's your favourite for the long jump?"

"Ah!" said Wharton, and drew his chair close in. "That's where I may have to ask your help. Didn't you run across a doctor here? An old fellow named Mannin?"

"Yes," said Travers reflectively. "I called on him in a nursing home at Seaborough. He'd been attacked by a man and had his leg broken."

"Ah!" said Wharton again, and gave a roguish look. "A car, wasn't there? And a wicked man hit him on the head with a spanner."

"Just a moment," said Travers. "By the way you're talking, any one would think it never happened!"

Wharton nodded heavily. "So you swallowed it, too. Ah, well! We all have our little lapses." Then he snorted. "Happened! Of course it never happened. A bigger cock-and-bull story I never heard in my life." He drew still nearer. "Listen to this."

So Travers, with much show of astonishment, heard how Mannin must have fallen down those steps—all the theory, in fact, at which he himself had arrived.

"By Jove! you're right, George," he said. "But what did Mannin say when you taxed him with it?"

Wharton gave a prodigious wink. "I'm too old a bird for that. When I get my hands on a man, they're on for good. When I'm ready for Mannin, then I'll make my grab."

He adjusted his antiquated spectacles, and with much peering over their tops consulted his notes.

"As a matter of fact, I've been making full inquiries into his alibi. Just listen to this, will you? I don't find any flaw, but I'd like your opinion as an independent judge." He laid the notes momentarily aside. "As to his movements that night, I ought to tell you that I've since discovered he was seen approaching Mrs. Diddy's house at just before 7.45. My authority is the local constable, who saw him and spoke to him, and happened at the same time to consult his watch. So that gives us a starting-point."

Then he gave a queer smile.

"Doctor Mannin went to see old Mrs. Diddy because her grandson played her up over taking his medicine. That sounds reasonable to you?"

"No," said Travers. "I can't say that it does."

"And it doesn't to me either. Taking a sledgehammer to crack a filbert. My grandmother'd have given me a clip over the ear. Still, that was Mannin's excuse for calling—that, and to ask for a bunch of the violets that were growing in the front garden. Don't forget that; the *front* garden. I've worked it out that if the watch was right, then he was there at 7.45. And now I'll tell you what happened."

Now he read from his notes.

"First of all he looked in the living-room, where the boy was reading a book. Then he and Mrs. Diddy had a look at the violets, after which they went to the kitchen and the Doctor said it was time for the medicine. He was wearing a wrist-watch, by the way. The boy came in and the Doctor himself poured the medicine out and the boy took it. The Doctor praised him, and then produced a bag of sweets, but the bag burst and the sweets were scattered all over the floor. The boy and his granny picked them up, and then the Doctor said it was time for bed. Up went the boy. Usually he went up alone, but the Doctor suggested to Mrs. Diddy that she should put on a hat and coat and fetch the new medicine from the surgery. It was just gone eight o'clock when she came down, and she and the Doctor went to the gate together. Then the Doctor mentioned the violets again and Mrs. Diddy said she would gather a bunch. The Doctor was delighted, she was to do so and bring them to the surgery. He had a patient to see first, but he would meet her there."

Wharton laid the notes aside. "There are certain peculiar differences," he said, "between that statement and the one I was given by Tempest—"

"I noticed that for myself," Travers said. "I did the first interviewing of Mrs. Diddy in connection with that supposed attack on the Doctor But I wouldn't say there are differences. I'd say that what you've just read places emphasis on different things and throws light on others. In any case, what's all the worry? What you've just read merely proves that Mannin couldn't possibly have done the murder."

Wharton held up his hand. "Just one minute! You're talking about proof. I've got proof that Mannin did the murder. That fake assault affair is proof enough for me. It's also proof enough that Mannin planned the murder carefully and had a defence already planned. What we're now doing is to find the flaws in that defence. To bust his alibi, if you like to put it that way."

"I don't want to obscure the main issue," Travers said, "but just why do you think Mannin killed Trowte?"

"Mannin's motive?" He shrugged his shoulders. "They'd had words about the child. Mannin had guessed what that devil was up to and he decided to stop it in his own way."

"But *how* did he guess? Not a soul here suspected that Trowte was doing what he was. The Yardmans thought the old man simply doted on the child."

"That fellow Howcrop knew a thing or two," Wharton said. "He did the snooping and passed the information on—once the Doctor became interested."

"Have you seen Howcrop?" Travers asked. "Did he tell you that himself?"

"I can't say that he did," was Wharton's admission. "As a matter of fact, I put certain things to him—quite tactfully, of course—and he swore blind he hadn't the faintest idea anything was wrong about the child."

It was Travers's turn to give a shrug of the shoulders. Wharton countered with an airy wave of the hand.

"Which was why I knew the contrary! Tempest told me Howcrop was an elegant and consummate liar. From what I've seen of him I have no reason to modify Tempest's opinion."

Travers gave a little chuckle, and beamed at him with all the affection of years.

"George, I believe you're putting up a monstrous bluff. What does it matter what you think or what you suspect? It's what you can demonstrate in a court of law that counts, as you've often told me. Howcrop would be a godsend for any defence. You can't even disprove Mannin's account of how his leg got broken. And what about his alibi?"

"If you hadn't interrupted me at the very beginning," said Wharton piously, "you'd have heard all about that alibi. That alibi, on which you keep harping, isn't all it seems on the surface. In fact, my friend, I think there's been a good deal of jiggery-pokery going on. And I think I can make you admit it yourself."

"Splendid!" said Travers. "I'll play fair with you, George. If I'm convinced I'll say so frankly."

"Very well," said Wharton. "Now let's go back to that night. Misty, wasn't it, and dark very early? Take the cottage, for instance. That kitchen and the sitting-room were both very dark. Mrs. Diddy spoke to the grandson about his straining his eyes, and mentioned lighting the lamp, and then said it wouldn't be worth while, as the boy would soon be going to bed. Remember those two rooms? No clock at all in one, and an ordinary tin clock in the other—on the mantelpiece, facing north!"

Travers nodded thoughtfully. "Yes, Practically invisible."

"The Doctor had a wrist-watch," said Wharton ironically. "He could glance at it, and then at the clock. He could *dictate* the times, and I say he did so."

"Carry on," Travers told him quietly.

"The boy came into the kitchen for his medicine. I admit there's nothing in that, became the medicine was kept there. And now I'd like you to think of this. The doctor had volunteered to come in and supervise the ceremony because the lad had been playing his granny up. What was the correct procedure, then? I say this: the doctor should have been listening and watching *unknown to the boy*, and then he could have stepped into the kitchen when the tricks were in full swing. But no. He was there, and so there couldn't be any tricks. And not only that. He didn't give the lad a talking to. Oh, no! He gave the boy some sweets, which was just what the old granny could have done without his help!"

"Yes," said Travers. "But carry on, George. This is getting interesting."

"I'm carrying on all right," said Wharton grimly. "I've got something to say about those sweets, for instance. *The bag broke*. Wasn't that a peculiar thing! And the sweets scattered all over the floor."

"Sticky sweets, were they?"

"Ah!" said Wharton triumphantly. "You've thought of that, have you? No,' and he nodded to himself delightedly, "they weren't the sticky kind that might have been spoiled by rolling about on the kitchen floor. They were sugar-coated Brazils; hard as iron and very little susceptible to dirt. Now do you see the point?"

"I think so," Travers told him. "While the old lady and the boy were looking under tables and things, the Doctor manipulated the clock."

"Exactly! A hand round the back and he could alter the time in a flash. I say he did, and he slipped the clock on to eight, which was the boy's bed time."

Travers's fingers were fumbling for his glasses. "But just a moment, George. How much did he gain? Ten minutes? And why?"

"I consider that no more than five minutes need have elapsed since he set foot through the front gate," Wharton said, "and therefore he could have slipped the clock on from ten to eight to eight o'clock."

"But why?"

Wharton shrugged his shoulders and spread his hands.

"I don't know why. Amn't I asking you to try and help me out? All I'm doing is to point out certain queer actions and coincidences, and to assume chat they happened for very definite ends. By the way, there's more to come. Consider that eight o'clock had been established in that cottage as being the correct time. Granny and the boy go upstairs, and then the Doctor moves the hands back again to ten to eight, so as to make the clock once more right. Now it's still darker in that cottage, and when Granny comes down in her hat and coat, he hurries her off to the front gate before she has time to try to look at the clock again."

"Wait a minute, George. She told me she did look at the clock."

"She's modified that to me," Wharton said. "She looked at the clock through the Doctor's eyes. He said it was still not five past eight. Then at the gate he remembered the violets and asked her if she'd gather some at once and bring them straight to the surgery. No more going back to the kitchen, because the violets were growing in the front garden quite near the gate. And as he well knew, by the time she'd gathered them and had got to the surgery and waited and so on, she'd have lost all sense of time when she got back home. It could never conceivably have occurred to her that the clock had ever been tampered with. In any case it was dead right when she reached home again."

Travers gave a Whartonian grunt. "Well, I said I'd admit it if I were convinced, and I am—and I am not. I think your theory and the way you've worked out things are some of the best pieces of deduction you've ever done. They're convincing—and yet they're utterly useless. Counsel for the defence would simply pour ridicule on them. But, worst of all, they don't help. Mannin couldn't have done what you've made clear he did do. Why should he tamper with clocks at ten to eight, when the murder was actually being committed?"

"Heaven knows," said Wharton exasperatedly, and clicked his tongue as he got to his feet. "I've no reason to doubt that the local man's watch was right, and the clock at the house was right. As you say, if Mannin tampered with that kitchen clock—and I'm positive he did—then it's a mystery why he did it. Unless—"

It was a sudden idea that had occurred to him, and he scowled away for a minute or two while he tried to work things out. Then he shook his head. "I was just wondering. Is he holding something up his sleeve? I mean, is he shielding some one else whose alibi depends on the faked time?"

"You mean, something that happened in that short time between when he altered the clock and when he put it back again? That would be approximately between 7.50 and 7.53. It would also mean that he didn't do the murder, but he came later to the house while I was at the bungalow, and it was after that that he fell down the steps and broke his leg."

"If he came to the house he might have seen the child."

Travers shook his head. "That child's not to be questioned, George. It'd be criminal, after what she's gone through. Besides I'll give you my word that she knows nothing. She couldn't conceivably have seen him. What brought her downstairs was first my calling to her, and then the sound of Howcrop and myself talking at the gate and as we walked down the path."

"Well, I'll take your word for it," Wharton said. "You'll think everything over? You'll go into what we've been discussing and try and lick sense into it?"

"I certainly will," Travers told him.

"And you'll come along for a minute and have a word with Norris?"

Travers said he would, but only for a minute. He would also see the Yardmans before he left. Howcrop too, perhaps.

"He's a bad hat, that one," Wharton said as they took the steps down to the beach path. "I'm never one to harry a man who's been in trouble and who's tried to go straight, but Howcrop's a twister and a snivelling old liar."

Travers shook his head. "I've got a soft spot for Howcrop. I'd like to do something for him."

"Isn't that you all over?" Wharton told him exasperatedly. "Look at the double-crossing he was doing with that pianist. I'll wager he was supplying information to Mannin, and at the same time getting money out of the other one."

"Keep a sense of proportion, George," Travers said. "How could he supply information to Mannin? How could he know what was going on? Trowte had his ear glued to that phone during lesson time, and the Yardmans—even if Howcrop had been on speaking terms—would have told him something totally different."

Wharton shook his head doggedly and said it was a hunch. Travers switched the talk round. Wharton had not guessed a possible communication by means of notes, and with Howcrop in one place and Jeanne in another, that much of the truth would never be known.

He spent a quarter of an hour with Chief-Inspector Norris, and then said good-by to him and Wharton and made his way to the bungalow. The Yardmans had received their good news, but it was not their thanks or even reactions that were in his mind, but the wish to fill in certain gaps in Jeanne's daily routine, and so maybe get nearer to her mind.

"From when they came in from the walk, sir, to when she went to bed?" Yardman said. "Well, sir, they usually got in at about four, and then I took in tea. Then I saw nothing of them and never a sound till about a quarter to seven when I sounded a gong—"

"One minute," Travers said. "Why *about* a quarter to seven? Wasn't there a fixed time?"

"The old man wasn't so careful as all that, sir. He wasn't one to worry about time so long as we were somewhere near."

"And why the gong?"

"That was a sort of first dinner-gong," Yardman said. "He and Miss Jeanne used to go upstairs then. Sometimes he'd get down first and sometimes she would. A regular little woman, she was, looking after herself in things like that."

"Like what?"

"Well, sir, tidying herself and washing, and so on. She had to be. We weren't allowed to be with her."

But the Yardmans could throw no light on what Jeanne actually did with her time in that long period before the evening meal. The old man made up the fire himself, and neither of them was in the room till the two had actually gone upstairs. The only concern of Trowte—and indeed that had become so accepted a fact and happening that it could no longer be called concern—was that the Yardmans should leave for the bungalow as soon as the table was cleared.

So Travers shook, as he hoped, the dust of Seabreak off his feet, and resolved that the telephone should be for a considerable time the only link between himself and George Wharton. But as he drove towards Pulvery, with the case farther and farther from contact and reality, he all at once remembered something; and so strange was it that he drew up the car at the roadside, and with a pencil and paper began to reconstruct a certain set of parallel times, just as he had drawn them up some days before for the benefit of Tempest and Carry.

He jotted down a figure or two, then stopped. No sense in going into details. The figures had been a checking of the time when Howcrop supposedly left the house, in accordance with Mrs. Diddy's and the Doctor's statements, and the time when Howcrop should have arrived at Highways, as compared with the time when, according to Travers himself, he actually did ar-

rive. And those times had not agreed. There had been a difference of seven minutes, and those seven minutes, it had been admitted, might amount to ten. There was the curious thing. Ten
minutes to make two sets of actions coincide. And ten minutes,
according to Wharton, had been advanced by Mannin on that
kitchen clock.

But for the life of him Travers could hit on no connecting
link. And though somehow he was even more confident than
Wharton that Mannin had tampered with the clock, yet why the
tampering had been done was utterly beyond his powers of reasoning. For the first time in his life Travers was at a loss for a
theory. That long half-hour before sleep found him still puzzling
his wits and he woke in the morning to find no vestige of a solu-
tion spontaneously presenting itself.

"Did we wake you last night?" Helen said on his appearance
at breakfast.

"Why, what was going on?"

"Jeanne, walking in her sleep," Helen said. "Nanny happened
to hear her, and there she was in the corridor. Nanny just gathered her up and then she woke. She cried for a little while, then
we got her off to sleep."

"Poor little soul!" said Travers, and gave a doleful shake of
the head. "Do you know, I shouldn't be surprised if she used to
do a lot of that."

"What are you frowning for?" Helen asked.

"Am I?" he said, and smiled. "I was trying to work out why
she came downstairs that night with her clothes on and the
nightdress over them. Just an idea about walking in her sleep.
But it couldn't have been that, of course. She hadn't time to go
to sleep."

"She wouldn't sleep with her clothes on," Helen said. "But
any one can see why she wasn't undressed. She was afraid of
getting undressed and going to bed. She sat in the room in her
clothes as long as she could. Then when they did come down
that night she slipped her nightgown on so as to give the appearance of being undressed."

"That's it," Travers said. "She was expecting, perhaps that her grandfather might see her."

Tom came in to breakfast, and he pooh-poohed any idea of worry over the sleep-walking.

"I used to do it myself," he said. "No end of children do it. It's just a form of dreaming, that's all it is."

"If you ask me," Travers said, "it mightn't be a bad idea for most of us to take a holiday when Ruth goes back to school. What about it, Helen? Nanny can look after Jeanne, and you can play golf with Tom and me."

"Sounds rather a good idea," Tom said. "And I never refuse a man who offers to stand treat."

"Ludo didn't mean anything of the sort," Helen said.

"Oh, but I did," Travers cut in. "I'd love to stand the show. What shall we say? A fortnight?"

So they talked over the preliminaries, and decided tentatively on Bassett Warren, where there was a cottage that Helen had taken before. One maid, with Palmer, would be enough, and a stay in the country would be far better for Jeanne than the seaside.

Tom had a quiet word with Travers later, being anxious about Wharton and what Travers had let fall the previous night.

"I've decided not to do any worrying," Travers said. "Wharton's got more than his hands full, and it's my considered opinion he'll never be able to bring a case. All I'm determined to do is to dismiss the whole thing from my mind."

"Well, good luck to the bloke who did it," Tom said. "If he ever wants a fiver, hard up as I am, he can have it."

Travers spent an hour in the old nursery with Nanny and the children. Jeanne smiled shyly at him and seemed none the worse for a broken night's rest. By request, he contributed a story, and a cunningly introduced question or two at last induced Jeanne to speak. Once that first shyness was overcome, she seemed to find things easier, and she said "Good-by" with no prompting from Nanny.

"I think it's very good of you, Mr. Ludovic," Nanny later said, "to keep bringing into those stories of yours all about telling fibs. Miss Ruth is getting very bad."

Travers laughed. It was not Ruth at whom he was aiming. One day there might be questions to put to Jeanne, and it was the truth he might wish to know, though no other living soul might ever hear it.

"The way that Miss Jeanne looks at you is right affecting," Nanny also said. "Reminds me of a dog looking at its master. And how she talks about you when there's nobody there but me! A regular quarrel there might have been this very morning if I hadn't stepped in, both her and Ruth claiming you for their uncle, as if you wasn't uncle to both of them, as I told them."

Traven laughed again. "Well, you go on keeping the peace, Nanny," he whispered. "There's a special holiday in the air."

"A holiday, Mr. Ludovic?"

He told her all about it. Nanny said a holiday was just the very thing she could do with.

Travers had expected Wharton to ring up that very day, but it was not till the day following that he actually rang.

"Any ideas developed about that theory?" he asked.

"Never a one," Travers said. "That alibi has got me beat. But anything at your end?"

Wharton mumbled something and then said he might as well own up.

"I thought I'd try a bluff," he said, "so I went and saw Mannin. I put everything to him—you know, sort of suggestively. What do you think happened?"

"Don't know," Travers said.

"Well, before I was half through he wanted to know if I was attempting to make out he had anything to do with the murder. I tried to be tactful, but he virtually ordered me out of the house. Practically told me to go to hell and do what I damn pleased about it all."

Travers smiled dryly.

"And did you?"

Wharton begged that question and mumbled something

about getting at Mannin another way. But when he added that

Norris had gone back to town, Travers knew that the case was

as good as shelved.

XV
TEN MINUTES FOUND

TRAVERS HAD BUSINESS that took him back to town for a day or two, and the afternoon he returned he rang up the Yard and then dropped in on Wharton. As he had guessed, the case was shelved, though inquiries might go on for months.

"We've had a couple of conferences," Wharton said, "and that's what was decided. Norris is still nominally in charge, and I hope he'll have better luck than I did."

"But surely every one agreed that your Mannin theory was good?" said Travers, with a sympathy that was not wholly hypocritical.

"Well, yes," said Wharton modestly. "Howcrop is the main snag. He persists in that yarn of his that he saw Mannin in the car with the two men at just after eight that night. It's no use us saying there was a mist and be couldn't see. He's thought of all that, and he reckons the mist was a shifting one and it happened to swirl, or clear, just at that particular moment." Wharton spread his hands. "So that's that. We can't bring evidence to include the works of Nature."

"You couldn't get Howcrop to make a slip of any kind?"

Wharton shook his head. "He's a clam—that fellow. He'll talk and prate till the cows come home, but when you begin to get near to what I'd call business, he shuts up clean. You can see his mind working, and how he's telling himself there's something he mustn't give away."

"What about Mannin's alibi?"

"It's got us all beat," Wharton said. "What's more, we know pretty well by now that our opportunity's gone. If you can get an important statement from a witness straight away, then you've got something. The longer you have to wait, the harder it is to get that statement and the less value it has. That Mrs. Diddy, for instance. Suppose you'd had the luck to tackle her on the night of the murder, quite a lot might have come out. Now the Doctor's had time to put things into her mouth, and even if things didn't happen, she's convinced they did." He clicked his tongue exasperatedly. "No, we're up against a blank wall. That's the fact, and there's no denying it."

"Yes," said Travers, with suitable resignation. "It certainly looks like it. And haven't you any more private hunches?"

Wharton grunted. "Hunches? I'd call 'em convictions. I tell you I know Howcrop and Mannin worked the whole thing. They had it timed and schemed out to the last second. Even that accident when Mannin broke his leg wasn't enough to upset the time-table."

Travers nodded.

"I'd bet a thousand pounds on it—if I had it," Wharton said. "It's that damn ten minutes that's got us all beat. If that murder had only taken place at eight o'clock, everything would fit in as right as rain. We've even wondered if Mannin could have moved back the hands of the grandfather clock, but there you are—that's out of the question. The clock was absolutely right, and he hadn't time to slip back and put it so after you'd seen it, because he was lying on that beach with a broken leg."

Travers shook his head. "It's out of the question, George, as you say. That grandfather clock was never tampered with. I'll bet my head that Mannin had only just been admitted to the house—assuming for the moment it was he who did the murder—when I rang the back bell. After that he struck with the knife and bolted."

"Well, there we are," said Wharton resignedly. "If you should happen to get any ideas, perhaps you'll let Norris have them."

"I certainly will," Travers told him, and added that Wharton himself was looking a bit run down. He might do worse than slip down to Bassett Warren for a day.

"I can't manage it next week," Wharton said, "but I'd be delighted to drop in the week following. No ceremony, you say? Right. Then I won't even trouble to ring you up."

Holiday time came. Bassett Warren was a restful place, and the cottage a secluded one with the river at the garden end. Everywhere were lawns and trees, and spring flowers not altogether gone. A mile away was the little town with its golf course and picture house, and there were the loveliest little lanes for walks. There were rainy nights, but most of the days were warm and fine, and in that rambling garden there were always sheltered spots to cope with any shifting wind.

Travers spent much of his time with Jeanne. There was no more of that introspective analysis as to why he should feel so deep an affection for the child. Whatever the mainsprings—paternal, protective, or even response to her own sure worship of himself—he was content to take relationships for granted, and he would cease to wonder when he found himself looking forward to an hour in her company.

"No, Mr. Ludovic, it isn't right that you should look after her," Nanny would say. "It's what I'm here for."

"Oh, no, you're not, Nanny," he would tell her. "You're here for a holiday. You run along and enjoy yourself for an hour. Jeanne and I will keep each other out of mischief, won't we, Jeanne?"

"Yes, Uncle Ludo," Jeanne would say, and she would laugh because there was the implication of a secret. For they had all kinds of secrets of which no one had the least suspicion: the little notes they would still write; secret signs and mysterious signals, and a queer understanding of each other's moods.

Then one afternoon when Helen was out and Tom was taking his after-dinner nap, Travers knew the time had come to tell a story. It was one of his own composing; not too novel in plot, but with whimsical twists and touches of character. It was a made-to-measure story for her own fragile mind; a mind that had as background its shy humilities, its trust and gratitude, and its own keen and often strangely precocious perceptions. It was a secret story, he said, just for their two selves.

She had been lying on a rug spread on the grass at his feet, and when he had finished he beckoned to her, and she came and stood between his knees, as she often did, with his arm holding her and his cheek by hers.

"Do you know why Uncle Ludo told you that story, all for yourself?" he asked.

She thought for a moment, then shook her black head.

"It was all a big secret," he said, "and we're never going to think of it again. You see, you were once a little girl in a giant's castle." His arm held her still more closely. "Aunt Helen and Uncle Ludo came and took you away, and now the wicked giant is dead, and the castle's gone, and it's all like a nasty dream that frightens you when you wake up. But we're never going to be frightened, are we? we know it was all a dream. Everything now is going to be beautiful—always. Always Aunt Helen and Uncle Tom and Cousin Ruth, and every one—and Uncle Ludo."

There was silence in the garden for a long, long minute, while he let the thoughts move gently in her mind. Then he stirred.

"Who'd like a walk?"

Her face lighted up at once, and there little dimples in her cheeks when she smiled.

"And take Blanco, Uncle?"

"Well"—he frowned—"I don't know. Blanco wasn't very good the last time we took him."

"Oh, yes, Uncle—please."

"Well, we'll see," he told her. His hands went beneath her arms. "Like a ride? Or is it your turn to carry me?"

She laughed as he swung her up. In the kitchen Nanny nudged Palmer, and the two watched approvingly from the hidden window.

On the Saturday night the second post came, and with it Tom's copy of his local newspaper. After dinner he was glancing at it casually when all at once something caught his eye.

"Hullo!" he said. "Here's something to interest you, Ludo. There can't be two Mannins."

Travers, browsing peacefully before the fire, hoisted himself out of the chair at once.

"What, the *Doctor* Mannin?" Helen asked.

"Looks like it," Tom said. "Seabreak. Doctor Adrian Mannin, found dead in his bed. . . . Thought to be heart failure. . . . In his eightieth year. . . . Much respected in the district. . . . Recent victim of a strange assault. . . . You take a look at it, Ludo."

Travers polished his glasses and read the long paragraph, and he was shaking his head with a strange gravity as he put the paper down.

"A fine old fellow, and I liked him." He shook his head again. "There was something he said to me when I saw him that afternoon, about living till his next birthday. I think perhaps he knew. He was drawn and grey, and his lips were blue. I even think he was *trying to* tell me."

"You mean, tell you his heart was bad?" Helen said.

"Partly that," Travers said. "You see, I was trying in my blundering way to tell him I knew certain things. I think he was trying to tell me that he didn't worry about those things. He emphasized his age, for instance, like a man who owns he's had a long innings, and the time's near."

"What was he like?"

"Like?" said Travers, and smiled. "Typical old-fashioned country doctor, to look at. Shy, in his way, and pretending to be obstinate and even cantankerous. What I'd call a kindly man. You know—good by stealth and blushed to find it fame." Then he suddenly looked up. "Wharton will have had the news, if he died on Friday. I shouldn't be surprised if he turns up tomorrow."

But it was not till the Monday, just after lunch, that Wharton actually appeared, driving his own car by the coast way.

"You're just five minutes late," Travers told him. "The others have gone to golf. They'll be back by about five, though."

"I must be away and gone long before that," Wharton said. "I'm meeting Norris at Seabreak at five-thirty, but I wanted to have a word with you first."

"We'll go in the garden," Travers said, and led the way to the chain beneath the yew-tree. "It's poor Mannin you want to talk about?"

"Yes," Wharton said. "He had the laugh on us after all."

"You found something out?"

"Only the same old ideas." Wharton said, and gave a dogged shake of the head. "You've heard about the legacy, by the way?"

"What legacy?"

"He left Howcrop—'to my old friend Randolph Howcrop'—an annuity of two hundred pounds. The will was drawn up only a week ago."

"That was good of him," Travers said. "Howcrop's a free man again. He can go where he likes and do what he likes." Then he thought of something. "I believe Mannin knew the true story of Howcrop."

"Then I wish to God I did," said Wharton bitterly. "You can think all the nice, kind thoughts you like, but to me that legacy and when the will was made are just about the final proofs that Mannin and Howcrop did that murder between them. Each bolstered up the other's alibi, and they knew we'd never break one of them down."

Travers shook his head. "Mannin never tried to bolster up any alibi of Howcrop's. Be honest, George."

"He allowed Howcrop to perjure himself about his own, didn't he?" glared Wharton. "And what's all this affection of yours for Mannin? What's he ever done for you?"

"Nothing," said Travers quietly. "He treated me as a friend and he never lied to me. I take few friends at their face value, but I make an exception in his case. He was what I've called a kindly man. He was straight, honest as the day, and he loved his fellow-men. If he did that murder, then I regret it. Yet I don't think any the worse of him, knowing what I do—and what you do."

"He died well but he died luckily," Wharton said. "Sooner or later we'd have found the flaw in that alibi scheme of his and Howcrop's, and, kindly man or not, I'd have had him, just as I'd have my own brother. There's no sentiment in our game."

"Everything's conjecture," Travers said. "We shall never know who did it or how it was done. Far better wash the whole thing out of our minds."

Wharton clicked his tongue. "If I could only find the reason for that clock manipulation! Ten minutes or so—clean lost, just as if the sun stood still, or shot on ahead." He clicked his tongue again. "All the time I feel just like some one with something right on the tip of his tongue. One little extra clue, or hint, and we'd know. If, for instance, that actual killing had taken place at eight o'clock, instead of at about ten minutes to, everything'd be as plain as daylight. We'd know just why Mannin gave himself an alibi for eight o'clock. But why the devil he did so for a murder committed ten minutes before, fair gets me beat."

Travers smiled, and in the smile was a quiet affection.

"You've erected a building which you think is on rock. But it may be only on sand. Though every fact seems to fit, you don't know—and you'll never know—*if* the facts are even facts. Mannin may never have tampered with that kitchen clock."

"I see," said Wharton, with grim irony. "And he was never in the house, and he didn't fall down the steps and break his leg!"

"Exactly!" said Travers, "Mannin's story of the car may have been true. It may be Milovitch's alibi that ought to be broken, not some carefully erected alibi of our own devising."

"Milovitch!" said Wharton, and made noises of contempt. "Do you think I'd have sent him packing if I hadn't been sure? I tell you Mannin and Howcrop did it between them."

"Have you ever thought of something?" Travers said. "Let me put it up to you. It's something to do with Howcrop. You have hunches and believe in them; well, this is a hunch, and I'm sure it's a good one. Howcrop had been a pariah for a good deal of his life. Mannin became a friend of his, and Howcrop had a very deep regard for him. I'd say that Howcrop had two people whom he worshiped--Mannin, and Jeanne, his pupil. I'll say, therefore, that Howcrop guessed that Mannin had done the murder, and when he saw him in the nursing home that night and heard his tale, he at once volunteered confirmation. Howcrop was not trying to fake an alibi for himself. Out of the love of his heart; out of the pride, if you like, in a man who'd done a thing he'd have done himself if he'd only had the brains and pluck; I say out of those things came the wish to shield and cover that man. Through it he told the Doctor that he knew the truth, and approved, and was trying to repay. And that has been the thing that Howcrop has been trying to conceal; the thing to which you have persistently referred. You said he would shut up like a clam. He did. Once you began to press him for information that might incriminate Mannin, then he closed his mouth. No matter what the consequences might be to himself, he refused to talk."

"Yes," said Wharton slowly. "I don't know that you aren't right."

"If Mannin did do that killing of Trowte," Travers went on, "then I shall always believe that he had what seemed to him unanswerable reasons. We can debate what else he might have done to get Jeanne out of his hands, but I honestly believe that he'd debated all those methods and discarded them. He decided on what he knew to be the only way."

"Maybe you're right," Wharton said dubiously.

"When Howcrop let himself be the tool of Milovitch," Travers again went on, "it was the old Adam in him coming out. I don't think he intended to double-cross any one; it was just that he couldn't resist making a bit of money on the quiet. I'd say he never said a word to Mannin about it. What he might have done there's no telling, but things happened too quickly after that first day or two."

Wharton got to his feet. "Well, I shall have to be making a move. Perhaps I'll come down again on a private visit in a day or two, if you'll have me."

"A wasted afternoon, I fear," said Travers. "Professionally, that is."

"I don't know," Wharton told him. "You've given me a few things to think over. Not that I haven't got enough. Those damned, unnecessary ten minutes; that's the problem that's going to buzz in my brain the rest of my days."

Travers smiled. "Don't you believe it." Then he all at once stopped. "Oh, but you must see Jeanne! You can't possibly go without having a word with Jeanne. Stay here a moment and I'll find her. I think she's finished her nap."

Wharton looked positively startled when he saw the child. Then as she neared he screwed up his features into a grimace of joyful welcome.

"Here's a new uncle," Travers told her. "This is Uncle George. Say how do you do."

"How do you do, Uncle George?" she said.

Wharton took the little hand, and beamed affection.

"So this is little Jeanne. Quite a little woman."

"She *is* a little woman," Travers told him proudly. "And she's going to be a bigger one some fine day. Now run back to Nanny again, darling, because Uncle George has to go away."

"Ah! but I'm coming back in a day or two," Wharton said.

"There doesn't look much wrong with her now?" he said to Travers as they made for the car.

"She's getting on," said Travers. "But she hasn't forgotten, George, not by a long way yet."

"She's a pretty little thing. Be a rare fine-looking young woman one of these days."

Travers laughed. "Wonderful for me, don't you think? Like having a daughter all grown up." His face straightened. "My next move will be to get permission from the court to change her name. People have unfortunately long memories, Travers may be better than Trowte."

"It's a name she ought to be proud of," Wharton said, and held out his hand. "And you needn't look at me like that. I'm telling the truth. You're too modest; that's what's wrong with you. And too tender-hearted."

The blushing Travers was polishing his glasses and mumbling something about it not being right to hog all the virtues.

That early evening Helen and Tom took Nanny to the first house at the local pictures, and Travers, who felt scarcely in the mood for *Death Comes Creeping*, preferred a book beneath the bough. Then it struck him that the sun was still warm out in the open, and he sent for Jeanne, who lay sprawled on the rug at his feet, reading a book.

It was an evening of lovely quiet, with the young green a soft gold and the air all luminous in the westering sun. Now and again a bumble-bee would come lumbering by, and there were the near sounds of birds, and the rumbling of the little river over the near-by weir, but all those things were somehow part of the stillness, and Travers was aware of nothing but the evening quiet and a restful peace.

So soon he was lying back in his chair, the book closed on his knees, and was thinking once more of Seabreak and the actors in that strange case. It was Mannin who jumped first to the forefront of his mind: Mannin of the kindly, wrinkled face and the ragged, badger moustache, and the dry ironic smile. Single of purpose, and that purpose wholly good—that, thought Travers, might be the basis of his epitaph.

And whatever happened now, provided always that Howcrop maintained that dogged bravery of silence, nothing could match that epitaph. And then Travers smiled, and his fingers went to his glasses. By his silence he himself was as much a conspirator against the law as Howcrop had been, and as he thought of that he let emerge into open daylight the bolstering, incriminating facts which he himself had kept assiduously from both Tempest and Wharton.

Yet even then he refused wholly to admit, even to himself, that Mannin had actually done the killing of Trowte, or that Howcrop and Mannin had been confederates. But what he might have pointed out to Wharton was the perfection of the planning with which Mannin had apparently given himself *a wholly unnecessary alibi*. When Mannin and Mrs. Diddy parted at the gate, for instance, Mannin knew she would gather the violets and then go straight to the surgery without going back to the kitchen for another look at the clock. Then Mannin—on the pretence of seeing another patient—would do the wiping out of that maniac Trowte, and be at the surgery as soon as herself. And if he were late, then doubtless he had stopped or altered the surgery clock beforehand, or it might be the clock in the waiting-room to which she would be shown as a matter of routine by the maid.

"Am I to go to bed before Nanny comes, Uncle Ludo?"

He gave a little jump.

"Dear me! You frightened me out of my wits. And what was that about Nanny?"

"I needn't go to bed before Nanny comes, need I, Uncle?"

"Bless my soul, yes!" he told her. "Nanny's an old gadabout and mayn't come home till morning. Besides, I heard her telling Margaret to have you in bed at half-past seven sharp."

"But I needn't, need I, Uncle?"

He resisted the cajolement of the pleading eyes.

"I'm afraid you must. You see, Nanny's a very important person and I'm ever so afraid of her—"

"Oh, Uncle, you're not!"

"But indeed I am," he said severely. "Though perhaps, if she were here, I might ask for an extra five minutes—"

"Oh, Uncle Ludo!"

"Or I might not. It would depend on whether or not a certain little girl went on reading her book."

By way of example he opened his own book again and settled down to read. Five minutes and it lay closed again on his knees.

Howcrop and Mannin—had there been collusion or not? For his own part, he thought not. When Howcrop had blurted out that night in the nursing home chat he had seen the car and the Doctor in it, Mannin had accepted with some deep inward irony that tribute and repayment. After that, each had tacitly and with no false affectation accepted the other, and each had been a natural part of the unspoken trust. That legacy had no taint of blackmail; it had been Mannin's last gesture of recognition.

Travers smiled to himself as all at once he remembered Howcrop as he had seen him first that far-off morning and had walked with him towards the village. In even the worst of us, he thought, there is a best and a something incredibly fine. And now he was at last beyond the reach of want, and even of mendacity. Interesting to have seen his pompous old face when he first heard of the annuity, and maybe Mannin himself had chuckled dryly at a gratitude which he would never see. A paining, shaming thing gratitude could be. Wasn't it old Wordsworth who had said it could hurt more than ingratitude? No paradox that—

"Miss Jeanne! . . . Miss Jeanne!"

Travers roused himself and smiled down at the figure so suddenly and so unhearingly intent on the book.

"Come on, young lady! There's the word of command."

Jeanne got reluctantly to her knees.

"But you said I could have five minutes, Uncle."

"Did I?" He smiled to himself as he inwardly discussed that sophistry, then shrugged his shoulders with an exaggerated resignation. "Well, if I did, I did." He called back to the house. "All right, Margaret. Miss Jeanne will be coming in with me."

Jeanne flopped down at once to her book, and Travers was once more weaving a hazy way among his ideas. Best perhaps to dismiss the case wholly from one's mind—even that queer attendant problem of the missing ten minutes; the problem which Wharton had said would haunt him the rest of his days. Mannin had done nothing, or everything. Mannin had worked alone or with a confederate. Mannin had never done an abnormal thing in Mrs. Diddy's cottage, or he had planned there a perfect and unbreakable alibi. He had planned that alibi in grim earnest or it had been a grim joke and a thing of neither consequence nor moment. He had given himself an alibi to no purpose save unknowingly to haunt Wharton the rest of his days.

Alternatives, all of them, and one man alone had their secret, and held it in that final darkness to which we all must come. As for that problem of the ten minutes, maybe it would haunt himself. Why, in the name of sanity, should the Doctor have tampered with the clock to make out that a certain killing was done at eight o'clock, when it was done at ten to? And then Travers gave a gesture of final dismissal. Mannin had not done the murder at all Mannin was the victim of circumstance, and of certain ingenious brains who had fitted into perfectly simple actions a whole series of diabolically mysterious motives.

His eyes fell on Jeanne, now poring with an uncanny earnestness over her book. Curious, he thought, that children should so love the company of books, and of humans, that no artifice was unexploited to delay the inevitable moment for bed. Stranger, too, in the case of Jeanne. No need now for fear of bed or dark, but once she must have shuddered as dark came on. All her days must have been shadowed and haunted by that dread, uncertain climax, and as she sat at the evening meal her whole body must have been one inward, clamant shriek as the hands of that grandfather clock moved inexorably round. What wouldn't she have given then and what trick or artifice would she not have employed in her terrified, tortured mind to have stopped these hands or to have set them moving back?

Then suddenly his breath was held as if a sound incredibly still might be enough to shatter a vital thought. Jeanne, sometimes first in to the evening meal. Aware of the old man's leering anticipation of some new terror in the night. That clock so natural a thing to Yardman that he saw the hands as hands and not as tellers of time—even if he was aware of them at all. And Trowte himself, not one to worry about times and the punctuality of meals, so long as the Yardmans left the house when the table was cleared.

Travers let out a breath, but his eyes still strained as if to view back that one misty moment of time. Jeanne, creeping frightenedly downstairs and into the empty room. A quick listen for Yardman, and then—the terror of the night already on her—a quicker step on the chair that stood by the clock, and then the opening of the face and a small finger moving back the hands. That *must* have been it. That clock had not been right, though his own movements that night had not betrayed the fact. The clock had been ten minutes slow. And yet it had *not* been slow. When Tempest arrived, the clock had been dead right.

"Jeanne!" he called quietly. "Come here a moment, darling. I want you."

She heard nothing unusual in that quiet voice and saw nothing strange in the gentle face. His arm held her as she stood within his knees, and all at once his cheek moved tenderly against her silky hair.

"What would you say if Uncle Ludo ever told you an untruth?"

She tried to wriggle round at that amazing question, but his arm still held her close.

"A fib, Uncle?"

"Well, yes—a fib."

"Oh, Uncle, but you wouldn't!"

"Well," he said, "perhaps I wouldn't. But I told you once that we were never going to talk about a certain something, and now

188 | CHRISTOPHER BUSH

I've got to." He smiled at the ingenious way out that was suddenly presenting itself. "I'm going to talk about little girls and going to bed."

"But you said I could have five minutes, Uncle!"

"Yes," he said, "so I did. But first of all I want you to tell me a secret—the biggest secret in the world. Something that even Aunt Helen must never know about—only you and me—and as soon as we've told it to each other, then we're going to forget about it too. It's about when you were living in that wicked castle and how you used to be all frightened about the time, and how you sometimes used to climb up on the chair and put back the hands of the clock."

He felt the quick shiver run through her, and his arm tightened and his cheek rested gently on hers.

"We're going to forget all about it, and we're never going to mention the castle or the giant any more because they're only a kind of bad dream, and it's silly to think about dreams. But it was strange how you heard me, that very last night when I called up the stairs. You never dreamed it was your Uncle Ludo who'd come to take you away. And then, like the brave little girl that you were, you slipped your nightie over your clothes and you came downstairs. Then when you got down you remembered something you had to do. Something you sometimes did in the morning very early, or even in the night, in your sleep. So you did it, didn't you?"

There was a silence, and beneath his arm he felt the warm young body trembling. His cheek rested tenderly against hers, and all the love in the world was in his quiet voice.

"Just whisper to me, darling, and tell me what you did. . . . It was something you had to do to the clock, and being frightened about some one finding out."

He felt the lips move, but still no sound came.

"A secret between you and me, and no one shall ever know. Just whisper. What did you do when you thought about the clock?"

Her lips brushed his ear.

"I moved the hands back again, Uncle."

For a moment he was silent, then some deep emotion moved him and all at once he held her to him as if she should never go.

"That was a brave girl. Only, you see, it never really happened at all. It was only a dream, and we're never going to think of it again. All we're going to think about is being happy, and growing well and strong again, and loving everybody just as everybody loves you."

He held her, with his cheek to hers, while the thoughts made a quiet lullaby and a new soothing for her mind. Then his own thoughts were moving quickly again. Wharton had solved the case, and yet would never know it. Eight was the murder hour, and at eight that murder had been done. Mannin had killed to save the child, and by that child his own life had been saved! There was the deep human irony and there was the secret that must be hidden close as the grave itself, though it haunted Wharton the rest of his days.

"Ten minutes. Wharton's ten minutes!"

It was instinctively that he had spoken, but Jeanne was at once wriggling round, her face beaming.

"*Ten* minutes? May I have *ten* minutes, Uncle?"

He laughed. "You've had ten minutes, young lady. You've had more like fifteen." His hands went to her armpits. "Now, who'd like a ride?"

He lifted her and swept her up to his shoulder.

"Still not so heavy as you ought to be," he told her severely. "However, plenty of food and plenty of sleep. Which reminds me. Who'd like me to come up and tell a story when they're in bed?"

"Oh, Uncle!" She clapped her hands. "The one about Ali and the carpet and how they went to the desert and how the three old men kept on dancing and—"

"Steady, young lady!" He laughed as he bounced her up. "As Nanny would say, who's telling the story—you or me?"

THE END

Ingram Content Group UK Ltd.
Milton Keynes UK
UKHW011303140523
421711UK00022B/777